"Only a well-seasoned traveler like Robi[n] ... tale of two kindred spirits exploring a [...] I've enjoyed a couple of interesting trips [...] her words ring wise and true about the preciousness of friendships shared between women. And the descriptions of wildlife and scenery on safari were amazing. My only complaint: now I want to go to Kenya too! Well done, Robin!"

Melody Carlson, recipient of a *Romantic Times* Career Achievement Award, author of *Just for the Summer* and *A Royal Christmas*

"Robin Jones Gunn brings the ravishing wilderness of Africa to life in *Tea with Elephants*. This gentle, beautifully written story laps around you like the warm waves of the sea, soothing away the day's stress, whispering a soft promise of hope and lasting friendship. An altogether delightful read."

Tessa Afshar, *Publishers Weekly* bestselling author of *The Hidden Prince* and *The Peasant King*

"It is a widely acknowledged fact that Robin Jones Gunn has a knack for creating unforgettable characters. Just ask anyone who grew up with Christy Miller, and no doubt they'll go on and on about what those books have meant to them over the years. Now those fans have two new characters to grow with. Fern and Lily, a.k.a. the Suitcase Sisters, will work their way into the hearts of readers from the very beginning of *Tea with Elephants*. As I read the story of these charming characters, I couldn't help but smile at their joys, grieve for their hardships, and wish that I could go on adventures with them."

Susie Finkbeiner, author of *The All-American* and *The Nature of Small Birds*

"Robin Jones Gunn pens a tender tale about the realization of dreams deferred by the twists and turns of life in this love letter to the beauty of Africa. Readers will be swept off their feet by this faith-forward celebration of friendship."

Amanda Cox, Christy Award–winning author of *Between the Sound and Sea* and *He Should Have Told the Bees*

"Robin Jones Gunn masterfully intertwines the splendor of the African wilderness with a captivating story of two friends on a trip that promises to transform them in more ways than one. Through the lens of faith, friendship, and the majestic wonders of nature, *Tea with Elephants* is a testament to the enduring power of love and the divine beauty that awaits those who seek it."

Sara Brunsvold, Christy Award–winning author
of *The Extraordinary Deaths of Mrs. Kip*

"Robin Jones Gunn sets the standard in books about female friendships. Thought-provoking, stirring, and often funny, *Tea with Elephants* is the moving read you've been waiting for. Gunn brings African settings to life and writes characters who will leap off the page and straight into your heart."

Liz Johnson, bestselling author of *The Red Door Inn*
and *Meddling with Mistletoe*

Praise for Robin Jones Gunn

"When you read a Robin Jones Gunn book, you know you're going to receive a tender lesson and you'll be blessed for it."

Francine Rivers, *New York Times* bestselling author

"Robin's storytelling is a breath of fresh air. Her tender heart and wisdom make every one of her books poignant and unforgettable."

Karen Kingsbury, *New York Times* bestselling author

"Robin Jones Gunn writes about everyday women with truth, tenderness, heart, and soul . . . while taking me on an adventure."

Rachel Hauck, *New York Times* and *USA Today*
bestselling author

"Robin's stories always make me feel as if I've actually visited another amazing part of the world."

Tricia Goyer, *USA Today* bestselling author

"Gunn is adept at denuding light fiction of its usual tics and imbuing it with the hallmarks of literary fiction. The characters are multidimensional and ring true at nearly every turn."

Publishers Weekly

Tea with Elephants

Books by Robin Jones Gunn

Victim of Grace

SUITCASE SISTERS SERIES
Tea with Elephants

CHRISTY MILLER SERIES

SIERRA JENSEN SERIES

KATIE WELDON SERIES

HAVEN MAKERS SERIES

SISTERCHICKS SERIES

GLENBROOKE SERIES

FATHER CHRISTMAS SERIES

SUITCASE SISTERS #1

Tea with Elephants

A SUITCASE
SISTERS NOVEL

ROBIN JONES GUNN

Revell

a division of Baker Publishing Group
Grand Rapids, Michigan

Published by Revell
a division of Baker Publishing Group
Grand Rapids, Michigan
RevellBooks.com

Printed in the United States of America

Library of Congress Cataloging-in-Publication Data
Names: Gunn, Robin Jones, 1955– author.
Title: Tea with elephants / Robin Jones Gunn.
Description: Grand Rapids, Michigan : Revell, a division of Baker Publishing Group, 2024. | Series: Suitcase Sisters ; 1
Identifiers: LCCN 2024003937 | ISBN 9780800744823 (paper) | ISBN 9780800745103 (casebound) | ISBN 9781493443536 (ebook)
Subjects: LCGFT: Christian fiction. | Novels.
Classification: LCC PS3557.U4866 T43 2024 | DDC 813/.54—dc23/eng/20240129
LC record available at https://lccn.loc.gov/2024003937

Scripture used in this book, whether quoted or paraphrased by the characters, is taken from one of the following:

The Holy Bible, New International Version®, NIV®. Copyright © 1973, 1978, 1984, 2011 by Biblica, Inc.® Used by permission of Zondervan. All rights reserved worldwide. www.zondervan.com. The "NIV" and "New International Version" are trademarks registered in the United States Patent and Trademark Office by Biblica, Inc.®

The New King James Version®. Copyright © 1982 by Thomas Nelson. Used by permission. All rights reserved.

The *Holy Bible*, New Living Translation. Copyright © 1996, 2004, 2015 by Tyndale House Foundation. Used by permission of Tyndale House Publishers, Carol Stream, Illinois 60188. All rights reserved.

Cover art by Art of Nora
Cover design by Laura Klynstra

Published in association with Books & Such Literary Management, BooksAndSuch .com.

Baker Publishing Group publications use paper produced from sustainable forestry practices and postconsumer waste whenever possible.

24 25 26 27 28 29 30   7 6 5 4 3 2 1

For Wambura.
Asante sana for introducing me
to your beautiful homeland.

Our safari with Alice, Yna,
and Jeanette was glorious.

Afternoon tea in the treetops
on Mount Kenya was unforgettable.

You are a gift.

Prologue

Learn to be a faithful friend to your soul.

Hildegard of Bingen

Some mornings I wake up thinking I've just heard the chittering call of the cheeky monkey that watched Lily and me from his loquat tree. I'm certain I can smell the spicy-sweet fragrance of a steaming cup of masala chai placed on the nightstand.

Then I squint in the half-light and see that I am in my own bed, with the soft glow of the hallway nightlight sliding under the door. I am not with my closest friend, back in the place of gentle mystery, of emerald tea fields, stampeding wildebeests, elegant giraffes, and an unobstructed view of a singular baobab tree silhouetted against an amber horizon.

I am home, nestled under my thick comforter, settled into my once-again ordinary life.

Nothing, however, is the same as it was two years ago when Lily called me in the middle of a stressful workday. Her unexpected and exuberant announcement stirred in me the long-dormant embers of a wish we had whispered to each other twenty years earlier. We had big hopes back then. Back when we were starry-eyed teenagers who had just experienced our first taste of another corner of the globe. We dreamed of traveling together and were naive enough to believe anything was possible.

Then we grew up and went nowhere.

Lily's surprise announcement broke the stalemate of our unfulfilled wishes. Her father-in-law had given her a gift. An African safari for two. She said I had to go with her. Simply had to. Her husband didn't want to go. He thought I should. If Lily and I did not use the all-inclusive package, it would be lost.

I resisted.

She insisted.

The trip was impractical. It made no sense. Not when things at work were so intense. I was the senior fiction editor for a publishing house and fully aware that our sales numbers for the last two years had been less than stellar. I couldn't possibly request more vacation time until next year.

Lily persisted.

Again, I resisted.

She pleaded with me in that winsome way of hers, reminding me that this had been our dream. Our sincere and eager wish to go somewhere exciting, back when we could still fit into our skinny jeans.

I softened.

She asked if I remembered.

Of course I remembered. How could I forget the summer she and I met while volunteering at a Christian conference center in Costa Rica? Our prayer of surrender at the final campfire had marked both of us. We meant it when we turned our faces to the heavens and told the Maker of the stars that we were His. We wanted to serve Him the rest of our lives, wherever that might be. Two girls, ready for anything.

Returning to our cabin, we whispered late into the night. Would spending our lives doing what God created us to do involve travel? Yes, Lord, please! Where would He send us? Europe. England. Ireland. Brazil. Or even . . . Lily had whispered the name of the mysterious continent with panache. "*Ahh-free-kaa.*"

Now I smiled at my desk when she said it again on the phone, and it brought back all the feelings of adventures that awaited us.

"*Ahh-free-kaa!* Think of it! We've been given a free trip. I forbid you to say you won't come with me. We've waited too long for a chance to go somewhere together again." Lily lowered her voice and asked the question that melted my resistance. "If not now, when?"

Without thinking, I answered, "You're right. Yes, we have to go. We need to do this."

I had no idea how I'd pull it off. With some careful planning, it might be doable next summer. Possibly in the spring.

Then Lily included a few minor details. The dates of the tour package could not be changed. We were leaving in three weeks, on November 7. Oh, and by the way, she had an aunt and uncle who lived outside Nairobi. They were expecting us.

Before I could alter my impulsive reply, she hung up.

My pulse throbbed like a beating drum. I sat back and blinked. I felt like Lily had burst into my cubicle and popped a cardboard tube of glitter, and shimmering possibilities were floating all around me. How could I put the invisible glitter back in the tube? I couldn't bring myself to call her and insist that my yes had been too hasty. Yet I knew I couldn't go. Not in three weeks. It wasn't possible.

And then, sadly, sweetly, unexpectedly, it was possible.

Three weeks later, I was on a plane headed to Africa.

Ever since our remarkable trip I have not stopped thinking of *her*—of Africa. Every glimpse of her remarkable beauty made me want to see more. Every vivid image and unique sound, every fragrance and new taste invited me to absorb the wonder.

In a small way, I caught the feeling behind these words in the book *Out of Africa*:

> If I know a song of Africa . . . of the giraffe and the African new moon lying on her back . . . does Africa know a song of me?

Lily and I spent only a week in Kenya, and yet, I'd like to think we heard a bit of her song. A low, unmistakable, contented hum. It caused me to wonder what the great gentlewoman thought of us.

In those first days, when my affection for Africa was forming, I remember feeling shy, the way one does in a new relationship when you fear your deep fondness might be embarrassingly one-sided. But then I felt enfolded in Kenya's womanly presence, and I was sure I could hear more than her hum. I could hear the rhythm of her heartbeat as she presented her large self to us and drew us closer.

Lily and I arrived in such a flurry that neither of us fully realized we had brought with us great lumps of hurt in our punched and kneaded souls. We had kept our folded-in feelings and fears hidden even from each other until we arrived on Kenya's doorstep.

When we were welcomed in without hesitation, we calmed ourselves and saw why we'd really come all that way. I smile now to think of the gentle, maternal manner in which Africa scolded us, and how she took us in and covered us. She gave us a place to rise, to prove, like a loaf of my own mother's best sourdough bread.

And rise we did. All the way to the top of Mount Kenya, where my best friend and I gazed contentedly upon the hushed arrival of the golden hour and calmly sipped tea with elephants. Two women, ready for anything.

1

There is no friend like an old friend
who has shared our morning days.
Oliver Wendell Holmes Sr.

*B*efore I tell you the story of Africa, I must tell you the story of Lily.

The summer after we graduated from high school, we did something brave. We boarded planes in two different states and flew to Costa Rica, where we found ourselves sitting on the same bench outside the airport, waiting.

After those first few awkward moments, Lily asked, "Are you waiting to be picked up for Campo Cielo?"

"Yes! You too?"

"Yes!" She smiled confidently and turned toward me. I read the words "Rancho Corona University" across the front of her vintage-looking hoodie. I had no idea where that college was located, but then I didn't have a lot of insights into the world beyond the farming community where I'd grown up in Michigan. That was why I'd volunteered to spend the summer serving in Central America. I wanted more. I wanted to see what was out there in this wide world.

"I'm Lily." Her sparkling gray eyes fixed on mine, waiting for a reply.

"My name is Fern."

I tucked my dangling brown hair behind my ear, anticipating her response. Lily did what most people do when I tell them my name. She repeated it with a tilt of her head, as if she wasn't sure she'd heard correctly.

"Yes, Fern, like the plant. My sisters and I were named after characters in our mom's favorite books. I got *Charlotte's Web*."

"Really?"

At this point in most introductions, I move on to a new topic, eager to quench the chagrin I always feel about my name. That day I overexplained, which is what I often did, being the youngest of five girls.

"I know. It's a strange name. No one ever remembers the little girl in *Charlotte's Web*. They remember the pig and the spider. If I'd been named after the spider, you know, Charlotte, at least that would be a normal name and—"

"Fern. I really like your name. It's part of one of my favorite words."

I could not think of any words that started with or even sounded like "fern." My expression must have made it clear that I was baffled.

She leaned closer as if she was about to tell me a secret. "Fernweh," she said.

The word sounded like the flutter of a bird's wings. I'd never heard it before and was hesitant to admit that or repeat the word in case I didn't pronounce it correctly.

"Fernweh means 'a longing to go to faraway places.'" Lily raised her eyebrow. "Sounds like us right now, doesn't it? I mean, we probably wouldn't be here if we didn't share a longing to go to faraway places."

All my apprehension evaporated. Her words rested on me with a comforting sense of affirmation. It was remarkable. By uttering only a few sentences within minutes of us meeting, Lily had sealed my devotion. She gave my name, my identity, a touch of charm and mystique.

For the next seven weeks Lily and I roomed together and served in various positions at Campo Cielo, such as never-ending kitchen duty, organizing afternoon team games, and even a few first aid assignments when ice packs or Band-Aids were needed. I no longer felt like the forgettable farm girl who was forever linked to a talking pig and a spider. I was now the girl who dreamed of faraway places.

It was the happiest time in our young lives. We often laughed till we could barely breathe and always got teary during worship times. Lily had a sweet voice and sang with her eyes closed as if no one except Jesus was listening.

We especially loved campfire nights when we would lift our eyes and gaze at the thousands of stars just waiting to be wished upon. That summer we became ourselves, and that summer we became us.

My favorite photo of Lily and me is one in which we're walking into the airport, headed home at the end of our glorious summer. Our arms are linked, and we are taking long strides in our faded jeans. Our battered suitcases are trailing behind us on their wobbly wheels.

Lily's head with her wispy blond, free-as-a-feather hair is tilted toward mine. My long, thick brown hair is folded into a single braid trailing down my back. We were so young. So on fire! We carried with us the afterglow of the closing campfire when we were ready to "go into all the world" and dreamed of more adventures in faraway lands. Costa Rica had been a mere taste of the excitement that awaited us.

I still feel a lingering touch of joy every time I look at that classic photo of us.

Our moment of innocent beginnings and tender goodbyes was captured by Tim Graden, the camp lifeguard who took our photo. Tim took something else that day. Lily's phone number.

He didn't ask for mine. Only Lily's. I noted that he waited until the last moment to ask, when she and I were tearfully hugging before going to our separate departure gates.

Four days later Tim called her. He lived less than two hours from Nashville and had come up with a reason to make a drive there the next Saturday.

Lily was still a little breathless when she phoned me immediately after he hung up. I found it endearing that she was surprised Tim was interested in her. Of course he was. Of course he wanted to see her again. All the signs had been obvious at camp. But since the staff had relationship guidelines and since Tim and Lily were both rule followers, their mutual interest remained unspoken and untried until his call.

I knew right then, as she repeated his every word, that Lily and I would not be packing our suitcases for Africa the next June. We would not be carrying out our arm-in-arm wish to see another slice of any part of the world. Our summer in Costa Rica had been a one-and-done adventure, and I don't think I've ever felt so sorry for myself.

The next time I boarded a plane was less than a year later. I headed to Nashville for Tim and Lily's wedding. Soon after, my mom found an application for an intern position at a publishing house in Colorado through one of her literary interest sites. I flew to Denver in a thunderstorm and quietly entered the publishing world, staying on for two decades and working my way up to senior editor.

Aside from regular flights back to Michigan for holidays, weddings, and my grandfather's funeral, and a few trips to see Lily and Tim and their two boys, the "fernweh" spirit that once fanned its wings over me faded into a small, caged hope.

Then came Lily's call on that autumn afternoon, awakening our old dreams with a chirp.

That same afternoon, I went into my boss's office with invisible possibility dust in my hair. The cadence of my pulse had not changed from the drumlike pounding that began when I agreed to go. I hadn't called Lily back yet with my regrets because I'd come up with a plan to work extra hours at home so I could activate my unused vacation time on short notice.

Twenty minutes later I stepped out of the office. The answer I'd been given was unexpected and complex. I lowered my eyes and headed for the restroom. My vision was blurred by tears that were impossible to contain.

Over the next few weeks, Lily had no idea how hard it was for me not to back out of the trip. That was because I didn't tell her what had happened between her call and when I boarded the plane in Denver. I kept my head down and moved through the blizzard of obstacles. I kept telling myself that the moment I stowed my carry-on and fastened my seat belt, the storm would pass. The fog would lift.

But it did not.

The plane took off, and I felt as if I was still moving inside a dream. Not a cozy, happy dream. More like it's the first day of seventh grade and I can't get my locker open kind of dream.

As if I wasn't shaken enough from my job issues, one of my sisters, Anne (yes, Anne with an *e*), had been sending me information on the rise of attacks on international travelers. My dad sent news opinion pieces on how Africa would be ground zero for the next global virus.

Two decades ago, flying alone to Costa Rica had felt liberating and exhilarating. Now my flight to Heathrow, where I was to meet Lily, felt frightening, and I felt hollow.

I pulled out the paperback I'd brought with me. Reading in my youth had been my portal to other worlds. After editing fiction for a decade and a half, reading for pleasure was often difficult to achieve. I'd developed an occupational hazard of feeling the urge to change the structure of a sentence or enhance the qualities of the main character. Stories used to be a destination where I escaped to vicariously experience the adventures of a new imaginary friend.

Now I was the main character, caught up in a journey, suspended at the end of the first chapter by a cliff-hanger. I was the woman on some sort of hero's quest, moving through obstacles to an unknown conclusion. Everything before me, both in Africa and when I returned to Colorado, would be new, untried, wild, and strange. Reading only reminded me that when I returned home, I would have to find a new job.

I couldn't bear to think about it. Like Scarlett (not my second-oldest sister but the fictional one), I would think about that tomorrow.

Or, more accurately, I'd think about it later when my return flight brought me back to the now-altered world that waited for me in Colorado.

Danny would be there when I returned. He was the best thing about going home. He was my rock. Sure and steady. My sudden job loss hadn't troubled him. We had been through a lot since the blustery Saturday in April three years ago when we repeated our marriage vows, gazing deeply into each other's eyes. Danny had the most beautiful eyes. Sincere and alluring. He'd told me three days ago that he was convinced going to Kenya was the right thing for me to do. He believed everything would work out when I returned home.

I put aside my paperback, listened to two of the podcasts I'd saved on my phone, and somehow managed to sleep until the plane was far over the Atlantic. The respite, along with tea served in a paper cup, was enough to prepare me to navigate the massive Heathrow terminal. I found the departure gate for our Nairobi flight and spied Lily standing in the boarding line, waving both arms over her head to get my attention.

The moment I saw her infectious smile, I wished I'd already told her about the upheaval in my job situation. I wanted to feel as free as she looked right then.

She hugged me close and swayed for a moment. "Can you believe we're doing this? I am so excited!"

"Me too."

Lily held me at arm's length. Dozens of strangers surrounded us. Her sparkling eyes scanned my face, reading my expression. "Long flight, huh?"

I knew she was reading more than the effects of jet lag in my bleary eyes.

"Yes. Long. How was your flight?"

"Not bad. You okay?"

"Yeah, I'm good." I looked away, digging into my shoulder bag. "I was wondering, though, are we in the right line?"

"Yep. Direct to Nairobi."

I pulled out my phone and clicked on my boarding pass. "The sign for this line says first class."

"That's right," she said. "I told you, didn't I? First class is the only way my mother-in-law will agree to go anywhere. And since the tickets were transferred to us, we get to act like posh ladies."

I took a deep breath, feeling a more natural smile resting on my lips. "I don't think I've ever had to act posh before."

She grinned. "First time for a lot of things on this trip. For both of us."

21

In that moment, I stopped looking over my shoulder at all the uncertainties I'd left behind at home. I suddenly thought of the biblical account of Lot's wife, who looked back and turned into a pillar of salt. I didn't want to get stuck in what was behind. I wanted to look to what was ahead. Lots of hope. Many possibilities. With the companionship of Lily and the invitation to act like a posh lady in front of me, I set my gaze on Africa and all her welcome unknowns.

Twenty minutes later we were nestled into side-by-side leather reclining seats, being offered our choice of beverages and checking out all the swag in blue clutch bags handed to us. We found plush socks, satin eye masks, toothbrushes with coconut toothpaste, earplugs, and hand lotion. The blanket and pillow on our seats, like all the other items, had the airline logo prominently displayed.

"This is nothing like my last flight." I lowered my voice, even though I doubted anyone could hear me. The few scattered passengers around us were partially hidden in their own comfy cloisters.

"This is nothing like my last flight either," Lily said. "When I had to change our trip and move it up a few days so we could see my aunt and uncle, the travel agent had to adjust the existing tickets. This flight wasn't confirmed in first class until a few days ago. That's probably why I didn't tell you earlier. I know you hate surprises. I'm sure I forgot to mention it in the last-minute rush."

"Well, this"—I motioned to the luxury around us—"is the best sort of surprise. This will feel like a dream when we reach the village where your aunt lives."

"It's not a village. Did you read all the info in my long email? They live at a conference center. Again, sorry for my lack of communication. I had so much on my mind the last week and a half."

"I did too. As a matter of fact, Lily, I—"

"Here, I have the info on where they live. I should have sent this to you."

Lily turned her phone screen to me, and I read the entry on her detailed itinerary. I'd forwarded a copy to Danny so he'd know where I was at all times, but I hadn't read through the pages. Lily's phone said, *Jim and Cheryl Lorenzo, Brockhurst Conference Center, Limuru, Kenya.*

My heart gave a flutter, and I looked at Lily with my eyes wide. "Brockhurst? We're going to Brockhurst? This is the camp I applied to go to."

Lily looked confused.

"Right after you got married, I sent my application for kitchen staff, and then my mom found out about the publishing internship in Colorado, and that won over the six-month commitment at Brockhurst."

"How can you remember things like that from twenty years ago? That's crazy if it really is the same place."

"It is. How long have your aunt and uncle been there?"

"I don't know. I've never met them. They've been in Africa their whole married life. My dad insisted we add on the extra few days to stay with them."

I leaned against the comfy headrest as the plane took off. My arms felt tingly, as if I'd just rinsed them in cool water. Enveloping me was more than the sensation of effortlessly rising into the air. After living with a sense of being in a free fall for the past few weeks, I now felt I was being lifted. Something more than a random invitation to go on an extravagant vacation was in motion. I felt seen. God had not forgotten me or placed me aside. The tenderness of that hope made my eyes tear up.

"Sorry I don't remember you applying to go to Brockhurst," Lily said once the plane leveled to cruising altitude.

23

"Or that I had relatives there. All I could think about during that time in my life was Tim."

"I know."

She nudged me playfully. "Hey, maybe they'll let you wash some dishes while we're there."

I grinned. Somehow the thought of washing dishes at Brockhurst made me happy. It was silly, I know. But it would be the completion of a possibility I'd timidly investigated long ago.

The slender flight attendant leaned into our seats and asked if we'd like to see the brunch menu. The variety amazed us. Belgian waffles with berries, omelets made to order, full English breakfast, pastries, fresh fruit, smoothies, and a selection of teas and espresso drinks.

"How can they prepare food like this on a plane?" I asked. "Or is it all premade?"

"I've heard," said Lily, "that some airlines have onboard chefs."

"You're kidding."

"So? What are you going to have?"

Both of us ordered the featured special: poached eggs on a croissant with Genoa salami and arugula, topped with pineapple cilantro salsa. I opted for the Assam tea with milk and a small strawberry smoothie. Lily asked for a cappuccino with extra foam.

"You know who would go crazy over all this?" Lily asked. "My boys."

"Really?"

"I know Tyler and Noah come across like a couple of jocks who don't care about much more than the next game. But their grandfather likes to spoil them, and they've acquired a taste for what my mother-in-law calls 'the finer things in life.'"

24

I lifted my glass and gave the last sip of my "welcome aboard" ginger ale a swish. "To the finer things in life."

"Yes," Lily said.

We took turns settling in before our meal came. That included trips to the shockingly large restroom that was bigger than the downstairs half bath in my first condo. Lily had already changed from her shoes to our complimentary socks when I returned to our seats. She had the sleeping mask pushed up, holding her wispy hair off her forehead, the blanket was over her legs, and the pillow rested against the closed window. I copied her with the socks and blanket and felt positively cozy.

"I believe I would make a very good rich person," she said. "Don't you think I was made to live this lifestyle every day?" She leisurely tugged the mask over her eyes and reclined her seat.

"Absolutely. You're a natural. The only problem is that you will never be able to go back to flying economy again. You'll always be leaning into the aisle trying to catch a glimpse of what's going on with the posh people up front."

"True," Lily murmured. "So true."

She probably would have drifted off to sleep if our meals hadn't arrived on a cart with a touch of flair. Our attendant used tongs to lift rolled-up steaming washcloths from a silver platter and offered one to each of us. They smelled slightly of lemongrass, and the warmth felt so good on my hands, I rubbed the back of my neck and under my chin before placing it on the small, empty tray extended to us. I hoped my mini washup wasn't a first-class faux pas.

Another attendant then placed cloth napkins on our laps and presented our beautifully plated meals. I felt like laughing at the luxury of it all.

We ate every bite of the delicious food and were soon

treated to another lovely presentation. Our beverages were a course in themselves. My loose tea came in a silver teapot, poured through a silver strainer. The milk came in a matching silver creamer, and I was offered four varieties of sweetener.

Lily closed her eyes after taking her first sip of cappuccino. With a contented smile she whispered, "Fernweh."

I smiled. Not only because she was evoking the word that had enchanted me so long ago, but also because when she lowered her cup, a fringe of foam clung to her upper lip. I pointed and she daintily tapped her mouth with her napkin.

"This plane," she said. "These seats. This is the most exotic faraway place I have ever been. I will spend the rest of my life longing for this plane. Not the destination of the flight. Just the flight itself, right here, in this seat, with this perfect cappuccino."

"Fernweh," I repeated, lifting my china cup and gently tapping the side of her cup.

We remained in a state of mellow bliss for the next half hour, content to comment on the flavor of the salsa on our eggs and speculate what the fabric blend was in our blankets. We were so relaxed.

However, my earlier thoughts tugged at me. I needed to tell Lily everything I'd kept from her, and I needed to do so before we arrived in Nairobi and were enveloped into the world of her aunt and uncle. I didn't know how much privacy we'd have then, or for the rest of the trip.

I leaned closer. "Lily, I need to tell you something."

"Let me guess." She summoned her best *Downton Abbey* accent. "You'd like for me to ring the attendant so she can prepare your baaath."

I laughed. Maybe this wasn't the right moment. Our flight was more than eight hours. Did I really want to ruin the delight of our opulent experience?

"Hold that thought." Lily raised her hand to catch the flight attendant's attention. "Could you show me how we can watch a movie? I saw in the program menu that you have *Out of Africa*." Grinning at me, Lily added, "Perfect choice, don't you think?"

With a few clicks, the attendant had the Meryl Streep and Robert Redford classic up on both our screens, ready for us to put on our noise-canceling headphones and hit play.

"This is perfect," Lily said with a contented sigh. "First, tell me what you were going to say, and we can watch this together."

I hesitated. She looked so happy. I felt so happy. Why ruin this moment?

I put on my headphones. "I'll tell you later."

There is no better mirror than a best friend.

African proverb

As our plane began its descent into Nairobi, I leaned closer to Lily, and together we watched for lights to appear below in the darkness.

"Weren't you going to tell me something before the movie?" she asked. "Or did we cover it when we were looking at the itinerary?"

After watching *Out of Africa*, we discussed the movie, and that led to talking about what we expected of our trip and reviewing the itinerary that I had only briefly glanced at. Then the flight attendants served us fancy snacks and beverages, which were followed by naps that came on us both like heavy cloud cover.

I almost forgot I had another life before this posh one in the cushy reclining seats. The time went by too quickly.

"Well, I . . ." I couldn't think how to ease into my news.

Lily reached for my arm. "Are you pregnant?"

"No!"

"Well, it's a possibility." Lily still looked hopeful.

"Yes, but I'm not pregnant." I drew in a breath. "I'm unemployed."

"What do you mean?" She had a half grin as if trying to understand a joke I'd just made.

"I lost my job. I was let go."

Her eyebrows caved in. "Are you serious?"

I nodded and was relieved that I wasn't tearing up or feeling the gut punch I'd anticipated since my first attempt to tell her hours ago.

"What happened? When?"

"Three weeks ago."

"Three weeks! Why didn't you tell me?"

"I should have. I know. I'm sorry I didn't. So much was happening. Every time you and I talked, we had trip details to discuss. I kept my news out of our conversations because I didn't want to spoil this. I wanted to feel like I had something to look forward to and that one person in my life wasn't feeling sorry for me. That probably sounds pathetic and selfish, but I wanted someone to talk to me about happy things, and that person was you."

"Fern, I want to talk about happy things. But you can tell me sad things too."

"I know. It became harder to say anything the longer I hesitated."

"I understand. No need to apologize." She reached over and gave my hand a squeeze.

I felt I should keep explaining. She would ask eventually, so rather than just tell her I'd been wounded, I might as well pull the Band-Aid off all the way.

"Our publishing house was acquired by a New York house,

29

and my position became redundant. I found out when I asked about vacation time for this trip."

Lily grabbed my arm again. "Is that why they let you go?"

"No, my boss was planning to tell me when she announced the news to everyone the next week, but I sort of forced her hand. I'm grateful now that I knew right away because I had a little more time to prepare my authors before turning their books over to the new senior editor."

"Oh, Fern, I can't imagine how difficult those conversations must have been. You love your authors."

"I know. I felt like I was abandoning them. One author is in the middle of a complicated rewrite of her second novel. She's kind of lost. After I told her I had to turn her over to another editor, I went down to my car and sobbed."

I could see tears forming in Lily's eyes. I didn't need words of comfort from her. The response from her heart was all over her face. She exhaled slowly. "I'm sorry I wasn't there for you."

"Lily, don't say that. You're here now. We're here now. Fresh start. New chapter. That's how I feel about this trip. I have no idea what I'm going to do after I go home, but for now, I want to be fully here."

Lily gently leaned her head on my shoulder. I rested my cheek against her hair and let out a long, slow breath. The moment exemplified the essence of our friendship. Tender hearts, side by side. Few words needed.

She lifted her head. "What did Danny say?"

A clear image filled my thoughts. Twenty hours ago, my husband was holding my face in his large hands and kissing me goodbye at the airport.

"Danny said, 'Aslan is on the move.'"

Lily grinned. "Nice analogy since we'll hopefully be seeing a real lion or two in a few days."

We felt the bump of the wheels hitting the tarmac as the plane rolled to our gate. Our view outside looked like any other large airport, lit up and alive with taxiing planes and cargo trucks.

Lily gave my arm one last squeeze before unbuckling her seat belt. "Please know that we can talk about this or not talk about it as much as you want. Okay? I'm here for you."

The concerned expression in her gray eyes was comforting. I knew I wouldn't need to explain if I had to find a place to have a good sob. I hoped that wouldn't happen. Grief and confusion had not been invited on this trip, and they were not welcome as stowaways.

We gathered our belongings, and Lily patted her headrest before getting up. "Goodbye, dear foreign land of comfort. I will dream of you on every flight I take for the rest of my life."

Her charming farewell put a smile on my face.

"I didn't ask you," she said as I reached into the overhead compartment to pull out our carry-on suitcases. "But did you have any trouble fitting everything into your wheelie?"

"Not really. Although I left a bunch of things on the chair in our bedroom. I hope I don't wish I had them. What about you?"

"I liked the challenge of traveling this light," Lily said. "We'll see if this was a good idea."

I hoped the "good idea" was referring to the traveling light part of this adventure and not the adventure itself.

An unexpected wave of eagerness followed by a strong sense of hesitancy came over me as we made our way to customs amid the crush of travelers funneling into jagged waiting lines. Our emergence from the bubble of first class into a swirl of unfamiliar languages, people, sights, and sounds was jolting. I felt glaringly White and out of place. I spotted a dozen other Caucasians as we moved through the terminal, but for the most part, this was a hub for Africans of every shade, size, and clothing style. I was mesmerized by it all. At least English was one of the languages used on the terminal signs. And thankfully customs went quickly since we hadn't checked baggage.

The local time was almost 10:00 p.m. when we stepped outside into the mildly humid night. The number of travelers and the backup of cars jockeying for position by the curb surprised me. Nairobi wasn't the remote, slow-paced, distant land I'd imagined it would be. The barrage to the senses was thrilling and jarring at the same time.

"We're supposed to wait here." Lily checked her phone. "Our driver from the tour company is named Wanja. She will be in a white van that has the name of the tour company on the side."

We tried to spot the van in the tangled cluster of cars, but the multiple headlights made it difficult to see. Some drivers honked repeatedly while others had their windows up and seemed to navigate the mob unbothered by the possibility of a sideswipe from another vehicle.

A couple standing beside us waved at a small blue car that edged into a precariously angled position. That blocked other cars from pulling away from the curb and incited more honking.

Lily and I watched as four enthusiastic children bounded from the back seat, followed by an older man who exited the driver's seat. A woman with a covering over her head remained in the front passenger seat.

The couple was ecstatically welcomed in a language I guessed to be Swahili. They were all talking at once as the older man shoved one of their large suitcases into the small trunk. The second suitcase and a plastic bin were hoisted onto the roof, where a thin rope was tossed over the top. I tried not to stare as both men removed their belts and hastily secured the cargo. The couple and the four children wedged into the back seat and closed the doors.

As the car drove away, all four adults held their arms outside the open windows, gripping the ends of the belts and rope, ambitiously holding the suitcase and bin in place.

"We're definitely not in Kansas anymore," I said.

"I hope they don't have far to go," Lily said.

"'If you want to go fast, go alone. If you want to go far, go together.'"

Lily looked at me. "Did you just make that up?"

"No. Haven't you heard that before? It's a well-known African saying."

"Where did you hear it?"

"I read it in a book years ago. I've heard it a dozen times since then. It's probably going to be my only cultural contribution to our trip, so there you go."

A set of headlights flashed in our direction.

"Do you think that's her?" Lily waved an arm over her head. I'd forgotten how she did that. She'd done it at summer camp and again when she spotted me at Heathrow. She would have made a good cheerleader.

A small white van with the tour company name on the side cut through the stream of cars and stopped at the curb about twenty feet away from where we were standing. A young-looking African woman got out and opened the side door, greeting us with a quick hello. We hopped in and pulled our suitcases behind us.

She looked back at the curb. "Is that your only luggage?"

"Yes," we answered in unison.

"What a surprise." Wanja pulled the door closed. Before

she scooted back to the driver's seat on the right side of the van, her face caught the light from the terminal just right, illuminating her smooth skin. I thought she was beautiful. Her hair was a cascade of long, thin, twisted braids that began at the crown of her head and flowed over her shoulders.

She expertly navigated her way out of the airport while Lily and I quietly fixed our eyes, as Wanja did, on the road ahead. The drivers around us seemed to follow a different set of traffic rules than any I'd ever seen before. The lines on the asphalt seemed to be merely suggestions for traffic lanes. And why use your turn signal when you can simply honk to announce that you're making some sort of unknown turn?

I held my breath and considered reaching over and holding Lily's hand.

Several minutes after we exited the airport, Wanja glanced at us in the rearview mirror. "Welcome to Nairobi! I didn't say that yet, did I?"

Her accent sounded slightly British but was distinct in its own way. She seemed more at ease now that we had merged into a straight line of traffic and were moving along slowly. What felt disorienting to me was that she was in the "passenger" seat, and the oncoming cars were on the right side of the road.

"I should greet you with 'Jambo!'" Wanja said. "Most visitors like to hear a bit of Swahili on our tours. But we're not on a tour yet, and your luggage tells me you are not typical visitors. Have you been to Kenya before?"

"No," Lily said.

"Almost," I added. "A long time ago."

"Why didn't you come then?"

"I got married," Lily said. "It changed everything."

"No!" Wanja's rebuttal came out in a high voice. "Please,

do not tell me getting married changes everything. I am getting married in forty-three days."

"Congratulations," I said quickly.

"Thank you. We have waited a long time for him to finish uni. I am finally believing it will happen."

"Uni?" Lily repeated.

"University. He is going to be a geologist."

"I wish you all the best," Lily said.

"Asante." With another glance at us in the mirror, Wanja asked, "Which one of you has family in Limuru? At Brockhurst."

"That's me. My aunt and uncle live there," Lily said. "Jim and Cheryl Lorenzo."

Wanja's voice elevated again. "Lovely people. My grandmother works at Brockhurst. I've met most of the permanent residents. Cheryl is one of my favorites."

"Did you say your grandmother works there?" Lily asked.

"Yes. She is only fifty-eight. She married young, and my mother married young. I am the one breaking the tradition by marrying when I am so old." Wanja laughed. "You might meet my grandmother. She is the queen of the kitchen."

"Well, that's convenient," Lily said. "Because if she needs help washing dishes, I happen to know someone."

"Oh? Is that so? I will say it again. You two are not typical visitors."

Lily leaned over and gave me a cheerful nudge as if to remind me of my missed opportunity to serve at the sink years ago. I think she also liked hearing that we weren't typical. Her arm happened to touch the spot where I'd gotten my immunizations, and I winced because it was still tender.

"I have washed many dishes at Brockhurst," Wanja said. "You would both be welcome in the kingdom of my grandmother's kitchen anytime, with or without an apron."

Lily asked more questions about the conference center, Wanja's family, and her hometown. We learned that we were heading "up-country." Limuru was nestled in a fertile farming area where Wanja's family had worked the tea fields for generations. As a tea aficionado, I was thrilled to know we would be staying near tea fields.

"Do you think we could see a tea field while we're there?" I asked. "Could we go on a tour?"

Wanja paused before answering. It struck me that my request must have sounded as silly as someone visiting where I grew up and asking if they could sign up for a tour to see a cornfield. I would have laughed at such a question.

Instead of laughing, Wanja said, "There is a tea farm about an hour away that I believe still offers tours on weekends. But you will be on your safari then."

I didn't want to admit that I'd be more interested in seeing a tea field than a wildebeest.

"You don't need a tour for the fields in Limuru," Wanja added. "Find someone at Brockhurst who will go on a walk with you. It's only a few kilometers from the conference center."

We hit a bump in the road that jolted us and made me wish I'd taken the seat up front with Wanja. It was dark on the uphill road except for the headlights of the oncoming cars. The air through the open front window felt cooler than what had greeted us at the airport. We continued to head uphill, and I felt as if my ears were closing. I tried yawning, and that helped.

"Your hair is beautiful," Lily said. "It's probably rude to ask, but you didn't do it yourself, did you?"

"Oh, no. I could not do this myself. I sat in a chair at my sister's salon for half a day while she did the weaving. Only about five inches of this is my real hair. I am having it taken out before the wedding, but I have not decided yet what I want to do with my hair for the ceremony. It depends on my sister. She will have an opinion, you see."

"It's really pretty," Lily added.

"Asante sana. That is Swahili for 'thank you very much.'"

"How do we say 'you're welcome'?" I asked.

"Karibu."

"Karibu," Lily and I repeated in unison.

"Well done. But do not worry. Everyone speaks English. Colonization, you know."

We hit two more sizable bumps in the road. Alongside us flowed a steady stream of buses, trucks, and cars. For this hour of the night, it seemed like a lot of activity. I was glad Wanja had picked us up. At one point Lily had said she could rent a car to drive up to Brockhurst and then back to Nairobi to catch our short flight to the Masai Mara for our safari. The tour agent had assured her that she did not want to drive, especially after such long flights and with the flow of traffic being opposite that of the US.

She was right. Driving this road at night, on the "wrong" side of the road, would have been a challenge.

"Thank you for picking us up and driving us to the conference center," I said. "Asante sana."

"Karibu," Wanja said with a laugh. "It is not a problem. I wanted to see my grandmother for a few days. I grew up in Limuru and have not been up-country for weeks. This is my last chance before the wedding." Her voice switched to a teasing tone as she added over her shoulder, "And once I'm married, I understand it will change everything."

I looked at Lily, expecting her to have a few friendly words of assurance for Wanja. Instead, she was staring out the window.

I leaned closer and saw that she was silently crying.

3

There is no moment of delight in any pilgrimage like the beginning of it, when the traveler is settled simply as to his destination, and commits himself to his unknown fate and all the anticipations of adventure before him.

Charles Dudley Warner

*W*e will get the key to your cottage from the guard," Wanja said as we approached the gated entrance of Brockhurst Conference Center. "Someone will come to your room in the morning and give you a proper welcome."

She leaned out her window as the security guard stepped out of his station and came over to greet her. They exchanged friendly banter that made it clear they knew each other.

I leaned close to Lily and whispered, "You okay?"

She nodded.

I tried to read her expression in the dim light and realized that the drawback of our long-distance friendship was our inability to read each other's body language due to so few face-to-face times together.

I almost went ahead and whispered, "Why were you crying earlier?"

It seemed best to curb my curiosity and concern. I'd ask her later. The emotional overload could be jet lag. I was sure feeling it. Or it could be something she had kept hidden from me the way I'd kept the news of my job loss hidden from her. I hoped we would be able to talk once the two of us were in our room.

The guard peered around Wanja and greeted us. "Cheryl and Jim look forward to seeing you tomorrow."

He grinned broadly and gave us a wave as Wanja drove onto the grounds of the conference center. It was too dark to see much around us when we parked and clambered out of the van. Lily and I pulled our suitcases behind us on a bumpy path to a row of attached cottages. I hoped the loud clacking of the wheels wasn't disturbing anyone who was trying to sleep in the other cottages.

"Yours is the one on the end." Wanja held out the key. "Would you like me to go in with you?"

"No, I'm sure we can take it from here," Lily said. "Asante sana."

I offered Wanja an informal, American-style side hug, which she exchanged for a real hug for me and then Lily. "I will see you on Friday, Suitcase Sisters."

Lily turned the key in the lock. We stepped into a dark room and felt the wall for a light switch. It toggled but no lights came on.

I reached into my shoulder bag and pulled out a small flashlight—Danny's goodbye gift when he dropped me off at the airport. He thought I should be prepared for anything and purchased an assortment of must-haves, including a global electric plug converter and sleeves for my credit card and passport that blocked potential identity scammers.

When he presented his array of travel gifts, I regret to admit I brushed them off and showed little appreciation for his precautions. He was right, though, about the flashlight. It was exactly what we needed right then and provided enough light for us to navigate around the twin beds. I tried to turn on the lamp on the nightstand. No success.

"Here." Lily reached for a small box of matches on the desk under the front window by the door. She lit the thick taper candle. Our room went from feeling like a mysterious obstacle course to a warm, enchanting cottage.

In the flickering light, we took in our surroundings. The wrought-iron bed frames curled into rounded loops on the ends. The bedspreads were a woven African design in earthy yellows and browns. The floor was made of large, rust-colored tiles, and the walls appeared to be a soft cream shade.

"Cold in here, isn't it?" Lily opened the door at the back of the room, which revealed an en suite bathroom. "This is nice. And guess what? We have a tub! I'm so glad we don't have to go outside to a shared toilet. This is a lot more comfortable than I expected."

"Do we have hot water?" I took the flashlight in with me as Lily tried the faucet.

"Nope."

"Maybe we will tomorrow. I like our room too. Do you care if I have the bed by the window?"

"No. Take it. See if extra blankets are in that dresser."

I opened two empty drawers before finding the prize in the bottom drawer. "Two more blankets. Heavy wool ones."

"Great! We are going to sleep well tonight," Lily predicted.

She was right. With only a few words between us, we readied our weary selves for bed and blew out the candle. The combination of the cool air and layers of heavy blankets worked their ministering grace. I asked if she wanted to talk a little about why she got teary in the car. She replied in a murmur, and I was glad she hadn't said yes. I would have had a hard time staying awake to listen.

I closed my eyes and whispered a prayer. I don't think I moved all night.

Morning gentled its way into our room with welcome light but not much warmth. Lily turned in my direction as I reached for my glasses on the nightstand.

She whispered, "Good morning."

My raspy voice echoed her greeting as she slipped out of bed with a blanket wrapped around her shoulders and padded into the bathroom. I rolled under the warm covers and peered out the window. That was when I noticed the dark green curtains we could have slid across the black rod for more privacy and more warmth last night.

What captured my attention was the large window with its wide windowsill. The twelve square panes of glass lined up like a see-through checkerboard and reminded me of an old English cottage. Beyond our front window was a tree, and in that tree, something was moving.

A flash of black fur leaped to a higher branch. I sat up and tried to get a better view.

A chittering sound came from the animal, and then the noise turned into a squawking cry. I spotted three more furry companions scurrying up to the higher limbs.

"Monkeys! Lily, you must come see this! We have monkeys right outside our window!"

"What are they doing?" she asked through the closed bathroom door.

"It looks like they're about to fight over whatever it is they're picking off the tree."

"Don't open the front door," she said.

"I won't. Besides, we have a clear view of them out the window. I think they're loquats."

"I thought you said they were monkeys."

I laughed. "No, the fruit. I think the fruit they're picking are loquats. They're small and orange. About the size of a jumbo green olive."

The monkeys broke into loud shrieks, and all four of them suddenly fled, jumping onto the roof, where the sound of them scrambling indicated they were heading to the back side of our building.

"Oh, you missed them."

Lily let out a shriek. She burst into the room, pulling the bathroom door shut behind her. "Oh no I didn't. One of those cheeky monkeys was staring at me through the bathroom window! I opened the shade to get more light. Big mistake."

I started to laugh but was interrupted by a gentle knock on our door.

"Should we open it?" Lily whispered.

"I don't think monkeys know how to knock, so yes."

Lily cautiously opened the door. A slender woman with short, silver-gray hair entered, carrying a tray with three ceramic mugs and a plate of toast. She smiled calmly, looking at Lily and then at me. Her gaze returned to Lily.

"I'm your aunt Cheryl."

"Oh, hi! Hello!" Lily turned to me. "This is Fern. Thanks so much for letting us stay here."

"Of course. We're glad it worked out. I heard a scream as I was walking up. Is everything okay?"

"I saw a monkey," Lily said. "Rookie tourist. Didn't expect

to have a squishy little face looking at me through the bath-room window."

Cheryl chuckled. "They saw me coming and fled."

"We could hear them running across the roof," I said.

"They won't bother you. Here. I brought you some tea." She placed two of the mugs on the bedside table, then rested the tray with the third mug on the desk before pulling out the chair and settling in to join us. "It's masala chai. A favorite around here."

I reached for my mug and drew in the sweet fragrance of cinnamon, nutmeg, and cardamom. A perfect layer of foamed milk floated on the top. My first sip was golden. Like honey, slowly flowing all the way to my toes and instantly warming me.

"This is so good. Thank you."

"It's chilly in here, isn't it?" Cheryl reached over to try the light switch. "Did you have electricity when you arrived last night?"

"No. We were fine, though," Lily said as she crawled back into bed. "Thanks to these blankets."

"I will ask someone to check on that for you. You'll want warm water for showers."

"Yes, please," Lily said.

I nodded and sipped the blessed chai. Cheryl handed me the plate of what looked like Melba toast with jam—loquat jam, perhaps? Our easy conversation included updates on Lily's family and our enthusiastic recounting of how we practiced being posh ladies in first class from Heathrow to Nairobi.

Cheryl gave us an overview of where things were located on the conference grounds and where to go for meals. Before leaving, she asked if she could do anything else for us.

I didn't hesitate to tell her I hoped to visit a tea field.

"Wanja said I should ask if anyone is going there and see if I could tag along."

"Sure. I'll let you know. Someone is always headed that way. Is there anything I can get for you now? Do you need more food?"

"We're good," I answered for both of us.

"I'll check on having your hot water and electricity turned on." Before Cheryl left, she walked over to each of us and said, "I'm glad you're here." Then she gave us a motherly kiss on the forehead. I felt as if I was being blessed.

"She's wonderful," I told Lily after Cheryl closed the door behind her. "So rugged and yet so tender."

"I had no idea she would be like that. I don't know what I expected, but I love her."

"I know. Me too."

Lily added, "Did I tell you she was attacked years ago when they were at a different location in Africa? I don't remember where. She and her son were stabbed."

My heart clenched. "That's awful. It seems like she's okay. Was her son okay?"

"Yes, he's fine. He's about our age. She almost didn't pull through, but look at her now. She's one tough and tender woman."

I slid all the way under my blankets, trying to warm my skin as much as my insides had been warmed from the masala chai.

"In all our planning, we never talked about the possibilities of anything terrible happening to us here in Africa, did we?" I asked.

"That's because terrible things can happen anywhere. I don't think we need to be especially frightened of anything here."

"Except maybe the little monkeys in the bathroom window?" I teased.

"Hey, he startled me. You would have screamed too. Did you get a good look at them? They have black fur everywhere except for a white circle around their faces. And those beady little eyes." Lily made a sinister-looking face.

"Lily, did it ever occur to you that neither of us has a great affection for animals?"

She paused, considering my question. The cute expression on her face said it all.

I laughed. "You and I are the two least likely women who would ever go on a safari or go anywhere expressly for the purpose of being around animals. Especially wild ones."

"True." Lily rolled into a round of laughter that reminded me of our many late-night muffled giggle-fests in Costa Rica.

"Promise me you won't shriek again when you see your first zebra," I said.

"I promise. Although you might hear a happy squeal when I see my first giraffe. That's the one African animal I hope we see up close. I have a fondness for giraffes."

"Good to know."

"What's your squeal-worthy animal?" Lily asked.

I thought for a moment. "Maybe a baby elephant."

"Good choice. Have you ever seen videos of them playing in the water?"

"Yes. So cute. And when they try to run to keep up with their mama and their ears start flapping. I mean, come on. It does not get any cuter than that."

Lily burrowed deeper into her layers of blankets. "Weren't you around a lot of animals when you were growing up?"

"Not elephants," I said wryly.

45

"No, I mean farm animals."

"We had chickens. And a dog. Did you ever hear me talk about Roger? He was a good dog. No barnyard animals or cows."

"What about the chickens?"

"What about them?"

"Were they like pets?"

"No. Well, my mom had a favorite one when I was in high school. She named her Maud. None of the others ever had names. We fed them, and they gave us eggs."

"Did you ever eat them?"

"Of course."

Lily made a squeamish face, and I laughed. "You really are a city girl, aren't you?"

Suddenly the overhead light turned on.

"Hooray! Let's hope the hot water is next." I slid my bare legs out from under the blankets. Lily and I had both opted to sleep in our undies and camisoles late last night so we could get into bed as quickly as possible without unpacking. The time had come to open my suitcase.

I lifted it to the end of my bed and carefully ran the zipper around the perimeter. I expected my suitcase to pop open, and I'd have to stand back as all my squished clothes catapulted across the room.

Instead, everything was in the same condensed order I'd packed it in a day ago. Or was that two days ago?

"I need to try to call Danny or see if my added phone service works for texting. I tried it when we were driving up here last night, but it didn't go through. Have you tried to call home yet?"

Lily murmured something, but her eyes were closed. She looked like she was about to enjoy a second sleep.

Hobbits can enjoy second breakfasts. Why couldn't Lily enjoy a second sleep?

She was still snoozing when I was ready to leave our room to go exploring. The water wasn't warm yet, so I settled for a quick washup in the sink and inserted my contacts. As I wove my hair into a single braid, I was glad I'd kept it long. In moments like this, I could get by with a braid or by twisting it up on the top of my head. Hopefully I'd be able to take a nice, hot shower that night, and I'd wash it then.

I looped my shoulder bag over my arm, left a note for Lily propped against the candle on the desk, and closed the door softly.

A lush, green, fragrant world unfolded before me.

I had to stop and draw in a deep breath. This moment was not among the first impressions of Africa I had carried in my imagination. With second sleeps and second breakfasts still on my mind, I felt as if I'd stepped into the Hobbits' Shire.

I trekked to the main lodge, taking my time so I could examine the abundant flowering plants. I recognized a few that I'd seen when Danny and I were on our honeymoon in Laguna Beach, California. I loved the lily of the Nile plants that lined the walkway. They reminded me of sparklers. From the tops of their long, green stems, flecks of bright blue flowers exploded.

On both sides of me, verdant grass stretched out. I paused to listen to the birds in the large sheltering trees. They sang unfamiliar songs, which made the grounds feel even more mythical. A cool breeze swirled through the outstretched branches of the tree I stood under, causing the pale green leaves to shimmy until two of the teardrop-shaped leaves floated down to greet me.

It was enchanting. All of it. I felt as if I'd stepped into a storybook.

The lodge came into view, looking like a massive, firmly planted manor in the English countryside. The long building had windows across the front and a pitched, faded red roof.

The image reminded me that years ago, when I'd found the original website for Brockhurst, this main building was the photo on the landing page. A short history of the grounds was included under the photo. If I remembered correctly, the first wing of the lodge had been built a century ago to accommodate wealthy British and Americans who came to Kenya to hunt exotic animals.

Another memory came to me of how, after learning about the lodge, I'd gone to my hometown library and found a battered copy of *Green Hills of Africa*, Hemingway's classic account of his safari after World War II. He went into fascinating descriptions of the local people and animals, as well as gruesome details of the hunts. I skipped most of the descriptions of the killing and skinning of the wild animals.

Hemingway and his wife, along with several privileged men, spent three months in the Serengeti, living in tents and being served by their guides. They stalked the finest specimens of lions, leopards, elephants, kudu, and rhinoceroses. The purpose was to have rugs made from the animal skins. They also had the creatures' heads stuffed to be mounted on the walls of the hunters' luxurious homes.

Now that I was standing on Kenyan soil, facing a place where men like Hemingway had once lodged with their bagged trophies, I felt sorrow for this startlingly beautiful corner of the world. The struggle for domination was ancient and global, and yet I wished this Eden had been spared from exploiters.

With a deep breath of crisp mountain air filling my lungs, I walked toward the front doors of the lodge, realizing that I, too, was here seeking a wild and memorable experience. Did that not make me a hunter as well? I figured it helped that I would only be shooting photos of the animals on my safari.

There are no foreign lands. It is the traveler only who is foreign.

Robert Louis Stevenson

When Lily sent me details about this trip, I anticipated that everything we encountered would feel foreign and unknown. I thought it would seem as if we'd landed on a distant planet. Yet, ever since we arrived, I kept thinking that people and places are similar the world over.

The truth was, Lily and I were the foreigners. We were the ones who were different and unknown.

As I took the stairs to the top floor of the Brockhurst lodge, I felt as if I was being silently welcomed not only into this building but also into the flow of life at the conference center. Tables lined the perimeter of the large meeting area. They were positioned under the tall, wraparound windows where guests were sipping coffee, their heads bent close in conversation.

I settled at an open table and gazed at the captivating view of the lush greens of the lawn and the forest beyond the cottages. Pulling my journal from my shoulder bag, I prepared to do what I love in moments like this. I was going to write out a prayer.

For most of my life I'd filled journals this way. When I was in high school, my mom had taken note of my habit and asked what I was writing all the time in my notebooks. A novel, perhaps?

When I told her it was "only prayers," she shook her head in hearty disagreement.

"Prayers are never just prayers. What you are doing is creating a collection of love letters to Jesus."

I think her poetic interpretation motivated me to keep buying journals and filling them with every whim and wonder as well as details of the complex heartaches I experienced as the years went on.

No one else ever read my journals. I occasionally pulled one off the shelf and reread parts from certain years so I could remember what was happening in my life at that time. Whenever I skimmed the pages, I was humbled to read my sincere cries to the Lord and know how God had answered those prayers. Often, I'd add a note in the margin with the date and a summary of how God answered that prayer.

Five years ago, right before I met Danny, I'd written one of many prayers asking God for a husband. My thirty-three-year-old heart was weary from waiting and wondering. My prayer on that winter night got right to the point.

Father God, I boldly ask You for a husband. I know I've asked this many times. I know You hear me. Please answer. Please send me a godly man soon. Amen.

Two days later I met Danny at a church Christmas concert. I hated going to things like that by myself and almost stayed home.

I was instantly drawn to Danny's eyes when he asked if the two seats next to me were taken. The look he gave me with his sincere and alluring eyes warmed me. I kept glancing at his thick black eyelashes. He glanced at me too. Months later he told me my smile was like a magnet to him. I told him he should thank my father for agreeing with my mother that I needed braces. I was the only one of his five daughters who had her teeth straightened, and the extra expense came during a lean year of farming.

At the Christmas concert I couldn't help but notice the disrespectful teen boy who was with Danny. They didn't look related. I hid my surprise when Danny introduced himself and Micah afterward, calling the boy his son. Micah made it clear he didn't want to be there.

I appreciated Danny's attempt at small talk, and my heart did a little flutter when he courteously walked with me to the parking lot in the snow. I'd taken note that he wasn't wearing a wedding ring. I guessed that he'd checked my empty finger as well. I started to think about what I'd say if he happened to ask me to meet him for coffee sometime.

But when Micah continued to be rude while we were trying to talk, I thought, *Nope. Not the answer to my prayer. I would never take on that combo.*

I drove home thinking I should be more specific the next time I prayed about a husband. I needed to remind God of my must-have list. Surely He remembered the fixed image I'd carried ever since I was twelve and read a novel about a blond surfer boy with mesmerizing blue eyes.

Danny was of Latino heritage. He had black hair, not blond. His eyes were brown, not blue. He didn't surf. He smelled good, though. Like warm spices baked in a pie. I felt comfortable around him. Calm. And his eyes were gorgeous.

Danny's son was Black and appeared to have no affection or even respect for Danny. I was curious about their story when I picked up a hint that Micah's birth mom was out of the picture and possibly had passed away. But how had Micah come to be Danny's "son"? That night I decided the details didn't matter. Danny was not for me.

Jesus must have been smiling that night. How many times had God answered my prayers with His exact and best answers, even though I'd been so sure I had a better plan for what I wanted and needed?

Thoughts of Danny and our unexpected love story made me smile as I gazed out the window at the lush grounds of Brockhurst. I reached for my phone and sent both a text and an email to the wonderful man God had sent to me. I was still muddled on the time difference, so it seemed best to wait until I heard from him before attempting a call.

A middle-aged man with what sounded like a French accent paused at my table. He politely asked if I was Cheryl's niece from America.

"No, that's Lily. I'm her friend, Fern."

He placed his hand on his chest. "Philippe. Pleasure to meet you. I understand she wants to walk in the tea field this afternoon."

"That was me. Yes, I'd love to see them."

"I'm going with a colleague after lunch today. You are welcome to join us. We will meet at the entrance downstairs."

"Thank you. I'll be there."

He nodded, took a seat at a table across the room, and opened his laptop.

Smoothing back the first page in my brand-new journal, I put my pen to the crisp white paper and began my first letter to Jesus from Africa. It started out rather mushy. I searched my internal dictionary to find the right words to tell Him how much I appreciated the way He had showered me with so many good things. Danny, Micah, a job I loved for sixteen years, this trip, Lily, and now a promised trek in the tea field. I ended the prayer by telling Jesus that I wanted to trust Him for whatever was next for me. I wanted to be at peace about the unknown.

Then, before closing my journal, I reread my expression of gratitude. My letter felt unfinished. I'd only written about half of what was embedded in my heart.

The other half, the part that had been stifled over the last three weeks, was still aching and bruised. The feelings over the loss of my beloved job had not yet been given a voice. I'd kept the pain inside for the past three weeks, where it was conveniently hidden in a thick haze.

In the same way that I'd held back from informing Lily of the major change in my life, I had held back from talking to God about it. He knew, of course. I just didn't know how to talk to Him about it yet without wanting to throw something.

I also didn't want any of my hurt feelings and jaded thoughts to mar this grand adventure. I wanted to be free. Danny and I had been through enough family therapy with Micah to know that the only way to move forward is to start dealing with the pain. The only way I knew how to do that was with words, and this seemed to be as good a time as any.

Part two of my letter to Jesus came pouring out. I wrote with my finger and thumb clenching the pen. The letters of each word were heavily etched in my journal.

Great God,

I know You already know this, but I'm angry. So angry. Deep down I feel betrayed. What happened to me was not fair. I put so much into my career. You know that. I gave my all. For years.

Where am I going to find an equal position considering where we live? I'm not, am I? Because there aren't any. I had my dream job, and now it has been ripped out from under me.

Even if another publisher offered me a job somewhere else, Danny won't want to move. His mom depends on him. We need to stay where we are for her. We're stuck. I'm stuck.

And I'm mad. Slow, white embers mad. I can't cry. I have no more tears. Only anger.

Why did this extravagant trip have to come on the heels of one of the worst experiences in my life? I don't want to feel this way.

It took me a while, pen still pinched between my fingers, gaze fixed on the green lawn outside, before I decided I didn't have anything more to say. The words were out. They could sit there undisturbed until I was ready to think about all this again. Right now, I wanted to ignore it all. I wanted to move about freely in this world. This other side of the world, where no one knew anything about my life or me. Except Lily. And she understood.

Closing my journal, I continued to stare out the window, watching the comings and goings of the people as well as the flitting birds that crossed the open grassy area.

To the right was a photo-worthy scene of an empty bench. The sturdy wooden bench was positioned just right under an old tree whose weighty branches seemed to curl above the seat in a half circle as if offering a comforting embrace to whoever sat beneath them.

Imagining that the bench and the tree were beckoning me, I went outside and rested there in silence for some time. My phone vibrated, and I saw that Danny had texted me. He said I should try calling.

"Hey!" His wonderful laugh filled my ear and rustled my heart. I knew he had tears in his eyes. He was such a softie it didn't take much to move him.

Tears filled my own eyes. They had been stored in a reservoir while I wrote in my journal and stared out the window at this tree. Now that I was positioned under the fixed embrace of the curved branches, hearing Danny's voice, a lock lifted and the tears were released.

"I miss you, mi conejita. How are you?"

It had been a while since he'd called me by his Spanish pet name. When we first started dating, he had called me a bunny. A conejita. That was because I always ordered salads. I knew everything was about to change in our relationship the first time he called me "mi conejita" because the added "mi" meant that I wasn't just a little bunny. I was *his* little bunny.

"I'm okay," I told him.

"You sound a little choked up."

"I am. I've been processing. But I'm okay. I'm good. It's beautiful here."

I told him about our luxurious flight, our stone cottage, the monkeys, and how our surroundings were like something out of an English storybook. As I spoke, the silent tears kept flowing, and I wiped them on my sleeve.

"There's a tea field nearby. I'm going there after lunch."

Danny chuckled. "I know that will be a highlight for you."

"Yes, it will. But what about you? How are you? How's Micah? How's your mom?"

"Good. We're all good. I miss you. But I'm glad you're there. Glad your phone service works."

We talked another five minutes as effortlessly as if this were an ordinary day and I'd called him at the high school where he'd been a head coach for the past fourteen years. Just hearing his voice soothed me, the same way his patient and kind words had brought me comfort over the past few weeks.

We said our "I love yous," and I leaned back on the bench with my eyes closed. During our conversation, a bird kept calling out "tee-oo, tee-oo, tee-oo" and then paused before repeating the triple cries. The unfamiliar call had been annoying during our chat, but now the cry had a rhythmic and calming effect on me.

My eyelids felt heavy, and I dozed off sitting under the leafy hug of the grandfather tree. I don't know how long I sat there, in a dreamless state of surrendered rest.

Cheryl's voice roused me. "You found our daughter-in-law's favorite spot."

I squinted to focus. Standing next to Cheryl was a distinguished-looking man with short white hair, a trim mustache, and a goatee. She introduced him as her husband, Jim. He and Cheryl looked like they fit well together. I'd seen couples like them before who have become so entwined for decades that they seemed to be a complementary reflection of each other in their posture, their expressions, and even their eye-to-eye height.

We chatted for a few minutes before we spotted Lily coming up the path. She waved her arm over her head, looking rested and ready to take on the day in her cute denim jacket, black jeans, and Tennessee boots.

"We're glad you're here, Lily." Jim gave her a broad smile. She slid next to him for a shy side hug for the uncle she was meeting for the first time.

Both Cheryl and Jim commented on her detailed leather cowboy boots. Jim teased that they could take the girl out of Nashville, but they couldn't take Nashville out of the girl.

"You got that right," Lily said with a grin. "Born and raised." Her short blond hair looked tousled. My guess was she'd taken a shower but due to the lack of a hair dryer had to resort to quick towel drying.

"Ready for lunch?" Jim asked.

We headed to the dining room, and I told Cheryl, "I hope your daughter-in-law doesn't mind sharing her favorite spot. I can't believe I fell asleep. It's such a comfortable bench."

"She wouldn't mind at all. She and our son and their three boys are in California doing fundraising for several months. I miss them and our grandboys more than I can say."

"Did they move to California permanently?"

"No. Only for a year. They're doing extensive fundraising for the ministry we work with here."

"I don't think Lily told me what you do."

"We organize volunteer service groups and equipment to dig wells that provide clean water in remote areas. A lot of people in the West don't realize how difficult it is for some people in Africa to acquire clean water. It changes everything when they have access to it. Health improves, use of resources can be multiplied since the women don't have to walk for hours carrying heavy buckets and jugs back to their villages. We offer a cup of cool water in Jesus' name."

I was familiar with ministries that did similar work. However, being at ground zero, so to speak, made the ministry feel larger than life. This hub was where the work was organized, and Cheryl, Jim, and their family were in the thick of it. I felt privileged to be around them.

Jim led the way up the stairs of the main building and

into the large dining room with its extensive buffet. My eyes feasted on the variety of food as Cheryl walked beside me and explained a few of the items to me. I chose from the gorgeous assortment of fruit and vegetables. Everything tasted freshly picked.

Lily and Jim were soon deep into a conversation about her family at the table. Cheryl leaned toward me. "Tell me about your family."

I gave her a quick summary, and the first question she asked was, "What college is your son going to in California?"

"Rancho Corona University. He's on a basketball scholarship. He settled in faster than we expected, and now he says he's never coming back to Colorado."

"That's good to hear," Cheryl said. "We have a lot of connections to Rancho Corona. My brother has been a professor there for many years. Our son and his wife met there. It's a wonderful school."

"That's right. I knew Lily had an uncle who taught at Rancho. He sent her a hoodie when she was in high school, and she wore it the summer she and I met in Costa Rica. I always thought I might want to go there. But I started interning in Colorado and went to school there while easing into my career."

I felt my throat tightening and almost added, "The career I used to have."

Instead, I quickly said, "We were glad Micah decided to attend there. He needed to find his place, and Rancho Corona seems to be the answer to many prayers."

"Is he your only child?"

"Yes. We've only been married for three years. My husband adopted Micah a few weeks before we met. Micah's actually my husband's nephew."

I paused before adding the additional details. I'd learned

how to condense them in a way that usually didn't invite a lot of questions. "Micah's mom wasn't involved in his life due to her drug addiction. She passed away when Micah was eight."

"That must have been very difficult for all of them," Cheryl said.

"Yes. But it got worse because that same year, Danny's father also died. I didn't know Danny yet. But I've heard lots from my mother-in-law about how Micah became too unruly for her during all that loss. That's when Danny pursued adopting him because Micah's birth father was never identified."

Cheryl leaned back. "That's a lot for a family to go through."

"It was. It's been a volatile situation ever since I met Danny. But things are much better now for all of us."

"Your husband sounds like an exceptional man."

"He is." I smiled and looked across the table at Lily. "If it weren't for your niece and her persistence, I'm embarrassed to say my relationship with Danny wouldn't have gotten very far. She kept telling me to give him a chance."

"Were you hesitant to get to know him?" Cheryl asked.

"Resistant is a better word for it. I thought it would be too much for me to commit to both Danny and Micah. It took months before my stubborn heart softened toward both of them."

"How old was Micah when you married?"

"Fifteen. The first year was terrible. Last year was difficult too. It's hard to believe how awful he was to both of us now that he's texting us from college saying he misses us. He's asking when we're going to go fly out to California to visit him. Danny and I never expected to hear those words."

"I love a good redemption story," Cheryl said.

"Well, if that's what it continues to be, then it's to Danny's credit, not mine. I mean, it's all because of God, of course. But I made a mess of a lot of things those first few years."

Lily turned to face us from across the table. Her softened expression made it clear she'd been listening. "Fern, the transformation in Micah is as much a result of your consistent love as it is due to Danny's persistence. The two of you together are gold. Pure gold. Micah is finally realizing that."

I felt my face warming. Lily knew every detail of our challenging marriage and my big failures as a stepmom. Her friendship had been the greatest gift to me during the hardest times.

Memories flashed through my thoughts of the days when I'd call her on the way to work and sob. She always had the right thing to say. She assured me we'd get to the place where we are now, just Danny and me in our own condo with plenty of time to start fresh and figure out what it means to be married without a belligerent teenager stirring havoc.

Lily pointed at me and then looked at Cheryl. "You may think I'm exaggerating, but I'm not. This woman is a gem. Her husband is a saint."

"High praise," Jim said.

"And well deserved," Lily said. "I never could have done what she did. That's one of the reasons I was excited about having the chance to come here. It's a reset for her in more ways than one. Whatever she does next will be a new beginning. A new life."

I was glad Lily didn't include that I was now unemployed. That was a different sort of soul wound, and one I didn't want to talk about.

"I'm glad you gave Danny a chance." Cheryl smiled at me.

Jim added, "I like hearing about a couple who didn't give up on a son like Micah or on each other. It's becoming rare these days."

I smiled at Lily across the table as a nonverbal way of saying thanks for her kind words and encouragement. At that moment I caught a glimpse of tears pooling in her eyes. She looked away, focusing on the few bites of food left on her plate, and caught a tear just as it formed.

Something was wrong. Really wrong. I was convinced of it now.

5

The language of friendship is not words, but meanings.

Henry David Thoreau

I tried to convince Lily to come with me on the walk to the tea field. She declined, saying she wanted to spend more time with her aunt and uncle.

I understood.

Tomorrow morning Wanja was coming to pick us up, so today was Lily's only chance to be with them. I remained concerned about her and the puzzling cause of her quickly dabbed-away tears. Whatever was bothering her had to be more than jet lag. I hoped Cheryl would have the right words to help Lily sort out what she was feeling. If not, we'd have plenty of time to talk in our room after dinner.

Even though I felt a little strange about going off with Philippe and his colleague, Viola, I was also excited.

Viola was shorter than Philippe and me and seemed to be quick stepping to keep up with our long strides. She wore a floppy hat over her dark hair, and her sunglasses covered half her face. I wondered if she had an aversion to the sun or perhaps expected the trail to be more exposed to the elements than it was. Most of the way we were shaded by tall trees.

We tromped along on a red-dirt trail and exchanged the expected questions of where we were from and what we were doing at Brockhurst. Philippe and Viola surprised me. He was from France; she was from Hungary. I couldn't believe it when they told me they were publishers.

Both were at the helm of publishing houses that specialized in books written by Christian authors. They had come early for a gathering of international publishers who met at Brockhurst every year.

I found it unsettling that I'd been trying to extract myself from the angst I had toward the publishing industry, yet here I was, on the other side of the world, back inside a small circle of those who understood.

I hesitated to reveal to them my severed connection to their area of expertise. I was an editor. Not a publisher. I fell below their rank in the hierarchy of publishing. And now I wasn't even an editor. I was a former editor. I hated that truth and didn't want to speak it aloud.

The problem was, I had a feeling that if I didn't say something, Lily might innocently share details of my life at dinner, the way she had at lunch. If that happened, I'd be even more embarrassed for not having mentioned it first.

With a quick breath I blurted out, "I used to work at a publishing house. I was a senior fiction editor. All my authors wrote for the Christian market."

"Really?" Viola asked. "Amazing. You are no longer there?"

"No, I'm not."

"What are you doing now?" Philippe asked. "Do you free-lance?"

"No. I'm . . ." The words felt thick on my tongue. "I'm on a break. A short break. I'm praying about what's next."

"How long did you say you were staying at Brockhurst?" Viola asked. "You would be welcome at our conference. It begins tomorrow."

"We leave in the morning. That's when our safari tour begins. We came early so Lily could meet her aunt and uncle."

"Let's exchange contact details," Philippe said. "You might be able to join us another time. Here or at a regional workshop."

I doubted that would ever happen but took my phone out of my pocket to share contact information.

The three of us continued walking at our uneven pace. The conversation slid into how much the publishing world had changed over the last few years and what the predictions were for the future. I liked listening to their international insights. I somehow felt disqualified to add my opinions now that I was no longer employed.

I told myself I shouldn't think that way, but the layoff felt very final, as if there would never be another place for me in the realm where I once thrived. I'd been dismissed. Sent away. Not because I'd done something horribly wrong or because I'd failed to produce quality, strong-selling books. My only fault was that I was no longer needed.

I realized that being canceled and becoming redundant to the publisher was the biggest rejection I'd ever experienced. It was, in a way, the downside of growing up in such a kind and loving family. I'd always felt wanted. Danny was the one who pursued me from the beginning. He'd never rejected me, nor had any other guy because I'd never had a real boyfriend before Danny.

For a moment, I felt a twinge of the magnitude of hurt Micah had talked about in several therapy sessions. He had known many rejections. The bitterness had festered in the deep holes hollowed out by his birth mother and father when they chose to distance themselves from him.

Feeling unwanted is terrible. Losing a job is also terrible, but it's not unusual. What took place wasn't personal. It happens. I knew I couldn't dwell on it. I had to pull out of my emotional nosedive.

Several locals passed us on the path and greeted us warmly.

I thought about how easy it had been for one of my sisters, Emma, to be the first family member to call and tell me that God had a purpose in the job loss. I agreed with her, of course, but her summation had come too quickly. She had never experienced rejection on a large scale. She didn't know the extent of my hurt, just as I didn't know the depth of Micah's hurt.

Viola broke into my thoughts, asking if I had considered working remotely for a publishing house.

My reply came out with a rasp in my voice. "I am considering different options."

"Do you speak French?" Philippe asked.

"No."

"Pity. We are looking for freelance translators in the US who can also serve as acquisition editors for us."

I turned to him and shook my head with a tight-lipped smile, hoping to convey that I was not the person they were looking for and this was not the conversation I was looking for.

"If you think of someone who might be interested, please let me know."

I nodded, grateful that Viola had stopped walking, creating

a natural break from the topic. The path before us split. Viola pointed to a handwritten sign that said *Trail 1 km.*

"Does that mean the trail to the tea field?" she asked.

"Yes, we go to the right. It will soon change to a narrow trail," Philippe said.

It was good to know he'd made this trek several times and knew where we were going. We were in the thick of beautiful, rain-kissed foliage growing along the uneven path. The narrow trail continued and soon led uphill. We came around a curve, and within a few steps we were out of the dense overgrowth and able to see down into the valley without obstruction.

I stopped and drew in a long breath.

Spread before us, as far as we could see, were acres of tea plants. Acres and acres. They covered the rolling landscape like waves of green on an uncharted sea. Between the plants were long, narrow rows for workers to walk along at harvesttime.

"The valley looks like it is breathing," Viola said. "It is alive."

I loved her description. The deep-green shade of the sea of leaves caught the afternoon sunlight in such a way that, as the gentle wind rolled over the tea plants, they seemed to release a sigh of contentment.

"Come," Philippe called over his shoulder. He was twenty steps ahead of us and heading down the open path into the valley. Once again, I was glad he knew the way.

The closer we got, the more the details of the vast green ocean came into perspective. The individual bushy plants were only about three feet high, but they had grown close together and formed a hedge. Philippe described how, on a stroll through the fields during another visit to Brockhurst, he'd watched the workers handpick the leaves and toss them into side pouches they carried over their shoulders.

"They take no more than a few leaves and a bud," he told us. "It's quite specific."

Viola and I followed Philippe into one of the narrow rows between the plants and slowly turned around in a full circle. We were surrounded by emerald leaves in every direction.

I leaned closer to see if the plants carried a distinctive fragrance. They didn't. The only scent I caught was that of rich earth. I knew that tea was created through a process that included several steps to dry and press the leaves, but that was all I knew.

Right then the "how" didn't matter to me. I loved being in the center of the "where." It intrigued me to think that someone, somewhere in the world, would one day drink a cup of tea made from these very leaves I was now skimming with my palm.

My companions seemed to be having their own contemplative moments. They were spaced a distance from each other, lost in thought.

I took pictures and thought of how Wanja had swallowed a laugh when I said I wanted to visit a tea field. I'd have to be sure to tell her about this, because what I was experiencing now was exactly what I'd hoped for.

Standing among a growing crop brought back fond memories of my childhood summers. I used to traipse through our cornfields every morning with our dog, Roger. I checked to see if the cornstalks had topped my height. When the weather grew hot, our sweet corn could grow three to four inches a day. Those were the best mornings, seeing the overnight transformation and listening to the muffled rustling of the stalks as Roger and I brushed against them during our inspections.

Cornfields whisper. Tea fields sigh.

I never would have known that if I hadn't come here.

The pristine stillness of the tea field blended with my sweet childhood memories and had a remarkable effect on me. I felt as if something new was resting on me. It was as if I'd gained something. The impression had come to me not at my bidding, but I received the invisible mercy nonetheless.

Was it hope? Was that the comfort that seemed to envelop me? Had I been hope-starved since being let go from my job? What did hope feel like?

If this was it, then hope was filling a deep well within me as I extended both arms, palms downward, and strode between the waist-high hedges. My spirit felt buoyant among the tea leaves, floating along to who-knows-where, but doing so with an unexpected sense of strength.

I was adrift in a living daydream of unimagined beauty.

We'd become separated in the field—Philippe, Viola, and I. Philippe's whistle brought me back. He waved for us to head for the opening of the narrow trail that led back to Brockhurst.

I snapped two leaves and a bud off one of the plants and twirled them between my fingers as I fell into step with my partners on the trail. I wished Lily had come. I was curious if she would have experienced any of the same feelings that came over me. Would the walk have had a ministering effect on her as well?

As our merry trio picked up our pace, the conversation returned to the topic of the upcoming conference. Philippe gave us a summary of the keynote message he would be delivering tomorrow night. The theme was fighting for the freedom to publish. He had examples of obstacles that writers and publishers had overcome throughout history as they made the written word available to people everywhere. He was passionate about Christians not being censored in print. His conclusion was that in our lifetime we would see more underground publishing of Christian materials in nations where the government was opposed to what those writers wanted to say.

Philippe stopped walking, faced Viola and me, and concluded his summary with what I guessed were the closing lines of his presentation. He looked over our heads as if he were addressing a crowd and raised his right arm, making staccato motions with his hand in sync with his key words.

"We must no longer see publishing as a potentially lucrative career where we have free rein to create whatever content we wish. The time is coming, and in many places of the world already exists, when our vocation will be under attack. Freedom of speech must be defended. Our most valuable weapon in this war is prayer. Pray and keep doing what God has called you to do. Print the word. In season and out of season. Proclaim His truth clearly to all people in every language. Rise up, Christian writers and publishers!"

Viola and I glanced at each other, as if we shared the same question of whether we should applaud. Neither of us did.

Philippe lifted his chin and walked ahead of us in silence.

We were nearly at the conference center when I said, "Philippe, your message is very powerful. I appreciate your sharing the main points with me. With us."

When he didn't reply, I added, "Merci."

He looked over at me with a grin. "I thought you didn't speak French."

"That's the extent of my vocabulary. That and *croissant*, which is my all-time favorite French word." I'd added an exaggerated accent to the word *croissant*. I'm sure it sounded ridiculous.

Philippe laughed, and I was grateful that we were entering the gates to Brockhurst on a light note. I said my goodbyes and took the path back to our cottage. No monkeys greeted me from the loquat tree. I was a little disappointed about that.

Our room was empty, and the temperature was still chilly inside. The stone walls seemed to guarantee year-round cooling. I slipped out of my hiking shoes and opened the door so I could clap the mud off them outside. It was warmer outside than it was in our bungalow. I still adored our hideaway and felt glad to be "home" after all the hiking.

Dinner would be served in the dining room in an hour and a half. All I wanted to do until then was close my eyes. The deeply personal experience in the tea field had filled me and emptied me at the same time. I wanted to let my weary spirit marinate in all the thoughts I'd processed that day.

After plugging in my phone and setting the alarm, I slid beneath the layers of heavy blankets.

Sleep itself tucked me in.

I'd been warned about the dangers of what happens if you don't push through the entire first few days of daylight when arriving in a new time zone. When my alarm roused me, I could verify that all those warnings were valid. I could barely open my dried-out eyes. Instead of getting up, I stayed where I was, watching. The longer I watched, the more I smiled.

On the walls, a performance had begun. Slender, graceful sunset shadows were moving across the wall in silence. I was mesmerized by their dance and stayed under the warm blankets, yawning and blinking. I hoped they knew I was a more enthusiastic audience than I appeared to be.

The door opened, startling me out of the moment. Lily entered and flipped the light switch. It worked this time, and the entire cast and crew of the twilight ballet fled in the commanding presence of the overhead glare.

6

A true friend sees the first tear,
Catches the second,
And stops the third.

Unknown

"Fern, I didn't know you were here! I hope I didn't wake you."

"No. I napped a little, but my alarm went off a few minutes ago."

"How was the tea field?"

"Enchanting. I wish you'd come. I loved it." I was about to tell her more about my glorious afternoon, but she looked worried. "How about you? How was your time with Cheryl?"

"Good. I think it was important. Cheryl and my dad used to be close, but they didn't keep in contact after my parents divorced."

"That was a long time ago."

"I know. Just two weeks after you and I got back from Costa Rica."

I nodded, remembering the long phone calls Lily and I had when she was trying to decide which parent to live with.

"Why do you think your dad and Cheryl disconnected?" I asked. "Do you think she sided with your mom or something?"

"No. Nobody sided with my mom. Not if they knew the details. Cheryl didn't know about the weird guy my mom got tangled up with." Lily sat on the edge of her bed. "I also told Cheryl how my dad was never home because he was working all the time. That was the start of their problems. My dad told me he was faithful to my mom, and I believe him. He also admits that he was putting all his effort into his job, and he regrets that now."

I turned on my side and adjusted my pillow so I could see Lily more clearly. My contacts were dry, and I was having a hard time focusing on her face. I wanted to be able to gauge how she was feeling about all this by her expression.

"Cheryl appreciated me telling her some of the details. I was glad I did. Like a lot of people, she thought my dad was the one who'd been seeing someone because he remarried so quickly. She didn't know about my mom's choices. I told her that my dad didn't even meet Ilene until after the divorce was final."

"Did Cheryl know that your mom came to live with you guys right after Noah was born?"

"No."

I forced myself out of bed and headed to the bathroom to get some eye drops. As I leaned my head back for the first drop, I said, "Maybe you should tell Cheryl how you had an eighteen-month-old with asthma, a colicky newborn after an emergency C-section, and your mom showed up, expecting you to take care of her too."

"I didn't want to throw my mom under the bus. She was a mess. My brother refused to even let her in his house. If Tim and I hadn't taken her in, I think she would have ended up in a shelter."

"It was still the worst time of your life, in my opinion. I could not understand how a mother could be so self-absorbed."

"That's because your mom is the best mom of all time. She passed the kindness genes on to you. I'm telling you, Fern, if you hadn't come and spent your entire vacation with us, I don't want to think about what might have happened."

"I wasn't the only one who helped you guys. Your dad was there for you. He helped you stabilize your own little family. And the way he helped your mom get back on her feet was out of the ordinary for a divorced couple. I think he is the reason your mom is doing so well now."

Lily sighed. "I know. It was ancient history until I started telling Cheryl what happened. I told her she would like Ilene if she ever had a chance to meet her. It's just sad to remember how my parents' relationship unraveled."

"What did Cheryl say after you told her everything?"

"She said marriage is supposed to be sacred and that she wished my parents had found a way to stay together."

"Interesting." I returned to the bed and sat with my back against the wrought-iron headboard with my legs crossed. "What did you say?"

"I told her I didn't know if every marriage is supposed to last a lifetime."

I heard a catch in Lily's voice and saw a painful expression on her face before she looked away from me.

"Lily, what are you feeling right now?"

She paused. "Do you think marriage is sacred?"

"Yes."

She turned and looked me in the eyes. "Is it? I mean, really?"

"Yes, of course it is."

She looked away again.

"Lily?"

Her focus remained on her clenched hands in her lap. "What if—" She cleared her throat. "What if I made a mistake? I mean, a big mistake?"

My thoughts raced with all the possibilities of what she meant by a "big mistake." I refused to believe she had done anything irreversible. Not Lily.

"What kind of mistake?" I shifted so I could see her better and waited for her to continue. When she didn't say anything, I repeated my question, sounding as concerned as I felt. "What happened, Lily?"

"I got married. That's what happened."

"What do you mean?"

"I don't know if Tim and I should have married. We were too young. I wanted to get away from my family and all the drama that was going on with my mom. He was the way out. I was barely nineteen. We weren't ready. We didn't know anything. And I missed everything."

"What did you miss?"

"This." She gestured with both arms over her head as if she were encompassing the entire world. Her gaze moved to the window, and she stared at the loquat tree outside.

I waited while she took long, slow breaths.

"I don't mean to be so dramatic," she said. "It's just that all these intense thoughts are on the surface after talking with Cheryl. It brings up so many horrible and confusing feelings. I feel raw." She turned back to face me. "I'm frightened, Fern. Really frightened that Tim and I are on the same path that ruined my parents' marriage."

"Why do you say that?"

She moved into a cross-legged position at the end of my bed and calmly went through a list that sounded as definitive as if she were reading it from a court document. "Tim is never home. We both work all the time. The boys' schedules and activities take up all our spare hours. I can't remember when we did anything, just the two of us. Tim could have come on this safari with me, but he didn't want to. I know this will sound like I'm whining, but I don't think he wants to be with me."

"Do you think he's pursuing another woman?"

"No."

"What about you? Are you attracted to another man?"

"No! We're both too busy and too tired to initiate something like that."

"I had to ask."

"I know. But that's not the issue. It's us. We're flatlining."

I moved closer and sat beside her.

The edges of her gray eyes glistened with rising tears. "I feel like we are stuck on the path of my parents' lives, and I can see how this plays out. Tim is going to leave me, and I'm going to become my mother, moving in with whatever relative will have me until I remarry just so I won't be alone."

"Lily, stop." I reached over and placed my hand on hers. "Stop. You are not going to become your mother. You did not make a mistake when you married Tim. You got triggered by all the talk about your parents, and that's what created these thoughts. None of them is true."

"Some of them are true."

"Okay, yes. Some of them are true. You are both busy and don't spend enough time alone together. That can be fixed. Your marriage is not ending. Tim is not leaving you. It sounds like you guys are at a crossroads. This is your chance to make changes. Good changes. That's all this is. You can work together to make your marriage the best it's ever been."

Lily's complexion seemed to change from a shade of fevered red back to her usual fair-skinned, peachy tone. The fire in her belly had been contained. In a faint voice she responded, "Sorry to throw all that at you."

"Hey, you and I never apologize for venting, remember? We are free to talk about whatever. Always."

She nodded.

"I knew something deep was coming to the surface when I saw you tear up in the car last night."

"That was because Wanja was talking about her wedding and how they had waited until her fiancé finished university. I felt sick to my stomach that Tim didn't finish college. He wanted to, but we got pregnant so quickly. He had to work."

"He can always go back to school," I said. "Does he want to?"

"I don't know. He hasn't said anything about it for a long time. I think he gave up."

"So ask him if that's something he'd like to do now."

"It's not just that. When Wanja said her grandmother and mother married young but she and her fiancé had taken their time, all I could think was that I blew it. I married the first guy I ever kissed, got away from my family, such as it was at the time, and right away we started having babies. Why did we do that? Why didn't anyone tell us to step back and take in the big picture?"

I had never heard Lily sound remorseful like this. I always thought the timing of her life had been exactly right for her. She knew in Costa Rica that she didn't want to go to college. She was certain within a month of officially being Tim's girlfriend that she loved him and he was perfect for her, which I agreed with then and still did.

"Even if your parents hadn't divorced, I think Tim and you would have married when you did."

"I don't know. We might have waited. You and I might have gone to Paris or Morocco like we dreamed about. Tim and I never went anywhere together like we said we would. We got stuck on a fast track of jobs, babies, house. We checked off all our big life goals before we were forty. Now we're two old people, set in our ways and bored with each other, and we're not even forty."

Lily's phone alarm chimed. She pulled it out of her pocket and looked at the time. "We need to go to dinner. It starts in five minutes. I told Jim and Cheryl that we would meet them there."

"We can be a little late if you want to keep talking."

"No, I'm done. I don't have anything else to add. Thanks for letting me get it out."

"Of course. And if you want to hit pause on this conversation the way we do all the time on our phone calls, we can pick up on part two when we come back to our room tonight."

She nodded and smoothed back her feathery blond bangs from her forehead. "It's probably not a coincidence that we're away from home right now. I'm guessing we both needed this space and some time to sort things out."

I nodded.

"We both have big life pieces that are broken and need to be fixed. Like your elephant in the room of what you're going to do for a job."

I pulled back when Lily turned the spotlight on me. I was not ready to pick apart my problem.

"We can talk about that later." I knew I needed to vent more than I had with the summary of my hurt and anger expressed in my journal.

But not now. Not on the heels of what I'd felt that afternoon in the tea field. I wanted to believe God's Spirit had brushed up against my spirit and soothed something in me. Walking through the emerald waves of tea plants, I felt separated from the panicky feelings that had tossed me around over the past few weeks. I wanted to linger in that calm a little longer before entering problem-solving mode with Lily the list maker. She would want to go to work researching all job options and locations. Within an hour she'd have a spreadsheet ready for us to discuss. For now, I just wanted to be separated from the hurt. Not swimming in it again, trying to keep my nose up.

I hoped my desire for separation from the issue was a healthy first step and not simply denial.

Although, even if it was denial, didn't I have the luxury of resting in that for just a few days? If I were home right now, this would be my first day of not going into work. I'd be in my pajamas watching movies all day. I would have set up a snack station on the coffee table, and I'd be on the couch under the crocheted blanket my mom made for me when I moved to Colorado. I'd have a full box of Scottish shortbread cookies, and I'd be sipping loose-leaf English breakfast tea from a china mug my sister Anne had bought for me in London. I'd have my little ceramic cow creamer filled with half and half, and my favorite teapot would be refreshed between films.

Instead, I was in Africa.

I didn't need a diversion. This was it. And it was dreamy.

I put my muddy shoes back on, and we stepped into the twilight glow of the evening. Above us, the sky had softened to a fading shade of periwinkle blue with tinges of apricot edging the rim of a single puffy cloud.

We walked together in the comfortable silence that marked

the established sisterhood we shared. Nothing more needed to be expressed right now. We both knew there would be time for that later.

The main lodge filled our view. From the many windows across the front, amber lights broadcast their unspoken message of "welcome home, weary traveler." Leaving this place in the morning would be difficult. Spending one lovely day and two nights was not long enough.

I stopped on the path to the lodge, and Lily waited as I took a dozen photos of our surroundings. I wanted to capture it quickly before all the light faded from the sky.

A fresh thought shivered through me the way the first drink of ice-cold water shimmies down the throat. *Danny and I could come here. Together. We're free to do things like that now.*

I had no idea how or when that might happen, but it was a possibility, and I was a woman who could start collecting possibilities once again. My future was unwritten. I was well supplied with blank pages. Finding a new job was only part of my life. Until I married Danny, my work had been nearly my whole life.

"You know what, Lily?"

"What?"

"You know how I said you and Tim are at a crossroads?"

"Yes."

"I am too. We both are."

She raised her eyebrows, waiting for me to say more.

"That's it. That's all I wanted to say."

"That's why I was saying we both have big life pieces that are broken. And that's also why at lunch I told Cheryl and Jim that coming here is a reset for you."

"I think it's a reset for both of us."

Lily opened the door to the lodge. "You're probably right."

"*Probably* right?" I gave her a friendly nudge as I followed her inside. "Go ahead and say it. Say, 'Fern, you are right.'"

"Fern, you are right . . . probably. It remains to be seen."

"Fair enough. I'll check back with you at the end of our trip and savor the words when you say, 'Fern, you are right' and actually mean them."

Lily shook her head. "This thing you have about needing affirmation. That's a byproduct of being the last of five girls in your family, right?"

"Probably."

"Oh, so now you're saying I'm the one who is *probably* right?"

I laughed. "I see what you did there."

Once again, I was grateful to have Lily in my life. She let me be me. I hoped I'd always be equal in returning the gift of comradery. It's rare to find someone who can call you out on a playful level. I could remember only one time when we'd had a fight. In the end, it turned out to be a big misunderstanding over what both of us thought the other had said.

We entered the dining room, both smiling, and slid into line with Jim and Cheryl. They were behind two men whom I guessed were from West Africa because they were speaking French. Philippe had explained on our walk that along with keynoting at the publishers conference, he would also be translating some of the sessions into French for the francophone West Africans.

A woman greeted the men, and the three exchanged a warm reunion round of hellos in English and French. She was stunning. I tried not to stare. Her dark skin was highlighted by the brightly colored fabric in her headdress and a loosely flowing, matching caftan. She had high cheekbones and bright, penetrating eyes. Her posture and demeanor exuded a touch of royalty and poise.

Even after we were seated at our table, my eyes followed her across the room. I was certain she had to be an African princess. I'd never seen anyone like her in my life. Our small community in Colorado had a limited mix of ethnicities, so I was drinking in the beauty of variety.

The other thing I loved was listening to the swirl of languages, voices, and especially the laughter that echoed off the old, dark wood ceilings. If most of these people were here for the international writers and publishers conference, what a rich and varied time they would have. I wondered if I might be able to join them next year. Maybe Danny would come with me.

Something inside me was murmuring, *Don't dare to dream. Don't aim too high*. The murmur silenced my ponderings.

When we finished eating, Jim leaned in. His expression became stern. "I want you to know that Cheryl and I are glad you came to see us. However, there is a problem."

Lily looked concerned. "What's the problem?"

"Your stay was too short." He playfully pounded the table for emphasis.

"We wish you could stay longer," Cheryl said.

Jim smiled, looking pleased that he'd gotten a rise out of Lily.

"Do you think you could?" Cheryl asked. "The cottage is available all week."

Lily glanced at me. "We wish we could too. My dad will appreciate that we got to see you. But it will not make my father-in-law happy if we cancel the safari part of this trip."

"And what will make *you* happy?" Cheryl asked.

Before Lily could come up with a reply, a round woman

wearing a chef jacket bustled over to our table with a broad smile. Her hair had flecks of white and was shaved close to her head. She grinned at Lily and then at me.

With a teasing tone in her voice she said, "At last! I have found my long-awaited kitchen help."

Lily caught on immediately and laughed, pointing at me. "She's the one you're looking for."

"You must be Wanja's grandmother," I said.

"That I am. Also known as Njeri," she said. "Now, which flower are you?"

"Flower?"

"My granddaughter told me, but I've forgotten."

"You mean our names?" Lily laughed again. "I'm Lily. This is Fern."

"Fern and Lily. A grand name for a shop," Njeri said. "I would go there. You would not even have to sell flowers. You could sell soap. I would buy a bar of soap from 'Fern and Lily.'"

I loved this woman immediately. I had seen an African princess at the salad bar, and now I was smiling at an African fairy godmother.

"You could have something there, Njeri," Jim said. "But what did you mean by your long-awaited kitchen help?"

I quickly explained how I'd applied to come work at Brockhurst those many years ago.

"And I am here to say it's never too late. I can help make your unfulfilled dream come true!" Njeri said. "Follow me. I saved the pots and pans for you."

Without hesitation, I pushed my chair back, ready to excuse myself from the table.

"You don't need to go," Cheryl said, reaching for my arm.

"You realize she's only teasing you," Jim added.

I grinned at Lily. She explained to her aunt and uncle, "It's strange, I know. But trust me. You asked what would make us happy? Well, this will make Fern happy."

Jim said, "If you want to know the end, look at the beginning." He spoke it as if it were a proverb or well-known quote.

I didn't understand what Jim meant by his declaration, but I let it go and followed Njeri to the kitchen with a glad heart. At first I thought she was only teasing me, but I wanted to go along with it. However, there was evidence to the contrary. A large sink against the far wall was filled to the brim with pots and pans.

"Do you have an extra apron?" I asked.

Njeri laughed the most delightful, full-bellied laugh. "You are serious, then, aren't you?"

One of the kitchen helpers offered me an apron. I rolled up my sleeves and started. If it was possible to feel heat from the stares of a half-dozen people burning like the summer sun through your White-girl skin, that was what I felt as I reached for a scrub brush. I gave it a squirt of dish soap and noticed that it carried the faint scent of almonds.

No one except me could possibly understand what a sweet, holy moment that next hour was. Only Jesus knew. He knew I needed to stand in that kitchen and do what I'd once envisioned when my young heart dreamed of going to Africa and somehow being useful.

I drew it all in, thinking how surprised I'd been to see the lush surroundings of up-country Nairobi. But the monkeys had not surprised me, nor did the sky or the voices and the faces of the people. I had conjured up clear images of those elements of Africa many years ago, when I was curled up by the fireplace on a snowy afternoon in Michigan reading Hemingway's remarkable run-on sentences describing his impression of the deeper essences of this corner of Africa.

How he'd reveled in the hunt and the hike to where he knelt to feel the curled horns of the African kudu. The downed beast carried the scent of fresh grass on a drizzly afternoon below the equator.

The wildness and earthy, primal beauty were here in the air, the trees, the red dirt. I felt it. And yet I'd been here just a day and had only seen a British-colonized speck on this vast continent. Why hadn't the adventurous images dissolved into cold reality the way so many dreams from my teen years had as I grew up?

A rogue tear dove into the sudsy water. It was followed by only four or five more honest tears. That was all that was left of my years of wondering and regretting that I wasn't taking annual trips with Lily around the world. Those final tears plunged into the sudsy, almond- and chicken fat–scented water. As they dissolved, so did any lingering sense that I had failed God somehow by not coming here to serve as planned.

Colorado and the internship at the publishing house had been the best path for me. I had no doubts. Danny entered my life at just the right time, and I slowly slid into his at just the right time. Being released from the job I loved, though . . . How could that be the right next step?

As I balanced the last pan on the drying rack, Njeri returned to my side. I didn't expect to see such a serious expression on her face. She took my still-damp hands in hers and looked into my eyes. "This is what the Lord says—your Redeemer, the Holy One of Israel."

Her deep voice and her firm grasp startled me. I felt my heart rise to my throat and tears return to my eyes.

"I am the Lord your God, who teaches you what is best for you, who directs you in the way you should go. Wait for the Lord. Be strong and take heart and wait for the Lord.'"

Njeri tilted her head and looked at me as if she was listening.

I didn't say anything. I barely exhaled.

Another proclamation rolled from her honeyed voice, tenderly this time. "They will follow the Lord. He will roar like a lion. When He roars, His children will come—"

She stopped as if there might be more, but then her lips drew back and she smiled broadly, revealing a missing tooth toward the back of her mouth. She gave my hands a squeeze, saying, "Yes," as if it was a final agreement or benediction to what she had just spoken over me.

"Thank you," I said softly. "Asante sana." I returned her gentle squeeze.

She let me go and stepped away.

I removed my damp apron and returned to our cottage, floating on top of the mystery of what had just happened.

7

I never knew of a morning in Africa when I woke up that I
was not happy.

Ernest Hemingway

As I approached our bungalow, I smiled. Lily had lit
the thick taper candle and placed it on the wide
windowsill inside our room. The flickering glow
called to me like a favorite melody, an invitation to come
closer and enter.

No other lights were on inside our room, and Lily was
in bed when I entered. I whispered her name and quietly
removed my shoes. She didn't respond. Sleep had tucked her
in the way it had done for me that afternoon when I surrendered to a nap.

I tried to be quiet as I prepared for bed and reluctantly
blew out the friendly candle before snuggling under the thick
covers. I'd set the alarm on my phone, hoping I'd calculated
enough time for a shower before Wanja arrived to pick us
up. I hadn't had a shower since the morning I left home. It

would feel so good to wash my hair, even if it meant I had to towel dry it. I hoped we'd have hot water in the morning.

Falling asleep was more difficult than I expected. My afternoon nap could have been part of the problem. Or it could have been the swarm of thoughts that circled and hummed around me in the quietness of our room.

I gave in to the urge to pull out my journal, my ever-ready thought-catching net, and catch some of the buzzing memories of that day, pinning them to the pages.

With my husband's gift of the handy-dandy flashlight, I tried to describe the monkeys and the masala chai. I wrote about the perfect bench under the embracing branches of the aged tree and the waves of sensations that rolled over me in the tea field.

By the time I was trying to capture the words that Njeri said to me, my eyelids were heavy. I was ready to close my journal and my eyes and dream luscious dreams.

The sad thing about sleeping deeply is that I never remember anything I may have dreamed while my body rejuvenated itself.

My invasive alarm jolted me into waking thoughts. Lily rolled over and went back to sleep. With a low grunt, I shuffled to the shower and found that the water was tepid.

Tepid is a terrible word. When one of my authors included it in her book, I suggested she change it to lukewarm. However, as I stood under the tepid spray of shower water, I thought I should have let her keep her adjective of choice. If you've muddled through washing your hair in a tepid shower, lukewarm doesn't capture the soggy sadness of the experience.

I had just finished putting on fresh clothes and wrapping my wet hair up in a towel when I heard Cheryl's voice.

She had entered our room while I was showering and had brought her morning gift of steaming masala chai.

"Good morning," Cheryl greeted me.

"Jambo," I replied with a smile.

Lily was still in bed, propping herself up against the head-board. "How was the shower?"

I wanted to use the accurate word—tepid—but I didn't want to sound ungrateful. Not when Cheryl and Jim were spending their lives making sure people in Africa even had water available to them.

"The shower was good." I received the morning gift Cheryl was holding out to me. Eagerly circling both hands around the warm mug, I sipped the ministering elixir slowly with my eyes closed. "This is so good," I murmured. "Thank you."

"I also brought ugali." She nodded to the ceramic bowl she'd placed on the desk.

"I had some yesterday." Lily slipped out of bed and came over to the desk. "It's kind of like grits. Only it's made from white corn instead of yellow corn."

I looked at the white lump in the bowl. It resembled a mound of Cream of Wheat hot cereal my mom had often made for winter breakfasts on the farm. But the ugali looked like it needed a lot of milk added to thin it enough so it could be eaten like a hot breakfast cereal.

Apparently, milk wasn't needed. And this cereal wasn't hot.

Lily pinched off a small chunk and rolled it into a ball. She smiled and gave me a nod as if to say, *Go ahead*.

Following Lily's example, I took my first bite of ugali. The consistency of it made my throat tighten. It didn't have much of a flavor. I chewed until I felt hopeful that it would slide down easily. Then I reached for my mug of chai, grateful for the spicy and soothing drink and hoping Cheryl wouldn't notice if I didn't go for another ugali bite.

She didn't.

That was because Wanja arrived earlier than expected. She called out as she knocked on our door, "Hello, the house! Are the Suitcase Sisters awake?" She entered with a vibrant smile, carrying a basket. She stopped and surveyed the room. "Ah, I see I am not the only one who thought the Suitcase Sisters needed breakfast in bed. What did you bring, Cheryl?"

"She brought ugali," Lily said.

The answer brought a scowl to Wanja's lovely face.

"And masala chai," I added, holding up my mug.

"You brought them ugali?" Wanja laughed. "I see. Well, you do not have to tell me if they ate it because I know they did. These two are not typical visitors, are they? They must have ugali at least once."

"Twice for me," Lily said.

Wanja laughed again. "Practically a local girl already."

Cheryl was peering into the woven basket still hanging from Wanja's forearm. "Is that Njeri's banana bread I see?"

"Yes, it is. Still warm." Wanja pulled out the loaf along with a plate and a knife. "I will tell you something my grandmother will not tell you. Her secret ingredient is honey. Local honey from her sister's hives. She tells everyone her recipe is a secret, but it is not. Everyone here knows it. I will share it with you if you like her bread."

Cheryl already had cut thick slices and held out the plate to us. Lily and I reached for the plate quickly and at the same time. Our hands bumped into each other. Wanja and Cheryl both chuckled at our eagerness.

"This tells me a lot about what you thought of my contribution to your breakfast," Cheryl said.

"I loved the chai." I said it with sincerity and realized I

sounded as if I was offering condolences. Then I bit into the most moist and delicious banana bread I had ever tasted.

"Well, then it doesn't matter that I brought coffee, does it?" Wanja gave an exaggerated pout.

"Yes, it does!" Lily said. "I love coffee."

"Good. So do I." Wanja gave Lily a cute, over-the-shoulder smug grin. "All the more for us, then."

I settled cross-legged on my unmade bed and pulled the towel off my head. Shaking my elbow-length hair, I hoped it would dry quickly in the morning sunbeams that were gracing us through the window.

"I missed the monkeys this morning," I said.

"They've cleaned out all the loquats," Cheryl observed. "You may have caught them on their final day in that tree until next season."

Taking another bite of banana bread, I watched as Wanja lifted from her basket a large thermos, four ceramic mugs, a glass jar of milk, and a small, clear container that looked like it contained brown sugar.

"You have your very own Mary Poppins carpet bag." My comment flitted away without any sort of acknowledgment from Wanja. I wondered if Mary Poppins wasn't as universal as I'd supposed.

Lily sounded like she was cooing after her first sip of Wanja's special blend of coffee.

"I will take that as an affirmation of your approval," Wanja said.

"It's delicious."

"It's Kenya grown, that's why."

"My sister would love the recipe for this banana bread," I said.

"Which sister?" Lily asked.

"Jo." For Cheryl and Wanja's benefit, I explained my

abundance of sisters. "I always thought that of all of us 'little women,' Jo would have become a writer."

Neither of them seemed to make the connection between the name "Jo" and my emphasis on little women. So I explained why Jo would want the recipe. "She loves to bake and has a blog, which is very entertaining because she posts her disasters as well as her triumphs."

"I will email the secret recipe to Lily since I don't have your email," Wanja said. "Be sure to tell your sister it's even better with chocolate bits or walnuts."

Wanja made herself at home on the end of Lily's bed, and the four of us did what women the world over do when they have a moment to share coffee with friends. We fell into a relaxed rhythm, teasing each other, complimenting each other, and smiling because such moments are fleeting and wonderful.

We enjoyed our leisure a little too long, and Lily and I had to scramble to get ready to go. My hair was still wet, so I pulled out one of the handsewn, fabric headbands my mom made. Every Christmas my sisters and I received a new assortment of hair accessories from her as stocking stuffers. The one I chose was an animal print. Leopard, I think. I had never worn it in Colorado, but it was one of the two I'd packed, and today seemed the day to wear it.

Wanja hurried us along. Our suitcase wheels echoed off the cottages with the same clackety taps they'd made on the uneven path the night we arrived. I thought we'd sounded too loud on our midnight approach to our cottage. This morning our clicks only added to the concert of the birds and a gardener's blower that was headed toward us. Brockhurst was alive with morning sounds and motion, and we were removing ourselves from the hum of the lovely hive.

The sadness I felt over leaving seemed to squeeze my heart.

I tried to hold back the tears when I hugged Cheryl and thanked her for her generous hospitality.

She kissed me on the forehead, as she'd done yesterday morning. "May the Lord be with you."

My automatic response was "And also with you."

Lily didn't hold back her tears. She hugged Cheryl for a long time while Wanja loaded our suitcases into the mini tour van and started the engine. I climbed in and looked out the window as Cheryl handed something to Lily, and they exchanged their goodbyes.

As Wanja pulled away, both Lily and I turned to look out the back window of the van. Cheryl was still facing us, waving a handkerchief the way passengers did on ship decks a hundred years ago. I doubted she could see us both waving back, but we kept it up until the van exited the security entrance gate and we turned out of sight.

I knew that the image of Cheryl waving her handkerchief would stay with me the rest of my life. It seemed to be a lingering touch of the old-world charm that had clung to Brockhurst since its British-influenced beginnings. Cheryl embodied that charm. She was a woman who lived a life of purpose, kindness, and love.

Lily was still leaking tears. I reached into my shoulder bag to find a packet of tissues. She didn't need them. She quietly held up a fresh white handkerchief that she used to dab the corners of her eyes. I didn't have to ask where she got it. I knew Cheryl had slipped it to her during their lingering goodbye.

Such a sweet gift. It made me want to buy hankies and learn how to embroider initials and tiny flowers in the corner just so I would have them on hand to give as special gifts.

Not that any of the rare guests who stayed on the couch at our condo would understand the charm or intention of such a gift. Nonetheless, I wanted to be like Cheryl and give kisses on foreheads and slip hankies into departing hands.

Wanja drove on in a respectful sort of silence before asking if we were looking forward to our day. She told us we were going to take a tour of the house where parts of the movie *Out of Africa* had been filmed.

"We watched the movie on the plane," Lily said. "I'm curious to find out how much of it was about the actual events."

"Speaking of tours," I added, "Wanja, I wanted to tell you that I took a long walk in the tea field."

"Did you?"

"Yes, and I loved it."

"I see." Wanja caught my eye in the rearview mirror, and I could tell she was grinning even though I couldn't see her whole face. "I heard you also had another wish come true. In the kitchen."

"Yes, I did. I washed dishes in Africa. Well, to be precise, I washed pots and pans. Your grandmother saved the messiest ones for me."

"She has a way about her, doesn't she?" Wanja said.

"She does. She also did something I've never experienced before. She spoke over me as if she was giving me a blessing. I'm pretty sure the words were all from Scripture. I just don't know where the verses are in the Bible."

"Yes, she does that. She knows the Bible better than anyone I know. Scripture passages come out of her mouth at many unexpected moments. I am curious. What did she say to you?"

I tried to remember and pulled out my journal to see what I'd jotted down late last night. When I had time, I planned to look up the verses. For Wanja, it was enough for me to read some of the key lines to her.

"It sounds like the Lord wanted to assure you that He is

leading you. Are you about to make some changes in your life?"

I hadn't said anything to Wanja on our way to Brockhurst about losing my job. I wondered if Njeri knew. Could she have heard it from Philippe or Viola?

It didn't matter.

"Yes. I will have some big decisions to make when I go home," I told Wanja. "What she said and the way she said it was calming, you know?"

"Yes, I do know. She has spoken truth and blessings over me my whole life. God has used her words many times. I'm glad you wrote it down while you remembered. If you check your journal in a few months, you might see that this was to prepare you. To prepare your heart to trust God."

"I'm sorry I wasn't there last night," Lily said. She'd tucked her handkerchief away and seemed settled in her spirit. "If I hadn't been so exhausted right after we ate, I would have helped you. I promise."

I realized how little time Lily and I had spent together yesterday. She had been with Cheryl and Jim, which was exactly the way she should have spent her time. But I missed not sharing the tea field or the Njeri blessing with her. I hoped that the remainder of our trip would be more in tandem.

The three of us launched into a discussion about the ways we heard God. For Wanja it was often through her grandma. I said I wrote prayers in a journal.

Lily said, "The only thing I write are lists. Lots of long lists."

"Maybe God directs you that way," Wanja suggested. "Pros on one list, cons on the other."

Lily said she'd never thought of it that way, then changed the subject and asked Wanja how long she'd been working for the tour company.

We continued our trek down the mountain road, and I noticed that the world around us was wide awake. The drive was much more interesting now that we could see details in the morning light that we'd not been able to see in the darkness on our arrival.

Once we connected with the main highway, the ride was smoother and less green as we left the forested area. Traffic grew heavier. We were traveling at a fast pace, but cars, minivans, and several buses darted in front of us when they had a chance to pass. Everyone was in as much of a hurry on the road leading to Nairobi as drivers at home would be on their way to Denver.

"We are a world of people who are always in a hurry," I commented.

"Is it the same where you live?" Wanja asked.

"Yes. It's different, but everyone is rushing to get somewhere."

"The biggest difference," Lily said, "is the number of people here who walk. We drive everywhere."

I had noticed it too. On both sides of the road, people were walking to wherever they needed to be that morning. Women strode through the dirt along the edge of the highway, wearing dresses and carrying baskets on their heads. Men in slacks and white shirts pedaled bicycles. Children in matching school uniforms kept up a brisk pace.

Where I lived, people would be out walking their dogs or jogging but never carrying boxes or baskets or schoolbooks for whatever distance was required to complete daily routines.

I tried to take a few photos without being noticed in case it seemed invasive. I wanted to remember this rhythm of Kenya found in the everyday movement of the people. I also wanted to add more details in my journal. I wanted to find a way to describe what I was experiencing and not just make a list of the sights or the events.

I pulled my journal from my shoulder bag and wrote quickly. I wasn't sure I'd be able to read my own writing when I returned to these pages later. That detail didn't matter. What made me feel content was that I was grabbing my thoughts while they were fresh and putting them into words for safekeeping. Even if I was the only one who ever read these scribbled entries, I knew I'd be glad I had at least tried to preserve what I was seeing and feeling.

One of the authors I'd worked with a few years ago had a tendency to overdescribe in her novels. Before I went to work editing her first novel, she and I spent several hours discussing what she expected of the process. It took me a while to find the best pace for her long paragraphs and uneven chapters. Once I found the path through the forest of her writing, I trimmed her verbosity down to what was essential and yet still retained that extra touch of color and flair that became her trademark and delighted her readers.

She won an award for her third novel. I was so happy for her. I sent her a box of truffles to celebrate. To my surprise, she sent me flowers the same day. Her note said, *Thank you for making me look like I know what I'm doing. I was always a writer. You made me an author.*

The memory tugged at my gut.

I loved partnering with writers, helping them with their books. They had the ability to bring their story ideas to life. I was just the midwife who helped them deliver a healthy book.

Had that season, that privilege, come to an end? Or could I make enough income being a freelance editor and work at home?

I was a woman of possibilities. Wasn't that what I'd decided last evening when I told Lily we were both at a cross-roads?

What would make me happy? Wasn't that Cheryl's question to us at dinner?

My thoughts were about to hit overload when Wanja pulled into a gravel parking area. She was stuck behind a delivery truck, waiting to find a spot so we could get out. I closed my journal, thinking the decisive action would turn off the waterfall of questions. But my internal interrogation didn't stop.

What if I tried to write a book? Could I?

For the first time in my life, I let myself ponder what that would be like. Not editing someone else's creation but crafting my own tale. Was I capable of giving birth to a one-of-a-kind story?

The thought was persistent, and oddly it settled on me in Dr. Seuss style. I quickly opened my journal again and added the thought in free form.

> I do not want to read a book.
> I do not want to edit a book.
> I do not want to sell a book.
> No.
> I want to write a book.
> My own book.
> A book with a look.
> A look at Africa.
> Beautiful, vibrant Africa.

The notion seemed as ridiculous as the silly way I had snared the thoughts. My face felt flush with private embarrassment as I put away my journal along with the rogue notion that Africa needed me to tell a story of her.

Wanja turned off the engine, and Lily opened the van's

side door. Their actions halted my bouncing thoughts. We were at the Karen Blixen Museum and about to tour the home of a real writer who, over a hundred years ago, had moved to Kenya and successfully told the tales of beautiful, vibrant Africa.

8

Kind words are like honey—
    sweet for the soul and healthy for the body.
                    Proverbs 16:24 NLT

We are in the Karen district now," Wanja told us as we exited the van. "So named for Karen Blixen, the Danish baroness who lived in the house you are about to tour."

"Her pen name was Isak Dinesen." The random bit of literary trivia popped out before I could stop it.

"Then why was this area named Karen?" Lily asked. "Why not Isak?"

"Interesting question," Wanja said. "I don't know."

"I'm embarrassed to confess that my view of Kenya is highly romanticized," Lily said.

Wanja stopped walking, and together we gazed at the broad, bungalow-style house that appeared at the end of the gravel road. The entire front of the house was a covered veranda. Stretching out beside us was a large grassy area edged by mature shade trees. The scene looked as if it had been frozen in time and was very much like the house from the movie.

"Kenya is a romantic place for me too," Wanja said softly. "This land once belonged to my people. My tribe. Kikuyu. It is of irreplaceable value. But we were overtaken as a people, and this entire country experienced many bloody years. Most of my generation knows only about the gift of education and opportunities for growth. We no longer repeat the stories of our ancestors. My own grandfather was tortured by British soldiers during the uprising for independence."

I reached out and instinctively placed my hand on her shoulder. The brief communion seemed to bring her back to the moment.

"Well, enough history lessons from me. You need to meet your guide so you can experience a proper tour of this romantic house."

A man stepped off the covered porch of the house and raised his hand to greet us.

"Chenge," Wanja called out. "Come meet some of my favorites."

Lily and I offered a "hello" in unison. Lily added, "Jambo!"

Chenge nodded politely.

"Now, Chenge, I have promised the very best tour of the house and grounds to my favorite Suitcase Sisters because you are the very best guide. Is this not true?"

"As you say." He smiled. "It is good to see you, Wanja. How is your mother?"

"She is well, thank you. And yours?"

"Very well." The middle-aged guide turned to greet us. He nodded toward the grassy area in front of the house and explained that all the activity going on with the trucks, tents, and chairs was in preparation for a wedding on the lawn that evening.

"A wedding?" Lily perked up. "What a beautiful setting. That's what I do. I work at an event-planning company in Nashville. We scout locations for weddings all the time. If we had a place like this in Nashville, I would keep it booked continuously."

"I tried to convince Wanja to have her wedding here," Chenge said. "But she wants to marry in a church."

Wanja gave him an endearing shrug. "We like our church." Turning to us, she said, "I will leave you in Chenge's good hands and return later to take you to your hotel for lunch."

"Are we the only ones taking the tour?" Lily asked. "I thought we were going to meet up with the rest of the tour group here."

"The other guests chose to spend the morning at the hotel. Enjoy!"

"This way, please." Chenge's accent was thicker than Wanja's, and it took a while before I felt I could understand everything he was saying.

He started us outside, examining some of the coffee farming equipment.

"Karen lived here for seventeen years. She developed six hundred acres and attempted to grow coffee. The enterprise failed, and Karen was forced to return to Denmark, impoverished. She wrote about Africa after she left and was nominated twice for a Nobel Prize."

Chenge led us to the front of the long veranda, where Lily and I stood entranced. Even though we were told that the movie had used a different location for many of the scenes, the house felt familiar.

A beautiful portrait of an African man hung on the outside wall of the house. It was a painting done by Karen of a man who once worked for her. Around the side of the house was a small, round table with a thick wood trunk base. Chenge told us this was where Karen would meet with the local people most days. They would come to her with injuries, and she'd help care for them. She chose that corner of the property because of the view of the Ngong Hills in the distance.

"In Swahili, Ngong means 'knuckles.'" Chenge held up his fist so that the rounded tops of his knuckles aligned with the hills. "Do you see the resemblance?"

In the distance, the rounded "knuckles" were visible, rising above a thick glade of mature trees. This pleasant corner of the house offered an idyllic view.

Lily stayed behind, taking her time drinking it all in. I followed Chenge into the house as he explained that photos were not allowed inside. He pointed out the dark wood floors laid in a chevron pattern. "The wood has lasted so nicely because it is cedar. The termites do not destroy cedar."

Lily caught up with us in the living room. Another tour group was moving into a different part of the house with their guide. We could hear their muffled conversation.

"Look!" Lily said. "The old record player. Like the one in the movie. Remember when they played classical music for the monkeys?" She shot a look at me that enforced her dislike for monkeys.

I was intrigued by the way the light poured in from the large windows in the next room. I wished I could take pictures of the period-piece furniture, the leopard-skin rug, and the paintings on the walls.

"The two of you might like this," Chenge said.

He led us into one of the two brightly lit bedrooms. The area where the bed and dresser were located was corded off. He pointed to a large trunk against the wall with an ornate buckle and lovely trim.

"We believe this is one of Karen's original trunks," he said proudly. "She could be a Suitcase Sister with you."

I grinned back at him so he'd know I appreciated his attempt at customizing our tour. I wondered how Lily felt about our label. It was beginning to grow on me.

Chenge didn't linger. I wished he'd slow down so we could take in all the details. He led us on to the bathroom, where he pointed out the bathtub made of tin and the porcelain floral washbowl and pitcher on a wooden sideboard. We moved on to the elaborate dining room, where we paused.

"This table is beautiful," Lily said. "And so large. No one has large tables like this anymore. Can you imagine what it would be like to be a guest here at dinner?"

"Edward, who abdicated the throne of England, was a guest and dined at this table," Chenge said.

I wanted to remember that fact so I could impress my sister Anne, who had always been crazy about all things British monarchy.

Lily and I soon discovered it was easier to imagine being a guest dining on wild game and root vegetables than to be the cook responsible for creating a sumptuous meal for the guests. When we toured the kitchen located in a separate outbuilding, the sparseness was sobering. How did anyone ever cook on a clunky cast-iron stove like that?

Before Chenge left us, he directed us to where we could view a glass-enclosed bookcase with Karen's books along with some photos and other memorabilia. The first book in the case that caught my eye was *Babette's Feast*.

"I love this story," I told Lily. "The movie is one of my favorites."

"Is that like us being one of Wanja's favorites?" Lily asked with a grin.

"Yes, exactly."

"I like the way she calls us Suitcase Sisters, don't you?"

I nodded, still focused on the bookshelf. Such an interesting summary of Karen's life was contained between the covers of those books. Once again, thoughts of writing a book about Africa rose to the surface. I dismissed the notion, flicking it away as if it were a threatening mosquito. Writers were distinctly gifted. I knew many, so I knew they were disciplined. And creative. I was neither of those adjectives. I had other qualities and attributes. But becoming a scribe entrusted with the meticulous arrangement of twenty-six letters over and over for pages and pages in a way that would say something meaningful, well, that work was for others.

I checked the notion of writing a book off the list of future possibilities. It felt good to shake that one. No intriguing second possibility took its place, so I gladly let my thoughts return to the foggy place where it was easy to focus on only the here and now.

Lily was scrolling on her phone. "Listen to this," she said. "I was trying to find out what scenes were filmed here because I forgot to ask our guide. I found this quote from Meryl Streep on why she wanted to take the part of Karen Blixen. Apparently, she said, 'I think what attracted me to her personally is this idea that she expressed about herself, which was that you can bear any amount of suffering if you transform it into a story.'" Lily looked up. "Do you think that's true?"

Another tour group had entered the small space, so I suggested we go outside. We found two lawn chairs in the shade and sat in them side by side, facing the house. We were far enough away from the workers who were raising a covering for the wedding yet close enough to the house for Wanja to see us when she arrived.

"I don't know that turning suffering into a story is what helps a person bear a lot. I think God is the one who gives us courage and strength."

"What about the suffering?"

"It's inevitable. For every life. Don't you think?"

"Yes, but some people have more than others." Lily pulled out her sunglasses. "Didn't you tell me once that a lot of writers draw from their own life experiences when they write novels?"

"I probably said that. It's true for some writers. Not all."

"I think it would be difficult to write a book, especially if it includes your own personal suffering or struggles, even if it is changed to fiction."

"True. It is very hard to write a book."

"But it must be a sort of therapy, isn't it? A chance to get everything out and look at it."

"Yes. Or change the ending of something that didn't go well in real life," I added. "You can make something helpful and positive out of terrible events that happened to you."

"That was my point earlier when I read the quote," Lily said. "And you know what? Every woman I have met on this trip so far has surprised me. None of them is what I expected. Not Cheryl or Wanja or Karen."

"Or Njeri," I added. "You're right. The women are all pretty remarkable."

"Cheryl kind of reminds me of you."

"Me?" I didn't see the connection.

"It's the suffering part. You're both strong survivors."

"Survivors?"

"Yes. I think what you went through with Micah is a survival story. It's amazing that he's settled now after the many years of suffering he put you through."

"I would never say it that way."

"I know you wouldn't, but I would. Those were difficult years."

I couldn't disagree with Lily, but I also felt like that stretch of life was over now. I didn't want to think about it, and I didn't want to talk about it here or now. Danny and I had made it through. Best of all, Micah had made it through.

"You've had your share of challenges too," I said.

"Yes, but not the way you did. Although Tyler and Noah aren't out of high school yet, so future terror might await us." Lily released a long sigh. "I wonder how they're doing."

"Have you called Tim yet?"

"No, I've only sent texts. I didn't want to tell you this, but Tim and I had a big fight right before I left."

"Just like I didn't want to tell you I'd been fired?"

"Yes, like that. I didn't want to bring any angst on our trip."

"Same."

She lowered her sunglasses, and we exchanged knowing smiles. There is no gift like a friend who knows you by heart.

"By any chance was your argument about this trip? About me coming with you instead of Tim?"

"No." She leaned toward me. "Tim supported us doing this together from the beginning. Our argument was about buying another car. I mean, that was the thing we fought about because with both the boys driving, I'm the one trying to get rides all the time. I hate it."

I nodded, remembering the challenges we had when Micah started driving a few years ago. "I get it."

"I know you do."

I turned my chair so I could face Lily and have my back in the sun.

She lowered her voice as some visitors walked by. "The fight was really about how disconnected we are. Neither of us is aware of what's going on with the other. My problems don't seem like a big deal to him, and I have little understanding or sympathy for the pressure he's under. We both said terrible things. I apologized. He apologized. But I still feel like I don't want to talk to him yet. It's like I said yesterday, Tim and I are in a bad place."

"That can change. I think you should call him."

Lily turned away and let out a long sigh.

We sat together in silence for a few minutes, letting our thoughts settle. Years ago, Lily and I had implemented a strategy for our times of venting. We agreed that we always wanted to feel free to tell each other anything and everything and not be judged. To gauge the amount of input we wanted at the end of our rantings, we came up with a simple question. *Do you want sympathy or suggestions?*

I was pretty sure this was an outpouring, with Lily wanting sympathy. That was how I'd felt as our plane was landing when I told her my messy truth. Just to be sure, though, I asked our useful question. "Sympathy or suggestions?"

She paused before deciding. "Sympathy now, suggestions later."

"You got it. Sorry this stuff is weighing on you, my friend."

"Asante sana," Lily said.

I leaned back, and so did she. We watched the tour groups coming and going and checked on the time, wondering when Wanja might return.

"You know how I said the women we've met here are remarkable?" I asked.

"Yes."

"I wonder if you and I are living a different version of brave and kind. We face big stuff. We're exhausted, yet we keep going."

"I don't think we compare with them. I mean, having to

share my car isn't on the same level as Karen plowing her own coffee fields or Cheryl surviving an assault with a knife. My complaints are about first world stuff. The problems of the privileged."

"Problems nonetheless."

After a few minutes, Lily said, "You know what I want with Tim? I want to feel something again. I want to get some sweetness back in my life. I'm tired of always feeling numb and like I'm in a standoff with him."

"Honey." I wasn't sure if I'd thought the word or said it aloud.

"Yes, dear?" Lily replied playfully.

"Oh. So I did say that aloud."

Lily laughed. "Why did that pop out?"

"Because it was Njeri's secret ingredient. Think about it. Before this morning, when was the last time you had banana bread? At a café or some you made at home?"

"I can't remember. Ages."

"I know. Me too. I loved Njeri's banana bread."

"So did I," Lily said. "And what is your point, exactly?"

"Banana bread is just banana bread, and everyday life in our fast-paced Western world is just everyday life. But when you change something, like adding honey, the ordinary becomes delicious. So delicious it makes you smile and feel happy inside."

"You're saying I should call Tim and say something sweet to him."

"Yes. Why not?"

Lily let my random thought rest on her for a minute. "You do realize that you see life differently than most people."

"I don't know about that."

"I do. That's why I'm your closest friend. You need someone to tell you these things."

"And you need someone to tell you to call your husband and give the guy a few kind words. That's all. Just add a little sweetness to his day."

Lily didn't fire back a reply. She was gazing off at the Ngong Hills. Her hands were curled, causing her knuckles to protrude.

Turning to me with a teasing scowl, she said, "I thought I said suggestions later."

"Whatever you say . . . honey."

"Stop."

"Okay."

Lily kept scowling as she stood up. She reached for her phone, and giving me a teasing growl, she strolled across the spacious grassy area.

9

A good friend listens to your adventures. Your best friend makes them with you.

Anonymous

*W*anja didn't return to pick us up until almost noon. We knew something was going on when she arrived with a big smile. A big, mischievous sort of smile.

Lily teased her and asked if she'd snuck a visit to her fiancé while we were taking the tour.

"I certainly did not." Wanja gave us a playfully shocked look at Lily's suggestion and opened the door of the van for us to climb in. "I was at the hotel helping the other safari guests settle in and learned about a problem that now has a very pleasant solution."

Lily and I exchanged curious looks.

"Your hotel reservation for tonight was canceled when you changed your dates. You will not be staying at the resort. However, I was able to make other arrangements."

"I'm sure we could call Cheryl and go back to Brock-hurst," Lily said. "It's only one night."

"I believe you need to stay in the room I have reserved for you." Wanja looked elated with her secret. "You will see."

I found it difficult to believe there wasn't an extra room for us at the large resort. Their website showed pictures of their extensive grounds and the huge swimming pool. Many of the rooms had balconies. Lily and I had talked about how fun it would be to order room service and eat on the balcony. Why was it full? Was this high season for tourists?

Wanja turned the van into a parking area. I hadn't tried to read the signs because we'd only been in the van for a few miles.

"Where are you taking us?" I didn't see a hotel in any direction.

"Come!" Wanja was already out of the van and had the side door open. "You are just in time for lunch."

We followed her, perplexed, but soon saw why she was so tickled with the solution to our resort cancellation. She was leading us up to the entrance of the Giraffe Manor.

"Fern, this is the hotel I told you about where the giraffes come to your window, and you can feed them out of the palm of your hand."

Lily reached for Wanja's arm to slow her down. "How did you get us in here? I researched it, and they were booked for two years."

"I have friends in high places, and when you do favors for such people, they remember you and are pleased to return the favor."

"Wanja," Lily declared, "you are our favorite."

Wanja laughed. I agreed with Lily and said so.

"This is a special place," she said. "It pleases me that you will experience this good hospitality and meet the giraffes."

Once again, the English countryside influence was seen in the ivy-covered, red-brick buildings. As we approached the two-story manor, I looked around, hoping to see a giraffe sauntering about.

No giraffes were in sight, but as Wanja led us through a lovely patio area with lots of potted plants and empty tables, I spotted a warthog. He was a gruesome-looking character, furrowing on the outskirts of the garden with his threatening-looking tusks turned upward as if he were ready to charge at us. The interesting thing was that he had to kneel on his front legs to search for crumbs in the dirt. He paid no attention to us while shuffling around, looking for his lunch.

We entered the lodge-style lobby, and Lily and I exchanged gleeful expressions. The comfy-looking sofas and the large fireplace made the room feel homey. On the walls were paintings of scenery that I was sure had to be African locations due to the colors used and the telltale baobab trees. I noticed statues of animals on the mantel and paintings featuring giraffes.

"First the upgrade on the plane and now this," I whispered to Lily. "It's incredible."

"I know," Lily said. "Look at this place. I can't wait to see our room."

She pulled out her phone while I took a seat on the sofa facing the fireplace. The wide grate had stacked logs ready for an evening fire. It reminded me of the wood-burning fireplace in my childhood home, only this was three times the size. How grand it would be to settle in by the fire with a good book on a rainy night.

"The original manor house was built in 1932. It has only six guest rooms, and some of the rooms are named for the endangered Rothschild's giraffes that were brought here by the owners in the 1970s." Lily looked up from her phone, which she'd been reading from. "They went from only a few hundred Rothschilds left in captivity to nearly a thousand."

"They have a thousand giraffes here?" I asked. "Where?"

"No, they release them back into their natural habitat when they're three years old. This says a dozen are here, but I don't know how long ago this was posted."

"I still can't believe we got one of the six rooms," I said.

"Wait. Six more rooms are in a separate building that opened in 2011. The Garden Manor." Lily kept scrolling. "They have a pool! I didn't know that. And a spa. This keeps getting better."

Wanja headed toward us, her smile still radiant. "You are checked in to the Daisy room. I hope you enjoy your stay. It has been my pleasure to serve you, Suitcase Sisters. May God put us on the same path again one day."

"Wait. You're not leaving now, are you?" Lily asked. "Can't you stay and have lunch with us? I told you, you're our favorite."

Wanja laughed. Her laugh reminded me of the pleasant sound of a rolling brook. "I must leave you. I have other fires to tend. I meant it when I said it was my pleasure to serve you. One of our staff will pick you up here at checkout tomorrow and drive you to the airport for your flight to the Masai Mara."

Lily was fumbling in her shoulder bag, so I stood and initiated our farewell. "Asante sana, Wanja. We will miss you." This time my goodbye hug was one that I would give to my sisters. She returned the warm expression to both of us.

Lily slid her hand into Wanja's and said, "I don't know what the protocol is for tipping, so please don't be offended, but I would like you to consider this to be a little wedding gift from Fern and me. Also, watch for an email from me asking for your grandmother's banana bread recipe."

"I will send the recipe to your email today." Wanja tucked the folded-up money into her pocket without looking at it. "Asante sana for the wedding gift. It is our first gift. I will cherish the kindness that comes with it."

We hugged again, and as Wanja exited with her fabulous braids swishing, she called over her shoulder, "Blessed travels, Suitcase Sisters!"

A bellman appeared at our side. He introduced himself, but I didn't catch his name before he offered to assist with our luggage and asked if we had more.

Lily seemed to enjoy the satisfaction of saying, "No, just one piece for each of us."

On the way to our room, I wanted to stop and look at each picture hanging on the wall and touch the rich, dark wood on the doors. The name "Daisy" was carved into the door of our room.

When we stepped inside, it felt as if we'd stepped into an extension of both our cottage at Brockhurst and the rooms we'd seen at the Karen Blixen Museum. The floors were dark wood in a beautiful chevron pattern, and the windows were the checkerboard British style. The two beds had fresh white coverlets with sheer mosquito netting pulled back and ready to be dropped when needed. The charming double-door armoire had two full-length mirrors on the front, giving a long reflection and making the room feel larger.

In the corner by the crank-open windows was a comfy-looking reading chair, and next to it stood a side table with everything we needed to make a cup of tea or coffee. On the table sat a tall, potted orchid, and beside it was a handwritten note on Giraffe Manor stationery.

Fern and Lily,
Jambo!
We hope your stay with us at the manor is lovely
and that you will take home many favorite memories.

Afi

"The note is from me," our bellman said. "I will be available to you throughout your stay." He showed us the large bathroom, how the lights and windows worked, and pointed out the plugs in the wall, reminding us that we needed an adapter, which we had, thanks again to Danny.

Afi motioned for us to take the four steps up from the bedroom onto the large balcony, where a table for two awaited. Large potted plants lined the low divider wall between our balcony and our neighbor's. The ivy I'd admired growing up the side of the manor had crept along the edge of our wooden deck, looking like delicate green lace.

Directly below us was a patio area with tables, chairs, umbrellas, and a garden with a bench. To the right, beyond a grass and dirt field, was a thick cluster of trees with tall, slender trunks.

And tucked among the trees were giraffes. Three of them. I held my breath. They were right there! Giraffes!

"Lily, look!" I wasn't sure why I whispered. Did I think I'd disturb the noble, towering creatures?

Lily came to my side and slipped her arm through mine, giving me a squeeze. "I can't believe it," she whispered back. "They're so close."

"They will come closer," Afi said. "You may feed them from the palm of your flat hand, if you like." He filled us in on the details of what to expect in the morning when the giraffes came to our patio looking for breakfast. "As you can see, they are nearly six meters tall, so they can easily greet you at eye level."

"Six meters?" I questioned.

"Nearly twenty feet," Afi replied. "They only like grass pellets, so there is no concern that they might eat any other food you have. Your first meet and greet with our famous residents will be later this afternoon. They like to come visit downstairs at the backside of the manor at four thirty."

I was getting excited about "meeting" a giraffe.

"Now," he continued, "as for the two of you, lunch is served in ten minutes. Would you prefer to join the other guests downstairs or dine here on your patio?"

"I'd love to eat here," I said.

"I agree. Who wants to have lunch with people when you can have lunch with giraffes?" Lily reached to shake Afi's hand, and it looked like she was handing him a tip the way she'd given some money to Wanja. "Asante sana."

"Karibu. Your lunch will be delivered shortly." Afi closed the door behind him while Lily and I leaned on the low wrought-iron railing and took in the view from our balcony.

"You have to tell me how much you're tipping everyone so I can split it with you."

"I will. Later." She was lost in the view.

To our left, we could see the hazy skyline of Nairobi sprawling across the horizon. In the wooded area to our right, the three giraffes stood. Every now and then their tails flicked and their long necks slowly turned as they looked around.

"They're so calm," Lily said. "I wonder what they think of the people here who feed them and take pictures of them all the time. You know, you can only see the giraffes here at the manor if you stay overnight. At least that cuts down on the volume of humans they interact with."

"They're elegant, aren't they?" I commented. "This is amazing. I can't believe we get to stay here."

"As soon as my mother-in-law sees all my photos, she's going to want to come here. That's probably one of the reasons my father-in-law was eager to bless us with this trip. He wants to come to Africa. I'm sure he's counting on me to help convince her that it's quite civilized."

"Civilized?" I laughed. "It's extravagant. I had no idea it would be like this and that we'd be treated to such warm hospitality."

We pulled out our phones to take photos, trying to zoom in on the giraffes. It was remarkable how conveniently they blended into the tall trees. A small gray bird landed on our balcony railing and tilted its head as if to check out the newest visitors.

A knock sounded on our door. I opened it all the way so Afi and another server could carry in our lunch from a serving cart in the hallway. The other man went to the table on the balcony, spread a white tablecloth, placed a vase of red roses in the center, and set the table with silverware, folded cloth napkins, and crystal-cut glassware.

Afi placed our silver dome–covered plates on the table and offered us wine, water, or lemonade. We both chose water and lemonade, which the other server brought to us from the cart along with a basket of rolls and a dish of pale butter.

Afi removed the silver domes, revealing colorful salads made of mixed greens, avocado, cherry tomatoes, mango slices, cucumbers, and white chunks that I guessed were jicama. I could smell the balsamic dressing drizzled over the top.

"This is perfect," Lily said. "Thank you."

"And for dessert . . ." Afi placed on the table two slices of chocolate cake, gave us a nod, and exited with his assistant.

Lily and I lifted our crystal-cut glasses of cold lemonade, ready for a toast.

"I don't know what to say," Lily said. "'Cheers' is not adequate for a moment like this."

"Then let's borrow Danny's toast. To the King and His kingdom."

"To the King and His kingdom," Lily echoed.

We dined with delight, taking in the sound of the birds, watching the slow-sauntering giraffes, and allowing the soft mango slices to rest on our tongues before we slowly chewed and swallowed them.

Our afternoon continued at the same leisurely pace. Lily stretched out for a nap on her "princess bed," as she called it. I went down to the lobby and did a little more exploring around the manor.

Music flowed through the lobby. A wordless song with an African cadence. The steady rhythm of the drums seemed to invite my pulse to move with it. Or maybe my heartbeat was aligning with the sounds of Africa.

I found an old paperback travel guide to Serengeti National Park on a shelf in the living room. I'd been feeling bad that I hadn't taken the time to read more of the many lists and emails Lily had sent me before we left. She'd highlighted some of the things we anticipated seeing and doing, but I wanted to know more.

Inside the guide was a piece of folded-up, handwritten paper. I settled in one of the chairs and skimmed the paper. It looked like a class assignment because it began with statistics on how many billions of dollars come into Kenya every year from tourism. Then a paragraph stated that the Kenyans were reliant on this flow of income.

The next paragraph stated that Kenya had mountains, savannas, and animals. They did not have extensive mines filled with gold or deep reserves of diamonds. The ongoing conflicts in neighboring African nations were because of the valuable untapped raw minerals.

The conclusion was that surrounding nations might be wealthy in natural resources, but Kenya was wealthy in land. Therefore, surrendering the land, selling it, or sharing it has always been more desirable than being killed for it.

Insightful words. I was curious who had written the paper and how it ended up in a guidebook, so I checked with the clerk at the front desk.

"It may have been left here by a previous guest," he suggested. "You are welcome to borrow it."

With the book tucked under my arm the way I used to always cart books around when I was a child, I went outside to explore the garden we'd seen from our balcony. The giraffe-shaped topiary was the showstopper of the shaded, English-style garden.

I couldn't stop smiling as I ventured farther onto the manor grounds. I came upon the pool and the gorgeous spa retreat area. The long, rectangular pool was partially covered by surrounding trees and enhanced by stunning sandstone pillars. Lounge chairs lined the far side of the pool, inviting me to stretch out on a thick blue cushion.

I had every intention to learn all I could about the Serengeti. However, the humid air and serene setting had another idea for my afternoon, and I was soon lulled into a deep sleep.

My snooze was cut short due to the clouds that had gathered over the manor grounds as I slept. The rain began with a sprinkling of drops that tapped my face and bare forearms. Then the liquid symphony went from its shy opening bars to a full crescendo, complete with a clash of thunder.

I dashed back to the manor lobby and tried to shake off

a little before entering. I'd hidden the tour book under my shirt and crossed my arm around my midriff as if the world depended on my ability to save the book and return it in pristine condition. When you love books, that's what you do. I didn't once think of using it to cover my head.

I entered the lobby aware that I was sloshy wet. I stopped in front of the rousing fire that had been lit in the grand hearth. A few other guests were clustered there. I chatted with two of them about how quickly the rains came and how huge the raindrops seemed. I soon excused myself, deciding I'd be more comfortable in my own room with a towel around my wet hair.

Gingerly removing the book, I placed it on the front desk with an apology. The clerk examined it. "If you don't mind my saying, it has returned in better condition than you."

Lily was awake when I reached the room. She had donned one of the plush white bathrobes that awaited us on the back of the bathroom door. Her eyebrows rose when she saw my frizzed-out, drippy, mud-splattered appearance and said a single word. "Tea?"

I nodded and went directly to the shower, grateful for hot water. My first hot shower in days. The fragrant soap and shampoo made me feel as if I were receiving a spa treatment. I felt refreshed when I returned to our room in my matching robe with a towel on my head and sank into the corner chair.

"Why have I never owned a robe like this? I feel like I'm wrapped in a hug. These are so soft."

"I know." Lily finished preparing my promised cup of tea. "I put mine on right after the rain started."

She'd closed the door to the patio and all the windows. The rain was on a rampage, soaking our patio and dissolving our plans to participate in the giraffe meet and greet.

We didn't mind.

Lily had a playlist going on her phone, which made our room feel even cozier. She stood by the window, watching the rain, and started singing along.

"I don't think I've heard you sing since Costa Rica."

She gave me a "really?" look and playfully danced as she sang. I grinned from my chair, sipping my lovely hot tea and welcoming the rush of memories that came into our room. I vividly remembered how she used to sing with pure abandon at camp. Especially on campfire nights. I had followed her example by closing my eyes, swaying a little, and lifting my arms to the heavens as we sang the worship songs that had become the weekly standards. Those nights were a radical departure from my church experience of standing straight and holding a hymnal.

Lily and the campfire choruses that summer changed me. I had been at a crossroads then, exiting my teen years, confirming my faith, experiencing a growing love for God in my heart and an eagerness to know Jesus more.

Here I was with Lily again, both of us at new crossroads.

The next song on her playlist came on, and we both laughed. It was one of the summer songs from Costa Rica that we'd sung continually. I'd nearly forgotten it.

Lily had found a remix of the song that had an African beat. I watched as she moved to the new rhythm. She danced over to my chair with the best smile I'd seen on her since we had arrived. She reached out and pulled me to my feet.

I tightened the sash on my robe and let her lead. With the towel still wrapped around my head, I followed her to the balcony door. She opened it, and the sound of the rain filled our cozy space.

We exchanged questioning glances, and without hesitation, Lily and I stepped out into the rain in our robes. We laughed and turned our faces upward, catching the raindrops on our tongues.

With only God and maybe a few giraffes watching, we danced with sweet abandon and blessed the rains down in Africa.

10

The giraffe is so much a lady that one refrains from thinking of her legs but remembers her floating over the plains in long garb draperies of morning mist, her mirage.

Isak Dinesen

In the pale morning light, I peered through the sheer mosquito netting draped around my bed. Someone had knocked on our door. Lily was up, pulling on her robe, which she'd hung to dry while we slept. She padded across the wood floor in her stocking feet.

"Good morning," Afi said softly. He held up the bucket of pellets for the giraffes. "May I come in?"

Lily welcomed him and then followed as he led the way onto the balcony. I hurried to join them outside in the freshly washed morning light. The rain clouds had scurried along sometime during the night. The air was cool, carrying a faint scent of grass. A fine mist rose from the earth, draping the slender trees in a sheer veil the way the mosquito nets had enveloped our princess beds.

We drew our robes tighter and watched two giraffes

emerge from their ethereal camouflage in the wooded area. They sauntered toward us as if in a dream. As if they had just exited Noah's ark.

The closer they came, the more magnificent the prehistoric yet seemingly tame beauties appeared. In that moment, if Afi had told us they would talk to us, I would have believed him.

"Lily," I whispered. "You know how I said neither of us was crazy about animals?"

"Yes."

"I think I just changed my opinion about that. Look at these beautiful creatures!"

"I know," Lily whispered back. "I told you I had a fondness for giraffes."

"You also said you might squeal if we saw one."

In a cartoon-like voice, Lily gave a muffled squeal. I linked my arm in hers and echoed her sentiment.

Afi held out the pail, and as the giraffes came closer, he extended the palm of his hand, revealing two pellets. The first giraffe leaned her long neck over the railing and, with her surprisingly long, dark tongue, took the pellets.

Lily and I followed his example and were caught up in a fit of giggles as the giraffes calmly lapped up the pellets. Both giraffes seemed familiar with our reaction and didn't flinch. I was fascinated by the pattern on their skin.

Afi said, "These two are the gentle sisters."

"Are they your favorite?" Lily asked. I caught the grin she tossed my direction and mirrored it back to her.

"Yes, I believe they are. They are wild beasts, even though they have become comfortable with humans. The way I see it, we are their guests."

"May we pet them?" Lily asked.

Afi shook his head. "It's best to continue the way you are. Let them be the ones who come close to you."

"Would you take our picture?" I asked Afi.

He took some great shots of us gazing into the big brown cow eyes of our hostesses. Their black eyelashes were so thick and perfectly straight they looked fake. I smiled every time I felt the dry swipe of a dark purple tongue lapping up the pellets in my palm.

"You see how quickly they eat," Afi said before he left us. "If you want to take your time with them, continue to hold out only a few pellets at a time."

We took his advice, and when the bucket was empty, the gentle beasts backed up. They left us as gracefully as they had approached. We watched them stroll around to the other side of the manor with their distinguished gait, using their front and back legs on the same side at the same time.

"I will never forget this morning. Ever." Lily beamed in the softened sunlight that filtered through the haze.

"I'm glad we got so many pictures," I said. "Otherwise all our boys might not believe it when we tell them we fed giraffes out of our hands."

"I sent Tim a text," Lily said softly. "Yesterday. After your subtle intervention with the sweetness and honey hints."

We turned to face each other, and I raised my eyebrows, inviting her to continue.

"He hasn't texted back."

"He will. Time difference, you know. And phone service."

"I know."

"I'm glad you texted him a little sweetness."

Lily pressed her lips together and returned her gaze to the manor grounds before us. The morning mist had departed, leaving a clear view of Nairobi and the Ngong Hills. The grass seemed more vivid than it had the day before. The maroon-colored dirt pathway retained a few puddles from the rain. The puddles reflected the morning sun like rounded fragments of a broken mirror scattered across the walk.

"We should head down to breakfast," Lily said. "Do you want the bathroom first?"

"Sure. Thanks."

I think we were the last guests to arrive in the cheery breakfast room, where enthralled diners were seated at all the tables for two in front of the floor-to-ceiling windows. Every window was open, and through each one a giraffe leaned in, munching pellets and complying with all the photo taking. I took a few more photos while Lily found a table for us against the wall.

The server brought us a large round tray with carved giraffes embellishing the edge. It held two small bowls of yogurt with a fresh strawberry on top, a small glass canister of granola, a fancy assortment of mini muffins, two fruit kabobs, and my favorite accoutrement—a china cup filled with soil in which a small sprig of mint was growing.

"If I ever ran a B and B," Lily said, "this is how I'd serve breakfast to my guests. It's so cute."

Her latte was delivered to the table, and she looked at the server and said, "Are you kidding me?"

"Is something wrong?" he asked.

"No, something is good. So good. Fern, look."

The barista had somehow created a giraffe image in the foamed milk.

"I had a latte with a swan once, and I've seen plenty of hearts, but never a giraffe. I think I might cry." Lily turned to the server. "Thank you."

He nodded. "Karibu."

Lily had the same "this is too amazing" reaction when we went to the spa pool for a refreshing swim. She couldn't believe the spa center was so modern. After stretching out and doing side-by-side breaststrokes in the cool water, we made our way to the indoor hot tub. We watched a giraffe stroll by as we bubbled away.

"My mother-in-law must come here," Lily said. "She will love this. It's unreal."

"Have I thanked you enough for inviting me to come with you?" I asked.

"I'm not the one we should be thanking. Which reminds me. We need to find a gift for me to take back to my father-in-law. I have no idea what to get him. He has everything."

"How about a carved wooden giraffe? I saw lots of them in the gift shop yesterday when I was exploring."

"Perfect."

Two hours later, Lily had six carved giraffes of varying sizes tucked into her packed suitcase. She'd made space for them by transferring some of her clothes into her expand-able shoulder bag. We'd ordered the same bag for the trip. Hers was brown and white striped, and mine was black. Our theory was that we could fill our suitcases with heavier items as the trip progressed and fill our nearly empty shoulder bags with the lighter items when we hit overflow.

My single purchase was a tea towel. It was hand embroidered with a brown-spotted giraffe. I knew it would bring a smile every time I used it. Plus, it was flat and wouldn't take up much suitcase space. I didn't know what I was saving the space for in my shoulder bag, but whatever that might be, I had the room for it.

We seated ourselves at one of the patio tables, waiting for the tour company driver to arrive and take us to the airport for our flight to the Masai Mara.

"This is going to sound strange," Lily said. "But if we were headed to the airport because we were flying home today, I would be content."

I nodded slowly, trying to decide if I felt the same way. "I'd be almost content. I know it feels like we've been here for a long time, but we haven't even gone on our safari yet."

"I know. Maybe what I really want is more time right where we are. I'd love to have a whole day to lay by that pool and hit pause so I can think about everything we've seen and process the conversations I had with Cheryl."

"We'll be able to do that at the next hotel, don't you think?"

"I don't know. I hope so."

"I called Danny while you were in the shower. I wanted to check in before we left this area because I remembered something about not being guaranteed that we could make calls once we were on the Masai Mara."

"I should try to call Tim." She checked her phone. "He hasn't sent a message back to me yet." She shifted in the patio chair and said, "You know, I realized Tim and I have not been away from each other for more than three days since we got married. Can you believe that?"

"Yes."

"I feel like everything went on hold when I left Nashville. I think that's why it seems like our marriage is on hold. Or at least my emotions are. Everything we argued about is still there, under the surface, like it's frozen in time."

I had several things I wanted to say to her, but I read her expression and knew I should keep my mouth shut. The tension had returned to her face, and she looked sad. I didn't understand the depth of what she was feeling, but I did understand she would ask for my suggestions when she wanted to hear them.

Thankfully, she didn't deflect her issues by switching the topic to me and delving into solving my issues. I knew she'd have good job-option advice for me once I was at the suggestions stage. But I wasn't there yet.

For now, we gave each other the gift of being side by side during the sympathy phase. We'd been experiencing a disconnect from reality, and the distancing from everyday life had brought with it a strange sort of peace. The first wave had come over me in the tea field. A second wash of deep joy had covered me that morning when I submerged myself in the swimming pool, holding my breath and stretching my arms out as far as they would go.

I felt cradled.

In an attempt to guarantee my soul's protection for a little longer, I said, "I have a favor to ask. Could we not talk about my issues for the next few days?"

"Your issues? What about my issues?"

"If you'd like to talk about yours, that's fine."

"No," she said quickly. "I agree with you. I want to fully experience all of this. I want to be all the way here."

"Me too. I feel like I'm in a bliss bubble, and I don't want to leave."

I didn't know how good our plan was for our ultimate mental health. What was good was the way we both smiled at each other without a single worry wrinkle snaking across our foreheads. Maybe there's something to be said for denial.

Our tour van arrived, and we joined the three other people who would be part of our two nights and three days on the safari. They had taken the front seats, causing us to awkwardly stretch and twist so we could end up in the back seat.

Lily introduced us. The older couple turned to greet us pleasantly. White-haired John, with his impressive mustache, and fair-skinned Darla, with her noticeably large diamond ring, were from Arizona.

"Miss our cruise pals," John said.

"My in-laws?" Lily asked.

"Your father-in-law was the one who convinced us to go on this safari." Darla's voice was surprisingly squeaky.

"Last year. In the fjords," John chimed in.

"We hope they're both okay." Darla daintily pressed her designer-label sunglasses up on her nose. "The girl who checked us in to the hotel yesterday said they didn't come."

"They're both doing well. My mother-in-law wasn't convinced about coming, so I think we were sent to check it out and come back with a report."

"Disappointing," John said.

"For your father-in-law, he means," Darla said.

Lily addressed the young woman seated beside John and Darla. "Are you guys together?"

The dark-haired woman looked up from her phone and slowly turned to glance at us from over her sunglasses. "No. Are you?"

"Mia is not in a good mood today," Darla informed us.

"Boyfriend broke his ankle," John added in his clipped way. "Last night."

"It happened at the hotel bar," Darla added. "Poor Mia. If my John were in the hospital right now, I would be at his side."

"You realize I'm sitting right here." Mia pulled off her sunglasses and flashed us an unexpected bright smile. "He's fine. He'll be in the hospital for a few days. I couldn't miss work, so I had to come without him."

"You couldn't miss work? Don't you mean you wanted to continue your vacation?" I asked.

"My work is what others do for vacation." Mia's smile remained in place. She was a beautiful woman with perfectly balanced thick, dark eyebrows. Her lips were her second most noticeable feature along with her straight white teeth. Her skin was a rich chestnut shade. I guessed she was in her early twenties.

"What kind of work do you do?" Lily asked.

"What don't I do? I'm MoreMiaGlobal." She waited for us to react. "Seriously? You haven't heard of MoreMiaGlobal?" We shook our heads.

She let us know by her response that we were pathetic. "What SM are you on?"

"There she goes again," Darla said, giving us a glance that made it clear Mia was an enigma to them as well.

Lily—sweet, friendly Lily who can comfortably start a conversation and melt the ice with anyone—knew what Mia was saying. "Do you do social media work for the tour company? As an influencer?"

Mia kept her focus on her phone but answered more politely. "No, the hotel chain. Which has made my boyfriend's incident even more complicated. I need to somehow get the shots he was supposed to take of me."

She turned her phone so we could see one of her posts. She was seated by the hotel pool, wearing a marvelous floppy red hat and matching bright red lipstick, and looking up at the African server in a white jacket. He was holding out a white cup on a saucer that was balanced in the palm of his hand.

"This is the last one my boyfriend slash photographer took yesterday. I can't lose this hotel account. It pays better than the other accounts I work for. So, yes, I'm in a bad mood, but I'm doing what I need to do."

"I'd be in a bad mood too," Lily said softly. I think Mia caught her sympathetic words and look. It was hard to tell because she was riveted to her phone.

"A mystery to me," John said. "Young people and their phones."

Darla turned again in her seat and looked at us with her head tilted. "I don't believe I heard your answer."

"Answer to what?" I asked.

"Are you two together?"

"We've been best friends since high school," Lily said.

I added, "We wish we'd brought our husbands."

"Husbands?" John asked. "How many do you have?"

"Just one each," I said with a grin.

"My wife has had five husbands," John said.

Mia joined us in glancing at Darla for verification. Darla didn't flinch.

"And all of them have been me." John delivered his flat punch line to an unreceptive audience.

I wasn't sure I wanted to know what that meant, and neither did Lily by the way she nudged me. We exchanged open-eyed looks, and I knew she was thinking what I was thinking.

The next few days of our adventure were going to be nothing like the first few. With this crew, our bliss bubble didn't stand a chance.

11

Why is it you can never hope to describe the emotion Africa creates?

You are lifted.

Out of whatever pit, unbound from whatever tie, released from whatever fear. You are lifted and you see it all from above. . . . All you see is the space and the endless possibilities for losing yourself in it.

Francesca Marciano

*M*y stomach clenched as our small plane rose into the clear sky and carried John, Darla, Mia, Lily, and me toward our safari destination. We had two pilots, and they had checked and double-checked everything before we taxied down the runway. I was still nervous. The engine was so loud, and the plane was so compact. The only seat without a passenger was at the back, and it was occupied by a large box labeled with the name of the hotel where we were going to stay on the Masai Mara.

What calmed my nervousness was the view out the window. The airport and crowded city were soon behind us, and we were soaring over the beautiful green that had now become synonymous with my impression of Kenya. An enormous lake came into view, dotted with great clusters of pale pink. I was sure the pink was flamingos. Lots of flamingos. Lots and lots.

Astonishing.

I'd read about the Great Rift Valley years ago and guessed that was what I was gazing at as we soared over the canyon. I could barely comprehend the size of it. I tried to take pictures, but I knew they would be for my memory alone. No photo could capture the immenseness of the deep crevice in the earth and the way it split the landscape. If I remembered correctly from the little bit of reading I had done before our trip, the Great Rift Valley continued for thousands of miles. Nearly the length of the continent of Africa.

The farther we flew from Nairobi, the vaster and wilder the view became. I could see a herd of black-and-white-striped zebras grazing in a loosely circled group the way horses do. The plane flew closer to the ground, and the sun caught the side of the plane just right, casting our reflection onto a wide, winding river.

Lily was in the seat in front of me since the tiny plane had only one seat on each side and a narrow aisle down the middle. We had given up trying to talk soon after takeoff. Her hand reached over the back of her seat, and I smiled. She was undoubtedly reenacting the scene from *Out of Africa* in which Denys takes Karen for her first ride in a small plane, and she is so overcome by the beauty below, she reaches for his hand.

I clasped Lily's hand, and even though she couldn't hear me, I leaned forward and said, "Yes, I see it too. You're not experiencing this all alone. It's magnificent."

The bird's-eye view continued to captivate me. I'd never been in a small aircraft like this before, nor had I experienced this sort of exhilaration that came from soaring above it all. The view stretched out wide and far with a thrilling promise of what we might see once we were on the ground and traveling with our safari guide.

The flight took less than an hour, but it felt like ten minutes the way my senses soaked it up. Our landing came with side-to-side rocking at first but then smoothed out some. Our thump-and-bump landing was met with a group exhale of relief. We exited on a hot and windy airstrip that was merely a cleared stretch of red dirt.

Ours was the only plane. Aside from several tour Jeeps waiting for us, nothing else civilized or developed came into view.

"Look at this place. I feel like we landed on the last outpost on earth," Lily said.

"Do you mind?" Mia asked, holding out a selfie stick.

We realized we were standing in her shot of herself in front of the plane. Stepping out of the way, we watched as she put on a baseball cap, removed the cap, threw a fluttering scarf around her neck, and then looked off into the distance. It was hard to gauge how many shots she accomplished with her multiple poses. Not enough, it seemed, because as soon as the luggage was unloaded, she positioned herself on top of a large, designer-label suitcase. She pulled up the skirt of her long, flowing sundress and crossed her slender legs.

"She must work for a luggage company too," Lily murmured.

Mia turned to us and motioned for us to go over to her. Within seconds Lily was recruited to use Mia's phone to capture shots in the angles her selfie stick couldn't get. The name of the luggage needed to be prominent with the sun shining on it just right.

Next, Mia pulled an energy drink from her bag and went up the steps to the door of the plane, where she posed as if she were downing the beverage even though the cap was still on it. Lily was given directions on where to stand and how to hold the phone. She complied graciously while I admired her for her kindness. I wouldn't want to be ordered around by Mia. Lily's job as an event planner's assistant for the last decade had undoubtedly put her in situations like this in the past.

One of the drivers called our names.

"Lily, we need to go," I said.

Lily handed the phone to Mia, and we strode to the waiting vehicle where our suitcases were being loaded. In a melodiously masculine voice, our driver told us we had come on a good day, after the rains. He asked if we would be going out on the afternoon drive.

Neither of us replied. I think we were a little too captivated by his Kenyan accent and the richness of his voice.

He must have thought we didn't understand him because he spoke slower and more distinctly, explaining our options. "The afternoon drives run between 3:30 and 6:30. Morning drives are 6:30 to 9:00 a.m. You schedule them each day and indicate if you would like to go out for two hours or three hours."

"If we want to go today, it sounds like we need to leave as soon as we reach the hotel," I said.

"Is that okay?" Lily asked.

"Of course."

"Is that what you'd like to do, Fern? I saw so many animals from the plane. I'd love to go out now."

"I'd like to go now too." Turning to our driver, I asked, "Will you be the one who takes us on the drive?"

"No. You will have Samburu. He is—"

Lily finished the sentence for him. "He is your favorite, right?"

"My favorite?" Our driver's laugh was as warm and rolling as his voice. "He is my brother. Do not tell him he is my favorite. He will stop treating me with respect."

The three of us laughed, and I thought of Micah.

When he was young, Micah had often told Danny he wanted a brother. After Danny and I married, Micah changed his mind. During one of his darkest dips, he threatened to run away again if I got pregnant and we had our "own" child. He'd taken off once soon after our wedding. He was fifteen and had been missing for more than twenty-four hours before Danny found him in a bowling alley. Our family therapist handled the running away issue well in our next group session, and that was the last time Micah disappeared. He threatened but never carried out his threats.

I fished my phone out of the bottom of my shoulder bag to send Micah a text with a photo from the Giraffe Manor. After I typed a long message telling him I missed him, was thinking about him, and was praying for him, the message failed to send three times. I hoped it would automatically go through once we were at the hotel.

We approached the building's main entrance, and our driver dropped us off at the front. He assured us that our luggage would be taken directly to our room.

I paused before entering, wanting to take it all in. After experiencing British-influenced architecture, we were now being introduced to a tribal style with smooth, rounded doorways, clay walls, and rounded roofs. The wide and open entrance was painted with bold African markings in browns and yellows.

Once inside, we could see straight through the lobby out

onto a patio area. Beyond the patio, down the hill, stretched immense, flat plains.

I regretted not reading more of the book I'd borrowed at the Giraffe Manor. I wished I hadn't returned it without better understanding what we were looking at. Was the vast open space part of the Serengeti? Or were we in Masai Mara territory? I remembered reading that the two wildlife reserves shared an unfenced border, and the Serengeti was south, in Tanzania. I knew we were still in Kenya, so I guessed we had to be looking at the Masai Mara.

The interior walls of the building were smooth and painted a shade of sunny yellow. The high ceiling was an elevated dome with inset lights that had an orange glow. Around the top edge of the walls and over the open, rounded doorways a white line was painted. It was thick and wavy and gave the impression of an uneven river running through the space.

Chairs with plump orange cushions were placed in half circles around a coffee table, inviting visitors to make themselves at home. I sat down and gave in to my fascination.

I hadn't stayed at a lot of hotels, so I was not exactly qualified to make an experienced comparison, but this hotel seemed extraordinary. Every detail had been designed to give guests a distinct sense of place. For the first time since arriving, I felt as if I was truly in Africa.

A pleasant-looking woman in a tribal print dress greeted us and offered warm washcloths to freshen up.

I pointed to the breathtaking view and asked, "Is that the Masai Mara?"

Her reaction reminded me of how Wanja responded when I asked about taking a tour of the tea field. Polite, but with a hidden roll of the eyes. "Yes, you are looking at the Masai Mara Game Reserve."

"I thought so but wanted to be sure." I felt I should justify why a grown woman would come all this way and not have done enough research to know exactly where she was, so I added, "I feel a little overwhelmed. The beauty here is taking my breath away."

"Wait until you see your first lion." Her grin was adorable. Her words stirred in me another inkling that I might become fond of many animals by the end of our visit.

A server wearing a shirt in the same print as the woman's dress offered us cool bottled water. We checked in at the desk and told the clerk we'd like to go on a game drive that afternoon and again for three hours in the morning.

Within minutes all was arranged, and after a quick visit to the restroom, we climbed into a Land Rover. The side windows were the widest I'd ever seen in a vehicle, and the roof was open to the blue sky.

I looked up and said to Lily, "No wonder he said it's good that we came after the rain. No roof."

Our driver, Samburu, introduced himself. I was a little disappointed that his voice didn't have the same warm, butterscotch tones as his brother's. I whispered my observation to Lily.

"Were you expecting Morgan Freeman to narrate our safari?" she asked with a silly grin.

"Why, yes, as a matter of fact, I was." I tried to sound sassy. I wasn't sure how successful I was.

"We're not supposed to be like most travelers, remember?" Lily said.

I'd taken Wanja's compliment to mean that we were flexible and didn't need a lot of extras. Now I wondered if it also meant she hoped we hadn't brought our Western assumptions with us.

Samburu's companion guide approached our Land Rover and climbed in, ready to ride shotgun.

Literally, shotgun.

He had a rifle. A queasy shiver went up my neck. I wondered how often the guides had to use their rifles.

"Do you think it's just a tranquilizer gun?" Lily whispered.

I nodded, and my shoulders relaxed. I chose to believe it was a tranquilizer gun and watched as he securely stored it and checked the two-way radio between the front seats.

"Do we need to wait for anyone else to join us?" Lily asked Samburu.

I followed her line of sight and saw that the second vehicle from the airstrip had arrived. I knew what she was thinking. John, Darla, and Mia were climbing out of the vehicle, but none of them headed toward us.

"We are cleared to go now, if you'd like," Samburu said. "Another drive is scheduled to leave in thirty minutes. Would you like to go now or wait for the next drive?"

"Now," we answered in unison.

I noticed we'd done that often on this trip, replying in tandem. I also noticed we both kept our chins down so we wouldn't make eye contact with the other three travelers.

"This is exciting." Lily shot me a look that reflected her relief that just the two of us were heading out.

Samburu drove away from the hotel and soon turned onto a rutted dirt road that led out into the wide-open plains. I readied my phone to take pictures but still had no service. My text to Micah would have to wait until we were in our room, where I assumed we would have cell service.

In the far distance rose a long range of rounded foothills. It took me a moment to adjust my eyes as well as my thinking to grasp the vastness of the land stretched out before us.

We hadn't gone far before sighting a cluster of zebras. Lily and I pointed at the same time but didn't say anything.

The bumpy road and the wonder of being out in the wild had silenced us.

Samburu approached the zebras at a reduced speed, and to my surprise, they didn't run away. My guess was that we were only about forty feet away from them when we stopped.

"Horses in striped pajamas," Lily said. "That's exactly what they look like."

"Their ears are more like a mule, though. Don't you think?"

"Sort of. Are they identical?" Lily spoke louder. "Samburu? Do zebras all have the same stripes?"

"No. Every zebra has a unique pattern of stripes. It's the same with giraffes and cheetahs. Like human fingerprints, all are different."

"That's amazing." I adjusted the binoculars provided for us and tried to see if I could identify the differences. They looked the same to me.

"Are zebra herds usually this small?" Lily asked.

"This is a family," Samburu said. "One male, several females, and their young. When they join other families, they become a herd. Zebras mix well with other zebras. Sometimes we have seen herds with two hundred or more. It depends on where they can find food."

Lily and I were busy taking pictures. She had two more questions for Samburu. From his answers we learned that three species of zebra exist, and the purpose of the stripes is probably not camouflage but rather to repel biting flies that carry disease.

I had a question about why zebras hadn't been tamed and ridden the way horses were. Samburu might not have had the best narrator's voice for a documentary, but his accent was easy to understand, and he was enthusiastic about answering all our questions.

Before I could ask, the two-way radio crackled. Our shotgun guide spoke to the person on the other end, but we couldn't pick up what they were saying. He relayed a message to Samburu.

"I apologize for the inconvenience," Samburu said. "We need to return and pick up another person in your party."

Lily and I exchanged wary glances. Our private tour was about to end, and we had a pretty good guess who the add-on would be.

12

I have no notion of loving people by halves, it is not my nature.

Jane Austen

Mia stood at the entrance of the hotel with her hands on her hips. Her flowing yellow sundress had been exchanged for a khaki photographer's jacket with lots of pockets and tight army-green leggings with brown leather boots up to her knees. Next to her was a duffle bag that was larger than my suitcase.

When she saw us pull up, she put on the hat that had been hanging down her back by a loop around her neck. It was an outback-style hat with one side of the brim up and the other down. It was difficult to guess what style she was going for.

This time Mia had to wedge past Lily and me before plopping on the bench seat behind us. Samburu's companion carried her bag to the vehicle and slid it on the floor between Lily and me with an apologetic glance.

Mia had not only changed her outfit, but she'd also freshened up with a heavily floral perfume. I was grateful the windows and roof were wide open.

"Why didn't you wait for me?" she asked.

Lily and I glanced at each other. Was she speaking to us or Samburu? Samburu ignored her and drove out of the hotel entrance, returning to the vast plains we'd only begun to explore before the interruption.

"I need you to finish what you started, Lucy."

Lily paused a moment, glanced at me, then turned and politely said, "I'm Lily. Not Lucy."

I would've added, "And I am not your personal servant." Lily, however, had much better manners and people skills.

"What do you need, Mia?" she asked kindly.

Mia's tone softened. "I can't get all the shots I need by myself, and I doubt those two speak English."

"They speak perfect English," Lily said.

"Well, they would expect a tip."

With a wry grin and teasing voice, Lily said, "What makes you think I wouldn't expect a tip?"

I caught Samburu's glance at us in the rearview mirror.

"Lily." Mia's voice was low, and her words came out in a forced staccato. "Would you help me? I checked the shots you took at the airfield. They were exactly what I needed."

"Before I answer that, let me say something."

Mia waited.

"I'm willing to help you, but you need to show me some mutual respect. You are working, but we're on vacation. So, could we start over and could you be more considerate? To both of us?"

Mia had not made eye contact with either of us from the moment she clambered into the vehicle. She continued to divert her gaze, but her reply was an improvement over her earlier tone toward us.

"Yes, mutual respect is something I believe in. Thank you for agreeing to help me."

"You're welcome."

Lily's fists had been clenched while she was speaking. I noticed her hands relaxing as she settled back in her seat and looked out the window.

I gazed out my side of the vehicle and saw that we were coming up to the zebra family, right where we'd left them. Taking a cue from Lily's school of exceptional manners, I said, "Mia, there's a family of zebras ahead on the left. We saw two baby zebras with them earlier."

"Perfect. Driver? Get as close as you can."

When he didn't immediately do her bidding, she added "please" as an afterthought.

Samburu stopped about where he had earlier. Mia handed Lily her phone and slid past us, reaching for the handle to open the door.

"You must stay in the vehicle." Samburu's voice sounded forceful.

"I know what I'm doing. I'll only be a minute."

"Guests are not allowed to leave the vehicles without clearance from the driver."

"Do you want me to sign an insurance waiver or something?"

"No. I would like you to stay in the Land Rover and enjoy taking photos from the windows or the open roof."

"Fine."

The five-minute photo session was a failure, according to Mia. She was not able to position herself close enough to the zebras to get the up-close-and-personal photos she was after. She settled for a round of shots of herself standing up and using her selfie stick as she looked off into the distance.

We all waited for her to give the okay before driving on to seek out more wildlife.

Lily thought she saw some giraffes and asked Samburu if he saw them as well. The sun was lowering quickly and blinded us as we drove into the west. If there had been giraffes, they'd moved on too quickly for us to figure out which way they'd gone.

Samburu turned in a wide half circle before returning to the rutted dirt road. Several large birds flew over us. They seemed to have come from nowhere. Across the stretch of yellowed grassland a few trees appeared here and there. They weren't in a cluster but long distances from each other.

We were nearly to the area where we'd last seen the zebras, but they were no longer there. The tall grass was moving, and Samburu drove closer to see what animal was crouched just past our view.

"Could it be a lion?" Lily asked.

"Hyena," Samburu's copilot informed us.

Mia stood on the back seat, popping out of the top of the vehicle from her waist up. Lily and I stood and could see the hyena clearly from the open roof.

"What is he doing?" Mia sounded panicky.

It was obvious what the hyena was doing.

It was also so primal it brought tears to my eyes. The hyena had taken down a zebra. A baby zebra. The entrails had been yanked out and pulled away from the carcass, and the hyena was eating them. Three other hyenas crouched nearby, ready to pounce and tear into their pound of flesh once the signal was given from the victor.

"Stop them," Mia cried, waving her arms. "Honk your horn! Where's your gun?"

Samburu's shotgun companion didn't move. He simply said, "Vultures."

I looked up and saw the large birds circling, waiting for their chance.

"Aren't you going to do anything?" Mia pounded the palms of her hands against the side of the Land Rover. "It's barbaric."

Samburu remained silent.

I shifted my gaze to the horizon, feeling a little queasy.

"Drive on," Mia ordered Samburu. "This is not what I want to expose myself to. It's sickening. I need more photos before the sun goes down. Can't you take us to a lion or elephant or even a giraffe?"

"We will go out again in the morning," Samburu said. "Three full hours. We can go farther and see the wildebeest stampede."

"What about the elephants and lions?" Mia asked.

"Tomorrow," Samburu said calmly.

He pulled away, and we could hear the other hyenas making eerie yelps as they made their move. How had they garnered the reputation for being "laughing" hyenas? Their sound did not replicate any sort of laughter I'd ever want to hear again.

Lily and I sat back in our seats and were somber the rest of the ride to the hotel. Mia pulled a different jacket and hat from her bag and attempted to meet her quota for shots of herself in the back seat.

When we arrived back at the hotel, I wanted to go to our room, have a cup of tea if they provided in-room beverage service, put on a sweater, and catch my breath.

Mia had other plans. She requested Lily's help in taking photos in front of the hotel. Her indignation over what we'd witnessed lingered in her tone, but her words to Lily were almost respectful. I knew this would not be a good time to part ways with Lily, so in essence, I acquiesced to helping Mia too. My attitude about the role was not nearly as gracious as Lily's. I ended up being the second assistant and pulled wardrobe pieces on demand out of the big bag.

We weren't the only ones watching Mia as she leaned against the curved wall that led into the hotel lobby. She then posed by the carved wooden sign at the entrance, highlighting a different pair of sunglasses she put on and quickly piling her long hair on top of her head.

The sign listed the altitude as being 5,300 feet. That surprised me. I was used to altitude since we lived at almost 7,000 feet, but our climate was dry, and our winters were cold with snow. One of the few details I read in the book from the Giraffe Manor was that it didn't snow on the Masai Mara. I had to remind myself that it was November. Here, the evening air felt cool and a bit humid, like a mild summer evening at home.

Our final photo session was on the patio near the fire ring and deck chairs. As twilight came, the distant mountains turned into a wavy outline on the horizon and took on a deep gray hue that matched the color of the long, thin, uneven clouds that stretched as far as I could see. A faint hint of the blushing sunset buffered the line of clouds and the unmoving hills.

The green slope and outstretched land directly below us grew long shadows and gained subtle, butter-colored strokes where the tall grasses sprouted. It was as if this corner of the world had been told to hush. To rest. To wait for the dark cloak of night to cover its edges and continue the promise since the beginning of time.

And there was evening, and there was morning—the first day.

I thought of the creation verse from Genesis. I felt a lingering touch of Eden lost while staring out on the Masai Mara that evening. In the distance, a single baobab tree stood like a great umbrella, a tenacious survivor, a silent, simple tree of life.

"That's it." Mia's declaration broke into my mellow observations. "That's all I need. Thanks, Lily. Let's go eat."

"We haven't been to our room yet," Lily said.

"They're nothing special," Mia said. "You might as well eat first."

At that point, I didn't care what we did next. Lily gave me a shrug as a gesture of agreement or possibly of surrender, and the three of us returned to the lobby.

I motioned to Lily that I was going to the restroom, and she joined me. Mia went to the desk, where we heard her asking that her large bag, which she'd left on the patio, be taken to her room.

"Are you okay with this?" I whispered to Lily before Mia came into the restroom.

"Yes, but only for tonight. Let's eat quickly and go to our room. I'm going to tell her that tomorrow—"

Mia entered on the tail of Lily's comment. "What about tomorrow?"

"I'm going to just be on vacation tomorrow. I won't be available to help you."

Mia looked at me, and for a moment I thought she was going to try to recruit me. Instead, she said, "I'm leaving in the morning. There's nothing else I can do here. Not considering the unacceptable animal cruelty they allow. It is against my beliefs and beyond my tolerance."

Lily laughed and then quickly pulled back her reaction. "Seriously, Mia, you had to know that you were going to be out in the wild. It's a safari. Not a petting zoo."

151

To my surprise, Mia didn't seem to take offense to Lily's reality check. She ignored it, finished washing her hands. "I hope they have something here that I can eat. I'm vegan."

"I'm sure they do," Lily said.

The dining room decor continued the tribal theme but with the added touch of white tablecloths and white cloth napkins that stood at each place like a tall candle, welcoming us home.

I looked over the menu and remembered how I'd told Danny that I wanted to be open to all the newness Lily and I would encounter. I told him I didn't want to be afraid to try something different, including the food. So far, at Brockhurst and the Giraffe Manor, I'd selected only foods that were familiar.

Except for the ugali.

But that wasn't as awful as I'd expected. Time to try more newness.

I ordered something called nyama choma. It was described on the menu as "traditionally roasted meats." I also ordered sukuma, which was "local kale cooked with tomatoes, onions, garlic, and coriander."

Lily copied my order, and Mia decided the kale combination was all she wanted.

Every bite was delicious.

We didn't talk much during our meal. Mia was on her phone scrolling and tapping as we ate. After we finished, she told us she'd edited several of the best photos and posted them on her accounts.

"That was fast," Lily said.

"I must be fast. My affiliate companies have dozens of influencers dying to take my job. You'd think the competitiveness would have calmed down, but it's as intense as ever."

"Sounds stressful," Lily said. "I couldn't do what you do."

"You could be an assistant to an influencer, though," Mia said. "I'd give you a good recommendation."

"I'll keep that in mind."

How Lily continued to be so kind and keep a straight face was beyond me. If Mia knew the size of Lily's event company or the long list of celebrity clients Lily worked with, she would stop treating her like an intern. I wanted to say something. To brag about my talented best friend the way she had praised me in front of her aunt and uncle.

Before I could think of what to say, Mia picked up her phone and said to Lily, "Here. Let me tag you. You'll have a thousand new followers, guaranteed. What's your username?"

"I don't use my social media accounts to post anything," Lily said. "I just have them so I can follow other people."

"Her clients," I added. "She has some high-profile—"

Lily tapped my leg under the table. I left my sentence dangling as it dawned on me that she wouldn't want Mia to ask her for introductions to any of Lily's connections.

Mia's focus shifted to me, and thankfully, my near blunder evaporated. She nodded at my phone on the table. "What about your accounts? You could use more followers, couldn't you?"

I decided to embrace newness and handed her my phone. "I'm not very active on social media either. But I'd like to learn how to do a better job of posting updates."

Mia looked at the photo on my screen. She looked at me and back at the photo.

"That's our son," I said.

"Your son?" Mia looked stunned. "You have a son? Him?"

I laughed. I didn't mean to, but it was the same sort of laugh that had escaped from Lily in the bathroom when Mia ranted about animal cruelty. Her stunned facial expression was not her best look.

Curbing my reaction, I simply said, "Yes. Yes, he's my son."

"So, your husband is . . ."

"Mexican," I answered before Mia could finish. I'd been in conversations like this before and didn't feel the need to explain further. Out of the corner of my eye I saw Lily bristle, ready to jump in with her support and affection for my little family. I was glad when she followed my lead and kept silent.

"Interesting," Mia replied. She looked me in the eye for the first time since we'd met and tilted her head. "You surprise me."

13

It doesn't matter where you are going—it's who you have beside you.

Anonymous

Later that night, after Lily and I were settled in our mosquito net–enclosed twin beds, we talked about Mia. I wouldn't call it gossiping. We were processing. There is a difference.

We realized that Mia hadn't shared any personal details with us, such as her last name or where she lived. Not that we were particularly open about our lives with her, except for a short explanation of how Lily and I met in Costa Rica. I added that we had helped at a Christian camp for kids.

To our surprise, Mia asked us, "What is your opinion of God?"

"He's real," I said. "He made us. He wants us to know Him."

"Interesting" was Mia's reply.

Lily told her to look up an app that would send her a verse and short insight from the Bible every day. "I always read it first thing in the morning," she said.

"Are you an affiliate for the company?" Mia asked.

"No. I just like the app. I thought you might too."

Mia downloaded the app and told us she was curious about what people like us believed about God.

"Being curious about God is a good place to start," I said. "He promised that if we draw near to Him, He will draw near to us."

Mia's look had gone back to a camera-ready expression, and she'd made her exit.

"You were so gracious to her, Lily," I said now from my bed. "I sure didn't go out of my way to be nice. I wish I had. It feels fake of me to say that she should draw near to God when I did nothing to get close to her the way you did."

"I don't know that I tried to get close to her."

"You didn't avoid her like I did."

"I've had a few clients like Mia over the years. They are determined to have things go their way and are ruthless about gathering their minions to make it happen."

"I couldn't work with a person like that."

"I've only had a few. But they don't back down. Mia was next-level. I'm glad you changed your mind and took your phone back before she went into your accounts and started posting pictures of us and tagging herself."

"You saw her page," I said. "Did it really say she has more than 800,000 followers?"

"Yes. But you know what? Some of the women I work with who have businesses in Nashville have that many followers and more. Yet they are the sweetest women you'd ever meet. They love what they do and are good at it, and that's why so many businesses want them to promote their wedding services and venues. You can be an influencer and not be demanding."

"I've had a few authors with strong opinions. But I've never had to work with anyone like Mia. She seems to know what she's doing, though. The pictures she showed us were gorgeous. There was one she took of herself while standing up in the Land Rover, and I couldn't believe the colors. You and I were a few feet away, and that's not what I saw out the window."

"You know she uses filters, right? It also doesn't hurt that she's photogenic and knows how to pose."

"Maybe we should have asked her for pointers. It says something about our double-decade friendship when our favorite photo of the two of us is a picture of our behinds."

Lily laughed. "I love that photo. It tells a story. A wonderful story."

I pulled back the mosquito netting and stepped across the cool tile floor with my bare feet. "I forgot to get my charger so I can plug in my phone. I don't want the battery to run out while I'm trying to take pictures in the morning."

"Any cell service yet?" Lily asked.

"No. I was going to check on that before we came to our room, wasn't I? Let's be sure to ask at the desk in the morning and see if they can help us. They must have some sort of internet service we can connect to."

Before I tucked myself back into my sheer tent, I said, "I know Mia said the rooms weren't much, but I like our room."

"I do too."

"When we came down the path after dinner, I thought the cottage rooms looked like a village of individual beehives."

"They do. I like the colors and designs. Quite a change from the other places we've stayed."

I made a mental note to take pictures of our room. I wanted

to show Danny how unique this place was. I think he'd had the impression we would be staying in tents on the safari. I hadn't explained that Lily's in-laws only traveled first class. A few photos would be useful.

"Fern, were you offended by the way Mia reacted when she saw Micah's picture? You seemed so calm. I wanted to say something. I was ready to get into a catfight to defend you."

"I noticed."

"My aggravation with her had built up all day, as I'm sure you also noticed. But you didn't seem bothered by her comments, so I kept my lips closed. Trust me, though. My restraint was not easy."

"Many people, well-meaning and not so well-meaning, have made comments since the beginning. You know that. Remember when, after Danny and I had been seeing each other for six months, I finally told my parents I had a boyfriend? They wanted to see pictures, and when I sent them, well, you know. Then they heard about Micah. That's when my dad told me I was settling for less than I deserved."

"I remember. All your sisters married nice local boys with those familiar German or Scandinavian roots."

"Yep. Fifteen of my parents' sixteen grandchildren have blond hair and blue eyes."

"But they do consider Micah to be one of their grandchildren?"

"Yes, of course. My parents are kind. My mom sends him a card with money on his birthday every year. She always knits him a beanie for Christmas, like she does for all her grandsons. Everyone in my family is nice to Danny and Micah, but they are an insular tribe. Danny and Micah are the foreigners. Ever since I moved to Colorado, I've been a foreigner."

I realized I had never stated out loud how I felt about my

life choices removing me from ever again being in the inner circle of my family. It was strange to hear those thoughts verbalized.

"I always saw what you did as a gutsy move, to be so far away when you have such a lovely family."

"I think I wanted to prove myself to them because I was the youngest. I had to do something none of my sisters had done. Living in a different state felt adventuresome, I guess."

"And marrying a man of another ethnicity who had an adopted son? Was that considered adventuresome to your family too?" Lily asked.

"To my family, yes. To me, it was just Danny and Micah. It felt right after I opened my heart to them. And Danny's mom is part of our own little insular tribe in Colorado. I should include her since she's in our lives every day. Not to mention that we lived with Mamacita in her house for our first two years."

"Do you regret any of it? Marrying Danny, becoming a mom to Micah, living with Danny's mother?"

"No, not at all." I didn't have to think about it. My answer was instant, and I was glad it had tumbled out so easily.

"Really?"

"Yes, really. I don't regret any of it. Danny is the best gift God has ever given me. And you know what? Everybody must face difficulties sometime. Up until Micah, I had never experienced anything really difficult. Not like you went through with your parents. My first thirty years were fairly easy."

"Interesting way to look at it. We all have to punch our way through something." Lily turned on her side. "I hope Micah stays on the path he's on."

"So do we." I pulled the covers up to my chin and loved the way the soft sheets felt across my shoulders. "The counselor said his progress could be a fake normal, but she thought his week at summer camp had a big impact on his change of heart and adjusted behavior."

"Summer camp," Lily said in a fading voice. "It sure changed our lives."

"Yes, it did." I tried to figure out how to turn off the lamp on the nightstand without having to go outside the netting again. "Can you reach the knob on the light? It's on your side."

Lily didn't answer. She was already asleep. I decided to leave the light on all night since it was a soft, low light and gave the room a fireside glowy look. Minutes later I fell asleep.

My dreams were of a baby zebra running for its life with a hyena on its heels. I know this was what I dreamed because I woke in the middle of the night, breathing hard and looking around the room, feeling a sense of danger. I was glad for the amber glow from the light. I liked that it cast shadows on the walls that looked friendly.

I prayed for a while and tried to find a comfortable position again. When I was unsuccessful, I slipped out of bed and quietly opened the glass door onto our small balcony. The protected space was just large enough for two chairs. Across the way was the outdoor patio area with the firepit. The space was softly lit, and the large glass doors that opened to the lobby had been closed.

The rest of the world before me was dark. The rooms were built on the side of the hill, and far below was only blackness. The moon wasn't visible from where I stood. When I looked all the way up, I saw exactly what I hoped to see. An explosion of millions of stars burst across the heavens. I could barely breathe at the sight. The magnitude. The multitude. The magnificence of all those stars humbled my heart.

Lily joined me. "You okay?"

"Couldn't sleep. I wanted to see the stars. Look up."

Lily had the same response. Silent awe.

Our stargazing lasted only a few moments, as the air was cool and our feet were bare. But I knew that the image would last much longer.

"I was thinking," I told Lily when we were back in our beds with the mosquito nets encircling us. "If you hadn't been kind to Mia the way you were, I don't think she would have wanted to load the app when you told her about it. You showed her how Jesus loves people. I need to remember that."

"Hmm."

"Are you asleep already?"

"No, I'm just thinking. I feel like I've changed so much from that 'go into all the world' girl I was in high school. I want to get that zeal back, you know?"

"I do too. I feel like that's happening in quiet ways on our trip. Njeri's words, Cheryl, Wanja. They all have shown us that unjaded side of loving God."

"Mmm."

"You're asleep now, aren't you?"

Lily didn't answer. I smiled. I had never known anyone who could fall asleep so quickly.

Sleep came and went for me over the next few hours. Our alarm sounded, and I woke feeling a sense of release from the struggle of the restless night. It was a new day. Samburu would be waiting for us.

We brought jackets with us after stepping out on our tiny balcony to glimpse the vast plains in the day's first light. Even in the dimness, we could see the wide view and creatures moving in the distance.

Coffee, tea, and an assortment of breakfast breads were

available in the lobby before our 6:30 departure. We enjoyed the continental breakfast quickly and climbed into our familiar vehicle with Samburu at the wheel and his nearly silent partner beside him.

"Good morning, Samburu," I said.

"Good morning, Shotgun," Lily said, naming Samburu's companion.

The two of them smiled at Lily. I had a feeling the nickname was going to stick.

No other guests joined us, and off we went. Lily and I were quietly elated that it was just the four of us.

The ruts in the dirt somehow felt more rattling than they had yesterday. I wondered if I had a few bruises. If I did and if I was going to end up with more today, I didn't care. This day would be worth every bump.

I tried to take a few pictures between bumps. My sights were set on the sky because I wanted to catch the mellow light of the early morning. Long, thin clouds sailed across the horizon looking crisp and white, like sheets hanging on a celestial clothesline.

Lily moved to the back of the Land Rover, swaying unevenly. Planting her feet, she yelled, "Come on! Stand here with me."

I made sure Samburu didn't mind. His thumbs-up prompted me to join Lily. As I made the less-than-elegant transition from the seat to the back bench, he called out that we must hold on.

The wind snatched my breath as Samburu drove, swerving around rocks and ruts. Lily and I held on to the rim of the roof, and I used my cloth headband to tie my long hair into a ponytail. Lily's feathery blond tresses danced around her face. I felt my face and everything else jiggling as Samburu turned off the trail and powered through the grassland.

162

He called out something, but we couldn't hear him. Shotgun pointed to the right. Lily saw them first.

"Look!" she squealed. "It's *Ahh-free-kan* elephants!"

I burst out laughing. "You've been saving your *Ahh-free-kan* for just the right moment, haven't you?" I had to yell for her to hear me.

Her joyful smile told me the answer. She was having one of the "whoa, we are really in Africa" moments both of us had been experiencing at unexpected times over the last few days.

"More!" Lily cried out as Samburu slowed a little and got closer. "Look, there are six! Or is it seven?"

I counted six and held up my fingers for only a second before securing my grasp once more.

Lily called out, "Good morning, all you *Ahh-free-kan* elephants! You are amazing! And large!"

Samburu hit a rut, causing Lily and me to bash into each other. We started laughing and couldn't stop. The wonder of it all caught in my throat, along with a swirl of dust and probably a bug or two. There we were, bouncing and bumping along on the wide-open grasslands, heading straight toward a gathering of very large, very real elephants.

Samburu got closer. Not too close. He turned off the engine, and the world became still. The grand beasts had drawn closer to each other in a nearby clump of scrawny trees. The beasts' size dwarfed the trees. We could hear the crunching sounds of the twigs as the elephants snapped them.

Lily's declaration was right. They were large. Much larger than the Asian elephant I had seen a number of years ago at the Denver zoo. These elephants took my breath away. And we were so close to them. No chain-link fence separated us.

"The elephants seem oblivious to us," Lily said. "But they know we're here, don't they?"

"Yes, they know. They can smell up to twelve miles away," Samburu answered.

"Twelve miles! Is it true that an elephant never forgets?" she asked.

"More true than not true," Samburu said. "They are the largest land mammal and have a very large brain. They remember survival information. They know where to find food and water and who is a threat and who is not."

"I'm glad they don't seem to see us as a threat," I said. "I can't believe we're able to get this close."

Shotgun said something, and Samburu chuckled. "We have seen this herd before," he said. "Only a few days ago. South of here. It could be that they remember us."

I liked the possibility of the elephants "knowing" our drivers and having an easygoing ambivalence toward us, because their size and mass were daunting. But their movements were slow, and even though they were standing in one place, there seemed to be a slight swaying going on. I wondered if it was the way they used their trunks to effortlessly reach up into the trees and pluck the few remaining leaves and then swing the small snacks into their mouths.

One elephant was noticeably smaller than the others. It seemed more like a teenager-size elephant than a baby-size one. Not that I knew what size an adolescent elephant should be.

Samburu confirmed my theory. "It's been a while since we've seen a baby elephant with any of the herds," he said. "We are always looking and hoping for new life. Many young elephants didn't make it through the drought of the last two years." He went on to describe the importance of elephants to the ecosystem. "The next generation—all of us, actually—will suffer if there are not more babies."

The way he said it tugged at my heart and released an unexpected flash of a recent memory. I recalled Lily's exuberant expression on the plane when I was trying to tell her I was unemployed and she was asking if I was pregnant. I linked the impression to the happiness we'd all feel right now if we knew one of these elephants was about to have a baby.

"How can you tell if a female is pregnant?" I asked. "They are so large and so round already."

Samburu said he could tell. The elephants we were observing were not pregnant. Or if they were, they were not far along.

"How long does pregnancy last for an elephant?"

"Twenty-two months for African bush elephants."

"Ugh," Lily said under her breath.

"Are these all females?" I asked.

"Yes. The bull will return to the herd when he is in musth."

"Is that like being in heat?" Lily asked.

"Yes. If there was an adult male bull with them now, I would not get this close. They can become aggressive quickly."

I set my lens on zoom and took a dozen photos. The way the elephants' thick skin sagged surprised me. They were carrying around a lot of extra folds. No wonder they were clustering into the limited shade. The mama elephant closest to us was positioned sideways. Her body caught the faint sunlight in a way that made her skin look pleated down her hefty side. Even her legs had creases.

"Since the bull elephants don't stick around, who leads the herd?" Lily asked.

"The matriarch," Samburu said. "See the large one on

the right? That's her. She most likely is the oldest female. She will lead them to food and water, usually from memory of previous watering holes. They can travel in the open without fear of predators. Sometimes as far as forty miles a day."

"So, no other animals eat elephants?"

"No."

Shotgun said something, and once again Samburu filled us in. "Last year we saw a pride of seven lionesses take down a baby elephant. Food was scarce. Otherwise they would never attempt it."

I'd never expected to have so many visceral spikes in my feelings on this trip. If I'd let myself think about it, I could have cried over the baby elephant. My emotions had risen to the surface this morning, and Africa was managing once again to lead me down a primal path into deep places.

I felt a strange calm in the presence of these females. To me, they appeared to be gentle giants, and their slow, intentional movements were fascinating. Even their aloofness seemed majestic.

"I always thought elephants were gray," I said. "These girls are more of a rusty-brown color. Is that because of the reddish dirt everywhere?"

"Yes, the dirt helps keep them cool and can keep insects away," Samburu answered. Then he abruptly added, "Did you know that elephants are afraid of bees? If they hear the buzz of a beehive, they flap their ears and get loud. I saw it once."

"Can bees actually sting them?" Lily asked.

"The stingers would never penetrate their hide, but they can sting around their eyes and inside their trunks."

"Ouch," I said.

"What about mice?" Lily asked. "Isn't there a fable about elephants being frightened of mice?"

"Aesop's fable," I said.

"They don't like small animals running around their feet," Samburu said. "But mice are not a threat."

We watched the beasts in shared silence as they slowly continued to move into the shaded area behind the trees, reaching their trunks into the limbs and bringing down more leaves to eat. Soon they were nearly hidden from our view. I wanted to get more pictures, but none of them shifted back into the open where it would be easy to get a clear shot.

I considered asking Samburu to drive around so we could face them again, but I didn't want to come across the way Mia had. I also didn't know if this was one of many herds and if we'd see more before the drive was over so there would be lots of chances to snap pictures. Hopefully we could take a photo of a baby elephant.

Samburu started the engine and seemed to be doing my bidding without being asked, circling the herd. However, we caught only a quick last glimpse of the great, endearing elephants because Samburu's true purpose had been to return to the rutted path through the most open area where the ground was less rocky.

We drove on, seeing three other vehicles from the hotel and one from another tour company. I liked the way everyone waved as if we were all friends out for a jaunt. None of the vehicles was going the same direction we were. Soon we were off the rutted road and back in the open wild. Lily and I stood on the back seat and held on as best we could.

With another swing of my emotions, I laughed again. I found it hilarious being jostled back and forth and feeling all my wobbly bits wobble, yet knowing I was doing this by choice and didn't want it to stop.

Lily joined me in the wild laughter. We lifted our chins to the clear blue skies. At that moment, there was no place else I wanted to be and no one else I wanted to be with.

Like the matriarch elephant, I knew I would never forget.

The eye never forgets what the heart has seen.

African proverb

We rode on for some time in the bucking and swaying Land Rover, wind in our hair, sunglasses protecting our eyes. I felt so young. So enthralled by the waking world around us.

Along the way we spotted two giraffes in the distance, a few hyenas lying in wait in the grass, and several families of zebras. Lots of birds were out in the early day, swooping and searching for breakfast. Small herds of one of the many varieties of African antelopes stood perfectly still, staring at us as we passed.

We didn't stop for any of those animals because Samburu had a greater goal for us.

The ground turned greener than where the elephants had been, and the earth in every direction was covered with fresh grass. Samburu had returned to the main red-dirt road, which was muddy and pocked with puddles. Dark rain clouds sailed in front of us, having already blessed this portion of land.

In the distance we saw what looked like an outcropping of dark rocks. As we got closer, we could see that the objects were moving. There were hundreds. Maybe thousands.

"Wildebeests," Shotgun announced.

Samburu drove toward them, getting closer than he'd gotten to any of the other animals. He didn't stop until we were in the middle of the herd. They parted without challenging our position and continued to rampage around us on both sides. It was as if our vehicle was a huge boulder that had been dropped into the middle of a swiftly flowing river and the water simply adjusted its course.

Through the bottom of my feet, I could feel the rumbling vibration caused by thousands of hooves pounding the ground.

"Wow. They're everywhere," Lily marveled, looking right and then left.

I was more nervous than thrilled as the determined creatures moved around us on both sides. Certainly our trusty guides knew what they were doing, but these beasts were large and charged past us like an army.

"Is it okay to be this close, Samburu?"

"Yes, we are fine." Samburu rested his arms across the top of the steering wheel and peered out the windshield.

"They remind me of buffalo." Lily acted as calm as if we were watching a 365-degree movie with surround sound.

"We have buffalo and bison in Colorado," I said, trying to calm myself by talking. "They have larger-looking heads."

"These guys are shaggier, aren't they?" Lily said. "It's their long faces and beards that make them look like ancient cousins to a buffalo. Not to mention their scary horns."

"Are you sure they don't mind us being in the middle of their stampede?" I asked.

"They are not stampeding," Samburu said. "This is their migration."

I noticed a gathering of several dozen in the distance that were not moving with the procession. They grazed close to where we had stopped and didn't seem to be in a hurry to move along.

"Migration begins in the south. In Tanzania." Samburu pointed straight ahead. "They have migrated here for grazing. Some will go farther north. Some will stay here. Birthing season begins in January."

"There are so many." I steadied my feet on the back seat and leaned against the side of the Land Rover. If for any reason these beasts decided to ram into the side of our vehicle, I feared we'd topple. "They smell terrible," I said in a low voice. "Am I the only one smelling that?"

It didn't appear that Lily heard me over the constant rumble because she said, "Why are zebras grazing with the ones out there? Is that usual?"

"Yes, it's common," Samburu said. "Safety in numbers."

"Where did the name 'wildebeest' come from?" she asked. "It sounds like something from one of my son's old comic books."

Samburu's answer was brief. "Dutch settlers. Our people had a different name for them."

"Gnu," Shotgun announced.

"I like the name 'gnu' better," Lily said. Then she greeted the huge herd the way she'd greeted the elephants. "Good morning, gnus!"

She sounded as if she was announcing, Shotgun-style, to the thousands of animals surrounding us that their name had officially reverted to the indigenous one.

"Yes, I'm talking to you, Mr. White Beard Gnu. You and all your pals. We realize you're here on your migration, and we just want to say hello, and we're amazed by all of you. And I do mean *all* of you. So, God bless y'all and have a beautiful day."

Both Samburu and Shotgun turned to look up at darling Lily. They were grinning.

The winsomeness of her personality had not changed since the day we met. It had just taken several days on this trip before the free-as-a-butterfly side of Lily emerged from the cocoon that had bound her.

I was glad to see her flutter.

I was also glad when Samburu put the vehicle in gear and eased his way back onto the main road. I lowered myself into the seat and took a breath of dusty but fresher air once we were clear of the migrating gnus.

Lily moved closer to the front of the Land Rover and asked more questions about the rainy season and the migration paths of other animals. I was impressed at the way Samburu answered all her questions. Nothing seemed trivial to him. His respect for the land and the traditions came out in some of his answers. Even though his voice wasn't rock-star level like his brother's, he was the best guide we could have asked for.

Shotgun had been talking off and on with someone on the shortwave radio while we were asking questions. We had learned that the guides stayed connected with each other on the drives so they could inform the others where certain animals had been sighted. This time, instead of an animal report, we heard the word "rain."

We saw dark clouds coming from our right side. The winds picked up, and we knew it would be a race to reach the hotel before we were doused.

Across the expanse of green grass, against the darkening horizon, baobab trees sprouted like giant mushrooms with flattened tops. One here, one there. They were loners, separated from the other baobab trees, but each one served as a grand refuge station for birds and other creatures.

As the first drops hit the windshield, Samburu pulled into the hotel's circular driveway. Lily and I told him and Shotgun that if it wasn't pouring rain that afternoon, we'd be ready to go out again, if they were willing to endure us.

"It is our pleasure," Samburu said. "Truly."

We scooted into the lobby and went directly to the restaurant. Breakfast was being served buffet style, and the various offerings were labeled, which was helpful. I tried a little of almost everything along with a generous helping of scrambled eggs and, yes, ugali. When Lily and I saw the big white lump in the lineup, we gave each other nostalgic grins and knew we had to take some.

I liked everything I tried, especially the lemon mandazi. The deep-fried, triangle-shaped pastries had a hollow center. I liked the light puffiness, and that they weren't very sweet.

Lily liked the vibibi. They looked like small white pancakes. We found out they were made from coconut milk and rice. I'm not sure why those ingredients surprised us, but they did. I'd missed them the first time around, so I went back to the buffet for them and for one of the choma sausages that Lily recommended. The sausage was lean and a little spicier than my mouth was ready for after the vibibi and mandazi.

"This wasn't just breakfast. This was brunch," I told Lily. "It's all so good. I'm going back to the buffet for some fruit. Would you like anything?"

"I think all I could manage at this point is some coffee. When our server comes by, I'll ask him. Would you like some tea?"

"Yes, please. See if they have masala chai."

I returned with my plate of fruit and saw Lily waving to John and Darla, the older couple we'd met in our tour van. They were seated across the dining room from us and appeared to be about to leave. They came over to say hello to us first.

"Have you been out to see the animals this morning?" Darla asked.

"Yes, we went on a drive yesterday and again this morning," Lily said. "What about you? What have you seen so far?"

"We have a lovely view from our room. John saw some elephants and zebras with the binoculars this morning."

"Do you plan to go on an afternoon drive?" I asked.

"I don't think so," Darla said. "I brought a book to read by the lovely pool, but now this rain is sending us back to our room, I'm afraid."

"We heard it will clear up by this afternoon. It should be beautiful this evening," Lily told them. "I hope you can get away from the hotel to go see the wildlife."

"I don't know," Darla said wistfully. "We saw Mia last night, and she said she went yesterday and it was beastly. She said the road isn't paved, and John is concerned about his back."

"Might leave," John said in his clipped way.

Darla leaned closer as if confiding in us. "We're not sure this is the right sort of vacation for us."

"Your father's idea," John said.

Lily graciously didn't correct him and say it was her father-in-law who'd booked the safari. Instead, she seamlessly rolled into her customer service mode and suggested they take advantage of the other services offered at the hotel, such as getting a massage or checking out the board games and books in the library.

Darla shook her head. "We're content in our room. John made sure we had the largest suite, so there's plenty of room and enough to keep us occupied this afternoon. We did make arrangements to have dinner outside tonight. It's a poolside barbecue. They're roasting lamb. I'm sure that will be enjoyable."

"Might leave," John said again. "Tomorrow."

"Well, I hope whatever you do will be a great experience for you," Lily said.

Darla smiled. "Thank you, dear."

The two of them wove between the tables and left the restaurant.

"You know," Lily said, "I'm beginning to understand why my mother-in-law wasn't excited about this trip. When she goes on vacations, she likes to read books by the pool and get facials. Maybe it's a good thing she didn't attempt this. She would have been like Darla and not even tried to go out on a game drive."

"It's a long way to come just to read a book by a pool," I said.

"Or get a facial."

"Not that I would mind reading a book," I said. "It's always a good idea for a rainy day."

"How about getting a massage?" Lily asked.

"I'd need to let my stuffed belly rest a bit before I could lie face down on a massage table, but yes! That sounds good too."

"Let's book massages and hang out in the lobby for a while."

"Did you order the tea and coffee yet?"

"No. The waiter hasn't come by. Oh, there he is." Lily raised her arm and motioned to the server. She requested a mocha latte, and I asked for masala chai.

Our server brought a black coffee with milk in a smaller creamer and a cup of hot water with a chai tea bag.

"Not exactly what I hoped for," Lily said. "Yours either."

"It's okay." I dunked my tea bag in the steaming water and breathed in the slightly spicy fragrance. It was nice.

Lily took a sip of milk-laced coffee and nodded. "This is good. I shouldn't be so critical. After all, we are the Suitcase Sisters. We travel light and don't complain."

"Is that our motto?"

"Could be." Lily nodded at my phone sitting beside my place. "Are you going to call Danny this afternoon?"

I looked at my phone and showed Lily the screen, where it said the words "No service."

"I think I'll see if the concierge can help me figure out how to make a call," I said. "Maybe they have a landline available to guests. I thought I'd try to call Danny after the evening game drive. That's the best time for me to catch him when he's awake. If I called now, I think he'd still be asleep."

"I should probably try calling Tim then too. I thought of him today when the gnus surrounded us. He would have loved that."

I wanted to dive into a bunch of solutions I'd come up with that I thought would help Lily and Tim. But then I remembered our promise not to start giving each other suggestions until after the safari. It seemed like a good sign, though, that she was talking about calling him. It could be that her earlier apprehensions had dissolved. And if I started giving suggestions, she would do the same, and then the focus would be on me.

I wasn't quite ready to be the person we were processing. I was still processing all we'd seen that morning.

"Do you feel a little guilty that we're having all these amazing experiences?" I asked.

"Not exactly guilty," Lily said. "I'm in awe that we get to do this."

"Me too. But honestly, at least three times now I've felt like I don't deserve any of this."

"Then tell yourself you're blessed," Lily said. "That's what my friends in Nashville and I say when good things come our way. You tell God you're thankful for the abundance of riches and tell yourself you're blessed."

"Thank You, Lord, for the embarrassingly abundant shower of riches," I said. "I am blessed."

"Yes, you are." She took her last sip of coffee. "And now I'm going to bless you with a massage. Let's go schedule it."

"Oh no you're not. I'm going to bless *you* with a massage."

"I called it first."

"Too bad. My credit card works just as well here as yours does. So come on. Please, let me do this. I want to bless you."

Lily laughed. "Okay, fine. You cover the massages, and I'll bless you with something else later."

I didn't tell Lily, but I'd only had one massage before. And I had that one because my friends at work pitched in for a gift certificate at a local massage chain for my thirty-fifth birthday. I'd loved it and was looking forward to a repeat experience after the jarring game drives.

The two openings left for the day were back-to-back, with the first one starting in twenty minutes. Lily insisted I go first.

The massage I received from the local Maasai woman was nothing like the rubdown at the massage chain. Her technique was to use her forearm to iron out my tight muscles. Then she went after the tight spots with her unbelievably strong fingers and thumbs.

I felt like putty when she was finished. The room was

warm and fragrant from the oils she'd used. She said they were made from local fruits and flowers. I loved thinking that a small resource from the rich African earth was soaking into my Michigan farm-girl skin.

When she finished, I didn't want to move off the table. Sixty minutes was not long enough.

Lily was waiting in the candlelit spa lounge, reading a book. She laughed when she saw me as I exited the massage room. My whole body felt as if I could melt into a happy puddle right in front of her.

"You are going to love your massage," I said. "She has gifted hands."

"I can tell it did you a world of good."

I drank a large glass of water as the massage therapist had suggested and then slowly strolled back to our room. I went straight to bed, stretched out, and fell into the deepest sleep I'd had in weeks.

When I woke two hours later, Lily wasn't in the room. I pulled back the curtains and opened the door to our balcony. As predicted, the rain had cleared. The sky looked like an unwrinkled swath of purest blue cotton, unfurled and spread across the horizon.

On the valley floor, the rain had left a million diamonds poured out over the grasslands. They twinkled in the sunlight. An abundance of riches.

Four giraffes formed a line in the distance and calmly traipsed toward a lone baobab tree.

O Africa. You are a wonder.

15

No one can return from the Serengeti unchanged, for tawny lions will forever prowl our memory and great herds throng our imaginations.

George Schaller

Looking up from my chair on the balcony, I put down my pen and surveyed the immense view once again. I could see for miles across the vast plain and spotted several giraffes and lots of zebras.

A small herd of African antelopes must have found something tasty at the edge of the hotel grounds because they had come closer than any other large animals I'd seen while I'd been sitting outside. Samburu had told us earlier that more than seventy species of African antelopes exist. I zoomed in with the binoculars and saw that the antlers of these antelopes had a spiral twist. The largest one looked up. If I'd had a good camera with a great telephoto lens, I could have taken a beautiful photo.

The image would have to be a memory in my mental photo album, along with many other moments that had been impossible to capture as they happened. I think that was why I felt continual nudges to write about what we were seeing and experiencing.

Where should I begin? How could I describe so many extraordinary sights and moments? How do you take a fully rounded, 3D experience that stirs you deeply and find a way to funnel the moment into flat, linear sentences?

I glanced down at the fledgling attempt I'd just made at a poem in my journal. My spontaneous "Ode to Africa."

> O Africa!
> You captured my heart,
> You beautiful land of
> Soft skies and red earth.
> I waited twenty years
> to touch you
> And now
> you have touched me.
> Your echo
> Will forever reverberate
> in my soul.

That was when I realized it was a good thing my journal was for my eyes only! It brought me joy to try to express what I felt. I loved having the freedom to play with words and dabble in artistic composition without comments from experts or opinionated consumers. The expressions were for me. And for my heavenly Father, who created everything.

My respect grew for the many authors I had worked with over the years. They were brave. Every one of them. They had to be. When they put their art, their creations, out there, they were opening themselves to the scrutiny of agents, editors, publishing committees, and eventually the public.

It amazed me how my authors maneuvered through all the opinions and managed to keep going so they could finally finish a book. Or, even more miraculously, how they found the confidence to start a second one.

Earlier, when I entertained the fleeting thoughts about pursuing writing as my next career, I hadn't considered the toll that comes with the vulnerability of sharing your words publicly.

With a long sigh, I closed my journal. Once again, I knew I didn't have the fortitude to write anything for publication. My next job would not be writing. It would be something else.

But what?

Lily came into our room, and I put aside all ponderings of my inevitable career move. I was grateful she'd appeared before I went too far down a trail of self-reflection.

"I was wondering where you were," I said.

Lily sat in the chair across from me on the balcony with a Cheshire cat grin.

"What?" I asked. "Why are you smiling?"

"My massage was so relaxing, I fell asleep. The room was so warm and the music so soothing, I fell asleep and the massage therapist didn't wake me. She had another client but used the second room. I think I just had the best nap of my life." Lily stretched, still smiling, and asked, "What did you do?"

"I came back here, immediately flopped on the bed, and slept for two hours."

"Nice."

"It was better than nice. It was wonderful. Obviously, we both needed to recharge."

"We have needed to do that for a long time." Lily reached

for the binoculars and homed in on something she'd been staring at. "Are those antelopes?"

"I think so."

"Did you see their antlers? They're shaped as if they'd come out of a soft-serve ice cream machine. One of them is really big."

"It's funny how different it feels to be watching them through binoculars after having so many close encounters with other animals. They don't seem quite as real, do they? At this distance it's more like we're looking at movies of them."

Lily's watch made the sound of a soft wind chime. "Game drive in ten minutes."

We sprang into action and found Samburu, who greeted us with "Jambo."

Lily and I were too distracted to reply. Two women we hadn't seen around the hotel occupied the front seats in the Land Rover.

"Jambo," one of them said as Lily and I climbed in and slid past them to the back bench seat. We returned the greeting as Shotgun closed the door, and we were off.

A bumpy and loud ride followed, making it impossible for Lily to strike up a conversation with the other women as she was prone to do. I told myself to be friendly this time and not so critical or snooty as I'd been with Mia. We'd been spoiled that morning to have Samburu and Shotgun all to ourselves.

Both women had silky black hair. They were probably in their fifties. One of them wore large hoop earrings and had an expensive-looking camera on a strap around her neck. I secretly hoped she didn't have a commercial social media account and that her interest in taking photos would be for her personal enjoyment only.

Shortly we came upon a large gathering of antelopes and

stopped with the vehicle idling. Lily asked Samburu about the ones we'd seen from our balcony.

"Eland." Shotgun's sudden and short declarations were now familiar to us, but the other women seemed surprised. They talked to each other in a language I didn't recognize.

Once you've experienced something remarkable, you keep an eye on the newbies to see if they are noticing and reveling in the things that made a deep impression on you. That was how it was when Samburu located a family of zebras. They could have been the same family from the day before, sadly minus a baby. The memory made me press my lips together.

The two women were hushed in their appreciation. The one with the camera clicked dozens of shots. They didn't ask Samburu questions the way we had. They seemed content to simply observe and absorb the moment, barely talking to each other.

Samburu led us next to a gathering of giraffes, and Lily and I reverted to our squeals of elation. The lovely creatures appeared to be out on an evening stroll, slowly moving across the terrain with their sophisticated, unhurried gait.

They were so close. We took pictures as quickly as we could. One of them turned from the others and headed toward us. The women spoke excitedly in hushed voices while Lily and I called to them with cooing sounds as if they were our personal pets.

I wished we had some pellets to feed them as we'd done at the Giraffe Manor. Although these giraffes weren't used to poking their long necks into people's bedrooms and being offered a treat from the palm of a human hand. I was certain Samburu would insist we keep our arms inside the vehicle if they came any closer.

The giraffe was less than six feet from us when suddenly we heard the reverberating echo of a rifle shot.

I grabbed Lily's arm and looked around. The giraffes were fleeing. Their speed and agility were startling. They headed to a distant cluster of trees, and within a minute, we could no longer see a trace of them.

Shotgun was on the two-way radio, conversing with the other safari drivers. Samburu had stopped on the main trail and was listening to Shotgun's report. I guessed they were speaking to each other in Swahili and we'd get a filtered summary in English before driving on.

"What do you think happened?" Lily whispered.

"I don't know." I was watching Shotgun carefully to see if he would remove his rifle from where he'd safely stored it.

Samburu began driving, looking ahead. The chatter on the radio ceased. Neither of them said anything.

Lily and I exchanged wary glances. It didn't appear that we'd be privy to any of the details. I hoped it had been a warning shot and was part of the regular protection of the visitors, and that no person or animal was hurt.

"I'd almost forgotten we're in the wild," Lily whispered.

"I know." My heart was still beating fast.

The women were looking right and left as we drove on. Lily and I were on the alert as well. Our game drive felt different now. We weren't standing on the back seat with our faces to the wind, squealing with glee, as we'd done that morning. My reverence for our surroundings had grown with the sound of the gunshot.

Samburu slowed down. He and Shotgun had spotted something. We'd been driving through areas dotted with sprouts of short green grass. The terrain was now turning yellow and brown and was covered with large tufts of dried grass. It reminded me of a wheat field that had been left to lie fallow and yet still managed to produce clumps of unharvested yellow straw.

184

We turned onto the dry road and drove slowly over every rock and dip. Without a word, Samburu pointed straight ahead and then turned the vehicle to the right and stopped so we could have a commanding view of whatever had caught his attention.

I gasped.

"Lion!" Lily whispered in hushed awe. It seemed fitting that her announcement didn't come with a squeal.

"Lion," I repeated in a murmur.

No one else said a word.

I remembered how the hotel greeter had said, "Wait until you see your first lion."

She was right. I was breathless.

I rose and cautiously raised my head and shoulders above the open roof. The lion slowly moved toward us on his big paws. His tawny mane was wild and tangled. Through the binoculars I spotted a long scar across his right shoulder. He seemed to be panting as he walked with his great mouth open, revealing his spiked lower teeth.

"Wow," I whispered.

The yellowed hide that covered the lion's frame appeared thin compared to the full mane that encircled his wild face. I could see his ribs protruding along the taut sides of his torso and marveled at the regal elegance of his gait as he came closer and closer.

Lily stood beside me. We both took pictures, but neither of us spoke. Our shoulders pressed close as we shared the moment in an instinctive primal pose, finding a sense of safety in each other's nearness.

The Land Rover continued to idle quietly as the lion approached. I glanced at Shotgun. He and Samburu had their eyes riveted on the great king of the beasts.

The woman with the camera pointed wordlessly to the

multiple clumps of tall, dry grass that separated us from the lion. She fixed her telephoto lens on something and murmured a few words to her companion.

One of the tufts, the largest, was moving.

Out of hiding, five lionesses emerged with two cubs following close behind. Tears of wonder clouded my sight.

The lion halted his approach.

As we watched in awe, all five lionesses went to him. Two of them brushed against his side and nuzzled their faces into his mane. He stood still, receiving their adulation. The cubs stayed close to the females, weaving in and out around their legs. One of them butted his forehead against the lion's paw and curled up as if he'd found the ideal spot for a nap.

With a slow turn, the lion lowered himself to an open spot of dry earth. He placed his paws in front of him, tucking his back haunches in close. The grand ruler at rest. And yet, his muscles gave the impression he was ready to spring to action. His closed mouth formed a slight upturn at the edges.

One of the lionesses drew near and stretched out beside him. She rolled onto her side and leaned against her unflinching mate. Both cubs came to her and cuddled in between the mother and father for a moment before scampering over to where the other lionesses were settling into the dry grasses. They stayed in a close cluster within touching range of the lion.

The cubs kept up their playful antics. They sprightly bounded over and cuddled into the lion's mane and then turned to bat each other before taking their tumbling games to another spot inside their informal circle.

Circle of life.

The lion yawned. He looked as if he was roaring, but no sound came from his ferocious open mouth. He licked his paws and rubbed his head against the side of another female who had sauntered over to lie near him.

The warm sunshine that had accompanied us all afternoon departed. The world around us became still. The yellow and tan colors of the Masai Mara were subdued.

I turned to look behind us, where the Ngama Hills sprawled across the horizon. A long line of clouds had spread over them, hiding the late afternoon sun and leaving an uneven line of pale blue sky still visible between the clouds and hills.

With the same surprising dignity with which the lion had approached us, twilight was approaching the Masai Mara lands.

I shifted my view from the pride of lions to the sight behind me. With a series of taps on my phone, I tried to capture evening's arrival. It was too intense. My camera couldn't translate the depth or the colors. I took a video just as the sun slid into the open crevice between the cloud bank and the rounded tops of the hills. I was barely breathing at the beauty of the breakthrough moment.

Light flooded our views once again. In the vibrant glow, the silent dusk came, bringing the miraculous hues of the golden hour. Our Land Rover cast a long shadow over the resting pride of lions.

I drew in a slow breath. I could almost taste the scent of the savanna. Ancient earth, dried grass, mesmerizing beasts, and an unidentifiable hint of some wild spice. The moment settled on my senses the same way my first taste of Cheryl's rich masala chai tea had soothed its way down my throat.

This was Africa. I was in Africa. I was less than twenty feet away from a lion.

The shadow of my head sticking out of the Land Rover fell upon the rounded belly of one of the lionesses that had settled in at the edge of their cluster.

A hint of me was touching her.

Lily took pictures. The women in front of us took pictures.

I couldn't. I wanted nothing to come between my eyes and the glorious sight of the golden lion.

In the stillness, a twilight breeze skittered across the plains, rustling the tall grass. Our majestic lion turned toward the breeze and faced the setting sun. He raised his bearded chin, inviting the final sunbeams of the day to transform his tawny mane to golden bronze. The wind brushed the spun strands of gold away from his face. He closed his eyes.

In my storybook-infused imagination, the time of evening vespers was upon us, and the king of the beasts was lost in eventide worship to the true King.

My heart was full. So full I instinctively placed the palm of my hand on my chest as if I could calm the pounding and keep this moment inside me for the rest of my life.

The two-way radio crackled, and in a jolt of reality, Shotgun was back at his indistinguishable communication with the other safari guides. This time, though, the voice that came through the radio was speaking English. I didn't catch the first question, but Samburu answered yes and glanced over his shoulder at us.

The piercing words that followed came through the radio clearly. All of us heard them.

"Return now. There has been a death."

16

Have we come to the place where God can withdraw His blessings and it does not affect our trust in Him?

Oswald Chambers

On the uncomfortably jarring ride back to the hotel, Lily and I held on and kept our thoughts to ourselves. My initial deduction was that the gunshot we'd heard had been a warning to an aggressive animal. They didn't have to kill the animal. Only warn it. It would make sense, then, that the guides wanted to make sure none of the other drivers encountered the beast. Especially if it was a male elephant who had returned to the herd and was, as Samburu told us, ready to protect the females.

However, the voice on the radio said there had been a death. It couldn't have been one of the guests out on safari, could it? Maybe someone like Mia had climbed out of the vehicle to get an up-close photo. The thought horrified me.

I planned to ask Samburu what had happened when we pulled to the front of the hotel and were no longer in the noisy vehicle. Then I noticed several uniformed staff standing near the entrance. They came toward us when Samburu cut the engine. I wondered if the threat was close to the hotel and they were making sure the guests were escorted to safety. Or was it worse than that?

Lily and I scrambled out of the vehicle, and Samburu's brother asked in his deep, buttery voice, "Fern Espinoza?"

"Yes."

He turned to Lily. "Lily Graden?"

"Yes."

"We have a call for you."

We followed him into the lobby. A terrifying thought gripped me.

What if the death is someone in our families?

I felt sick to my stomach.

Lily must have had the same streak of terror come over her. She reached for my arm. We walked together, arms linked, hearts pounding, imagining the worst.

We were led into the hotel manager's office and were directed to the two chairs in front of his desk. I gripped the arm of my chair, looking at Lily, who had turned pale.

We waited an agonizing twenty seconds before the hotel manager entered. He closed the door, lifted the receiver on his desk phone, and placed it on the end of the desk. "Fern Espinoza. The call is for you."

I couldn't move.

The manager and Samburu's brother exited. I stared at the phone, feeling as if I'd been plunged underwater.

Danny? Micah? My mom? Who . . .

"Do you want me to pick it up?" Lily asked.

"No, I . . ." I reached for the phone and squeezed my eyes closed. "Hello?"

"Fern! Mi conejita. I've tried to reach you for hours."

The tears began to free-fall. "Danny."

"Yes, I'm here."

"What happened? Are you okay? Is it Micah?"

"I'm fine. Micah is fine. It's my mom. Mamacita. I went to see her this morning, and she was gone. She passed away in her sleep."

"Oh, Danny." I caught my breath and glanced at Lily, who was on the edge of the chair, her lips pressed together. "His mom," I whispered.

Lily leaned back but still looked as grieved as I felt.

"I'll come home as soon as I can, Danny. I can probably catch a flight in the morning and—"

"No. No, I don't want you to come home. There's nothing you can do. Stay there."

"What about you? I want to come for you."

"I'm okay. Really. I went through this with my dad, and I can handle all the first steps with my mom."

"Don't you want me to be there?" I wiped the tears and tried to think clearly.

"Yes, of course I want you with me, but not yet. Don't come. I'll need you the most after we receive the coroner's report. When you are home, we'll make arrangements for the memorial service. It's only a few more days."

"I don't know, Danny. I think I should come."

"No. Stay. Please."

I looked at Lily again. "Are you sure?"

"Yes. One hundred percent."

"Have you told Micah?"

"Yes. He's flying in tonight and will stay with me for a couple of days."

"Okay. Good. I'm glad he's coming. Oh, Danny. I can't believe she's gone."

"I know."

"Are you sure you're okay?"

"Yes, I'm okay. Micah and I have got everything covered. You stay there. This doesn't change anything, Fern. Aslan is still on the move."

I choked up. Danny had no idea what Lily and I had just seen. He would have loved the view we had of the lions at sunset. I wished he'd been there. I missed him so much.

"Fern?"

"Yes, I'm still here."

"I love you."

"I love you too." My voice cracked. "Danny, if you change your mind and want me to board the next plane, just tell me. We haven't had consistent phone service here, but we leave the Masai Mara tomorrow. Hopefully it will be easier to reach me then. Try texting or messaging or whatever it takes. You have the phone number to the next place we're staying."

"Yes, I have all the details. You gave me everything I need." Danny's voice sounded calmer. "Try calling me whenever you have cell service. It doesn't matter what time of day it is."

"Okay, I will. I'll call Micah too. Tell him I've been trying to text him, but it hasn't gone through. I've been thinking about both of you so much."

"I'll tell him. And Fern? I'm good. Honestly. I think Micah is too. Or at least he will be. Please stay there and come home as planned, with lots of stories to tell us."

"I love you." I hung up and leaned back in the chair.

Lily reached over and covered my hand with her cool palm. "I'm so sorry, Fern."

My response was a slow nod that I hoped said "thank you," because at that moment I didn't have any words to give her.

"Do you want to sit here a few minutes?"

I shook my head.

"Do you need some water? Some tea or something to eat?"

192

A tap sounded on the office door, and the manager entered. "Please accept my condolences during this difficult time, Ms. Espinoza."

I nodded.

"How may we best serve you?" he asked.

Lily went into planning mode. "Would it be possible to have some tea and toast brought to our room?"

"Certainly."

"We'd prefer to have dinner in our room as well."

"If you don't mind waiting here a moment," he said, "I'll bring a menu and you can let me know what you'd like for dinner."

The manager left, and I told Lily I was going back to the room.

"Do you think you'll want some dinner?" she asked.

"Maybe. I don't know."

"I'll order something for you." She gave me a long hug. "Love you, Fern."

"Love you too."

My steps out of the lobby and down the path to our beehive felt heavy, and at the same time I felt as if my footprints were invisible. My body was still in Africa, but the rest of me had been transported back to Colorado.

In my mind's eye, I could see Mamacita's bedroom with her chenille bedspread and floral sheets. I pictured Danny arriving at her house, as he'd done nearly every morning since we'd moved into our condo. His pattern was to go an hour before he had to be at work so he could check on her, fix whatever she asked him to take care of, and make sure she took her morning meds.

I tried to imagine what Danny must have felt when he found that his mom was not in the kitchen, making him a mug of her Mexican hot chocolate and talking in long sentences, all in Spanish. What had he done when he found her still in her bed and not breathing?

Tears clouded my vision as I inserted the key in the door. I wished I'd been there for him. I wished I'd been able to embrace him at that moment.

I stepped inside and stood like a statue. My body was still, but my mind was racing.

I should go home. I should be there for Micah too. Surely Danny will understand if I overrule his multiple requests that I stay in Kenya.

My feet took me through the room, out to the balcony. I needed some air.

The vanishing Masai Mara Reserve filled my view as night flowed across the land like a giant can of paint. Midnight blue.

To the right, the firepit on the hotel patio flickered with a red and yellow glow. I could see the shadowy forms of the guests who had gathered by the flame. A low echo of their conversations bounced off the covering of our balcony. A woman was laughing.

Her laugh wasn't a shrill, wailing sound like the eerie howling of the "laughing" hyenas that had waited to devour the zebra. To my ears, though, at that moment, it was equally horrifying. The circle of life felt too immediate. Too brutal and too full of angst. I always thought Danny's mom would live to be one hundred years old. At least.

When Lily found me, I'd given up on the balcony and was filling the bathtub with hot water. Baths were my solace. Baths with tea and toast were even better.

Without a word, Lily wheeled her suitcase and then mine into the bathroom. I watched, still numb, as she placed the stacked suitcases next to the tub so I could use them as a side table. It was the kindest gesture she could have shown me in that moment. She was anticipating my needs before I asked.

Lily had one more gift for me. She removed the small nightstand lamp, brought it into the bathroom, plugged it in, and placed it on the closed lid of the toilet.

Room service arrived just then, and she set up my private tea party on top of the suitcases. She turned out the bright bathroom light and closed the door. The soft amber glow took my memory back to the luxurious massage room. I slipped out of my clothes and surrendered to the ministering waters in both the tub and the tea.

Closing my eyes, I prayed a simple prayer I had learned as a child. This had been my pattern and process during the roughest times of Micah's teen years. I would retreat to the bathroom, fill the tub, light a candle, and lower myself into the water. My heart would offer up a single prayer. Tonight, it was the same.

"I am drawing near to You, Father God. Please draw near to me."

I thought about the night during my early childhood when I'd had a bad dream and called out in the dark. My mom came to my room, placed her cool hand on my forehead, and told me it was time I learned her "secret" prayer. She'd said this was the one she prayed whenever she was frightened. The prayer came from James 4:8.

I took a deep breath. I knew this feeling. This sweet peace. A sense of calm like this didn't come from anywhere but God's Spirit. I wondered if that was why James 4:8 was the verse that came to mind when we'd talked to Mia the night before.

I knew that I could rest, as I'd done for years with Micah. I could wait. I could trust God and His timing.

All my tightened muscles relaxed as they had during the

massage. I found it easy to believe that God was drawing near to Danny and Micah and giving them His peace as well. In a few days I'd be with them.

Lily was seated in the corner chair when I emerged from my cloister, wrapped in the hotel room robe. I sat on the edge of her bed and told her what I was feeling and how I felt after I prayed. She listened intently and teared up along with me.

"It's so hard," she said.

"It would be so much harder without Jesus. I don't know how people go through difficulties without crying out to the Lord."

Lily turned her gaze outside. The firepit and patio lights were visible from inside our room. They offered the only evidence of movement in the dark night. In a way, the fire seemed like a beacon. A welcome. I could picture the ancients of this land gathering at fires in the cool of the evening, eating, telling stories, drawing near.

"I looked up some flight options for us," Lily said. "In case we decided to leave in the morning after all."

"No, I need to stay. So do you."

"You're sure?"

"Yes."

"Okay. I tried to send a message to Tim. It didn't go through, which is a good thing because I told him I thought you'd want to leave, and I listed when my flight would come in if we changed our return plans."

"You can delete that," I said. "We aren't finished with Africa yet. I don't think she's finished with us either."

Lily nodded. She pointed to the room service tray on the small table. "I ordered you chicken and some grilled vegetables. It's good. Basic, but good. I'm sure it will be cold by now, though."

"That's fine."

To my surprise, I ate nearly all the dinner and slept deeply that night.

Our alarm woke us before dawn. We needed to pack and be in the lobby at six o'clock for our final safari experience. Lily said we were going to hike to a hippo pool with a Maasai guide.

It sounded like an odd thing to do, and I considered staying behind. Lily could go without me. After all, I'd taken the walk in the tea field without her.

Then I thought of how much I wished Lily had experienced the tea field with me. I knew I might regret not going on this final walk. Plus, our breakfast was part of the morning tour package. I remembered how much I hated going to restaurants by myself during my many single years. Lily wouldn't enjoy doing this last excursion by herself. I didn't want her to cancel it because of me.

So I left the quiet comfort of our room and went with Lily.

With our suitcases delivered to the lobby and our trusty guides waiting for us, Lily and I saw that the two women from yesterday were already waiting. This time they'd taken the back seat.

Before I slipped into the vehicle, Samburu quietly asked me, "Is all well with you this new day?"

I nodded.

He kept looking at me with a compassionate expression. I didn't know how much he knew, so I confided that my mother-in-law had passed.

He pressed his hand to his chest as if the news had been sharp enough for him to feel the loss with me. He didn't add any words. His tender gesture was enough to make me feel a touch of comfort.

"Asante sana for asking," I said.

Samburu continued to linger. His posture was one of respect. I felt he was giving me a moment of silence, so I joined him.

I had observed how family and ancestors were revered when Chenge, our tour guide at the Karen Blixen Museum, had asked about Wanja's mother, and she did the same for him. Even though the influence of Christianity and modern Western ways had brought changes to the traditional worship of ancestors in Kenya, a deep respect for those who came before us remained woven into the culture.

I didn't know if it was my heritage that compelled me to say something buoyant in that moment, but a line from a Robert Browning poem came to mind, and I recited it to Samburu in a low voice. "God's in His heaven—all's right with the world."

Samburu tilted his head questioningly.

"It's from a poem. Have you heard it before?"

He shook his head, so I recited a snippet of the classic Robert Browning poem to him with a nervous squeeze in my voice.

> "The year's at the spring,
> And day's at the morn;
> Morning's at seven;
> The hill-side's dew-pearled;
> The lark's on the wing;
> The snail's on the thorn;
> God's in His heaven—
> All's right with the world!"

"I see." His curious expression didn't change. With a slight bow, he headed to the driver's seat.

I settled in my seat, and Shotgun closed the door.

"Why did I say that?" I murmured to Lily. "That was a weird response."

"My question is, how do you know things like that? How can you recite lines from a poem?"

"My mom."

"Of course."

"She found it easy to memorize lines from verses, hymns, and poems. They flowed out of her, and some of them stuck in my brain." I felt chagrin over my literary nerdiness but also gratefulness for my mom's nurturing and poetic influence. All my emotions felt like they'd risen to the surface. I could laugh or cry at any moment.

Lily leaned closer. "I've thought this before and will say it now. I would give anything to be one-tenth of the mom to my boys that your mother was to you and your sisters."

"What do you mean? You are an amazing mom, Lily. I have learned so much from you. I've told you many times I'm glad you had your boys before I became a mom so I could watch and learn from you."

She didn't look convinced of my praise.

Samburu started the engine. Shotgun took his place. I leaned back, expecting the familiar bumpy, noisy ride. I was going to miss this routine. I was going to miss Africa. We hadn't even left yet, and I was feeling the sadness of separation. Tears began to cloud my eyes.

Lily reached over and put her hand on my arm. "Fern, I know the safari part of our tour isn't over yet, but I need to tell you something."

"Okay."

"Are you okay?" she asked, looking at me more closely.

"Yes. I'm okay. Really. What did you want to tell me?"

She hesitated and then spilled what was clearly on the surface of her thoughts. "I'm ready for more than sympathy.

I need suggestions. I can't go home the same person I've been."

I nodded.

"I want all to be right in my world."

I gave her my best and bravest smile. "So do I, Lily. For both of us."

17

All I wanted to do was get back to Africa. We had not left it, yet, but when I would wake in the night I would lie, listening, homesick for it already.

Ernest Hemingway

The drive on our final morning was not far from the hotel, and it wasn't too bumpy. A welcome relief. We'd seen glimpses of the Mara River from the plane on the approach to the Masai Mara Reserve and again on our earlier drives. This morning in the fresh, barely awake breeze of the dawn, Samburu drove us to the river and parked near a wooded area. Two slender Maasai men were waiting for us. Both carried wooden walking sticks with rounded knobs on top. They were dressed in traditional red robes that fell to their knees and wore simple leather sandals. Around their shoulders was draped a piece of red-and-black-plaid woven fabric. Around their waists, wrists, and necks were many strings of colorful beads.

The guide who greeted us wore his hair in long, skinny braids that hung past his shoulders in the back. In the front, resting on his forehead, was a tuft of short hair. It looked like a dark, soft pom-pom. On both sides of his head, starting at his temples and hanging to the ends of his ears, were short braids that reminded me of little zebra tails.

He appeared to be about the same age as Micah, and I liked him immediately. I resisted wrapping my arms around him in a substitute hug. The Micah hug would have to wait for a while before I could give it to my son.

The other guide had gone on ahead of us into the wooded area.

"Follow me," the young man said. Lily, the two other women, and I did as we were told and headed into the grove with our brightly clad guide.

Lily asked him if the plaid shawls had some sort of Scottish influence because they looked like a tartan. He replied in English, but all I understood was that they were Maasai, and the garment was not colonial.

"The beads you're wearing," Lily began and then halted, as if she realized that asking more questions about his distinct apparel might be rude. "They're beautiful."

"They have meaning," he said. "For age, marital status, social status, and clans."

His voice was surprisingly soft. Lily and I drew closer to hear more as he led us through an area forested by slender acacia trees.

"Red is for courage, bravery, and strength. Red scares off lions, even at a long distance. Our people herd cows. We need protection when we are tending them. White is for cow's milk and speaks of purity and energy. Blue and yellow are together because they are the sky where the rain comes from and the sun. We must have both."

"What about orange?" Lily asked. "What does it represent?"

He turned to her with a kind smile. "Friendship and hospitality. The black beads are for the people and the hardships we live through."

"The patterns are so intricate."

"Our women wear the most beautiful pieces," he said. "Come. This way."

The four of us kept up as the shaded trail curved and came out into an open space. A table had been set up under the largest tree, and a man stood beside it. He was wearing the familiar print shirt of the staff at the hotel and greeted us with "Jambo."

A dozen crystal flutes were lined up on the cloth-covered table. In two silver ice buckets, bottles of chilled juice waited for us. The sight was unexpectedly elegant.

"Are we having breakfast outside too?" I asked Lily.

She nodded. We were handed the freshly poured refreshment and delicately clinked our crystal flutes of orange juice.

"This is amazing." I was so glad I hadn't opted to stay back at the hotel.

The two other women offered to tap our glasses in a toast. We all smiled. The universal language of women.

"Where are you from?" Lily asked.

"Brazil," the taller one answered. She waved her finger between the two of them and said, "Sister."

"America." Lily duplicated the finger gesture and said, "Friends."

They nodded and smiled.

"Are you a photographer?" I pointed to the camera around the neck of the younger-looking woman.

She lifted the camera but didn't seem to understand what I was asking. Then, as if the question was suddenly clear, she handed her glass to her sister and motioned for Lily and me to stand close so she could take our picture. We smiled, and she snapped several shots.

"Email?" She handed me a small notebook and a pen. I warmed toward her, happy to see someone else in the world who still carried paper and pen with them and exchanged information this way instead of by phone.

I wrote both our names and emails. "I'm Fern." I pointed to my name on the paper. "This is Lily."

They nodded but didn't say their names. Or if they did, I wasn't catching them because they were exchanging a lot of sentences. I guessed they were speaking Portuguese, which I knew was the official language of Brazil.

Our Maasai guide stepped closer. "Will you come with me?"

He led us into the grove where five tables had been prepared. Each table had a wide-open view of the water. They were all covered with tablecloths and had folded cloth napkins at each place. Glistening white plates were flanked by full sets of silverware. Beside them were bread plates with a butter knife.

Five minutes ago, we were wandering through an untamed wood where we needed a spear-carrying escort to guide us. Here, elegant civilization awaited us. The sight was enchanting.

Two men and an older woman were already seated at the first table. Lily moved on to an empty table at the end, away from the others. The sisters from Brazil followed us, and Lily motioned with a smile that they should sit at our table.

A uniformed server asked if we'd like coffee or tea. He motioned to the far left where two men in white chef's hats stood at a table. One of them was preparing made-to-order omelets while the other rolled back the lids of the chafing dishes for a guest.

"When you'd like, please take your plate to the buffet," he said.

The sisters followed our server to the omelet station. Lily and I lingered a moment, taking it all in. The sun was fully awake now, and the warm light filtered through the trees that surrounded us. I watched the shadows dancing across our table.

"I can't believe this," I told Lily.

"I know. I love it. All of it. You know how I told you on the plane that I'd make a really good rich lady?" Lily grinned. "This confirms my suspicions."

"Indeed," I agreed, trying to sound formal. "I do feel a bit bougie, though. Like we're the privileged White tourists who are expecting fancy service everywhere we go."

Lily laughed. "Well, we kind of are, aren't we? Shouldn't we take it and be grateful? I'm certainly grateful. Very grateful."

"Yes, me too. Very grateful."

"Then let's just receive this. This whole trip has been an extravagant gift. We didn't earn it. We don't deserve it. We've been graced big-time."

I nodded at Lily's choice of words. They sounded like something a blessed person from Nashville would say, and they described this week perfectly. We had been graced big-time.

"Speaking of grace," Lily said, "maybe we should give thanks now before we select our food."

Lily bowed her head. I joined her as she offered a sweet prayer of thanks, but instead of closing my eyes, I fixed them on the sunlight that shimmered on the calm waters in front of us.

A familiar passage from my childhood came to mind. My mother often led us in reciting it around the dinner table.

When Lily said, "Amen," the ancient words rolled off my lips as if it were a favorite poem. In a deep corner of my heart, it was.

"The LORD is my shepherd;
I shall not want.
He makes me to lie down in green pastures;
He leads me beside the still waters.
He restores my soul;
He leads me in the paths of righteousness
For His name's sake.

Yea, though I walk through the valley of the shadow
   of death,
I will fear no evil;
For You are with me;
Your rod and Your staff, they comfort me.

You prepare a table before me in the presence of my
   enemies;
You anoint my head with oil;
My cup runs over.
Surely goodness and mercy shall follow me
All the days of my life;
And I will dwell in the house of the LORD
Forever."

Lily smiled at me on the line "You prepare a table before me." We were both teary when we said the final word in unison.

We reached over and squeezed each other's hands. The unity we had first experienced as teens rested on us more thoroughly than it had since those starlit nights around the campfire. The Spirit of the Lord felt so close.

My thoughts were of Mamacita. She was there now. In the house of the Lord.

Forever.

My heart ached for Danny. He and Micah were walking through the shadow of her death. And here I was, being led beside still waters with my cup overflowing.

I don't think I'd ever felt such an extreme juxtaposition of life and death. Of loss and abundance. It was the joy of the golden lion and the terror of the hyenas with the baby zebra. Both ever-present realities of life and death.

The unexplainable thing was that I felt peace. The peace was tangible, but not complete. The reality of pain and sorrow still floated in and out of the peace. Somehow, that was okay.

Without words, Lily and I rose, took our plates with us, and went to the food station. I ordered an omelet and moved along the buffet table, where I took a yam, a sausage, and a small round roll. I also said yes to something the server called chapati. It looked like a tortilla, and I knew I had to have one. It was another bittersweet touch of Mamacita in this place where the veil between heaven and earth seemed thin.

Lily was elated to discover that her coffee came in a small French press. She sipped it slowly and flashed a wide smile at me.

One of the women pointed to the water. Leaning in her direction, we saw what looked like floating gray boulders with small, pale, pink flaps on the sides.

"Hippos!" Lily announced.

One of them raised its head as if in response to her summons.

"Whoa! I would not want to meet one of those brutes face-to-face," she said. "Oh, look. There's a group of them on the other side of the river. I thought they were big rocks. A baby is heading to the water."

"It's amazing how well camouflaged they are," I said.

"They blend in to the rounded rocks on the other side. The baby is cute, isn't it?"

The sisters spoke to each other again and pointed to something in the water.

"Is that a crocodile?" A shiver of fear went up my neck.

Lily looked around for our guide and motioned for him to come to our table. He had positioned himself to the side, between the river and our table. Instead of our guide, the server came to the table, asking if we'd like more tea and coffee.

"I wanted to ask our guide if that's a crocodile," Lily said.

The server looked at the long, floating creature slowly coming directly toward us. "Yes, ma'am. That is a crocodile."

"I know this might sound very touristy," Lily said with a nervous laugh. "But is it safe for us to be sitting here so close to crocodiles and hippos?"

The server gave her a closed-lip grin. "You are well protected at all times. Please enjoy your visit here. It will come to a close soon."

If I'd had my journal with me, I would have written down his words. He seemed to summarize what I'd been trying to grasp earlier about the uncomfortable blend of life and death. I hoped I'd remember what he said the next time I felt fear approaching me from behind, ready to take me down.

We finished eating, and the whole time, I kept glancing over to where the crocodile had moved to the other side of the river and climbed onto the muddy shore. He was at least twenty yards away from the baby hippo, which appeared to be well surrounded by three enormous, lumbering hippos that plodded around in the mud and then took turns lowering themselves into the river. It was surprising how quiet the hippos were when they entered the water. They glided around close to the shore one at a time with only their broad nose, their eyes, and the top of their head with their cute little ears staying above the water.

The crocodile must have realized he was facing a rifle on our side of the river and a posse of protective hippos on the other side. With a noticeable splash, he returned to the water. I could see him making his way upstream, where he wouldn't have an audience and could possibly find easy prey for his breakfast.

One of the sisters began humming. I recognized the tune. The other sister joined in, singing softly in Portuguese. They began harmonizing beautifully.

I felt as if a touch of my childhood had come to us in that pocket of shadows and sunlight. Singing with my four sisters had been a constant in my youth, but years had passed since the five of us had sung together.

When their song ended, Lily hummed a chorus we'd sung often in Costa Rica. It was the song she'd played on her phone the evening we danced at the Giraffe Manor while the rain came tumbling down outside.

Lily's favorite worship song must have made it to Brazil because the sisters sang along, exchanging looks that indicated the song had a special meaning to them as well.

The sister with the camera cried. I felt tears swelling in my throat. Lily and the remaining sister finished the chorus in a melodious duet of English and Portuguese. They sang as if we were the only people left on earth and, if we didn't offer up praise, the rocks would cry out.

Lily rolled into another familiar chorus, and the four of us sang together, no barriers of language or meaning. The troubles each of us carried that morning didn't hinder us from drawing near to God.

I knew He had drawn near to us.

Those feelings of closeness remained as we returned to

the hotel and were taken on our final drive to the airstrip. The echoing harmonies and timeless words continued to roll around inside me when we flew above the Masai Mara and once again viewed the magnificence from the sky. The small plane didn't intimidate me as it had on our first flight. But glimpses of the animals below still thrilled me, and the jagged gash in the earth that marked the Great Rift Valley still astounded me.

The swooping dip and then quick landing at the airport didn't raise a sense of panic in me. I felt in sync with our surroundings.

The God of all creation and all humanity felt near. We were well protected, and our time here was coming to a close soon.

18

God made us friends because He knew our parents couldn't handle us as sisters.

Unknown

 surprise awaited us at the remote Wilson Airport on our return from the safari. The scenario was good news/bad news.

The good news was Wanja!

She met us when we entered the small terminal, and we threw our arms around her as if she was our long-lost sister.

"We have a small change with your itinerary," she began. "It is often the way here."

"Whatever needs to be adjusted in the schedule will be fine," Lily said. "Do you have time for coffee?"

"Perhaps," Wanja said.

"What's the change?" I loved the idea of sitting down for a chat too, but I wanted to know what her opening statement meant. What was the bad news?

"As your itinerary states, you were to board a shuttle

now and ride a few hours to the mountain lodge at Mount Kenya."

"Yes," Lily said.

"Tomorrow night you were scheduled to return to Nairobi and stay at our partner hotel downtown."

"The one where Mia's boyfriend broke his ankle," Lily said.

"Yes, but his ankle was not broken. Only a sprain."

"That's good," Lily said.

"Yes, very good."

Again, I tried to move the conversation along. "Where will we be staying tonight and tomorrow night? Have our flights home changed?"

"No, your flights back to the US have not changed. The hotels have simply been changed. Tonight, you will stay at the Aberdare Country Club. Tomorrow, you will be taken to the lodge on Mount Kenya, where you will stay for one night."

"That's not a problem," Lily said.

"The next morning our driver will bring you back to Nairobi, where we will be sure you have some lunch before going to the airport for your flights home."

"That's fine. And hey, a country club sounds good to me," Lily said. "You sounded so serious."

"Some guests do not like adjustments. But I know you two understand more than any guests I've ever had the privilege of hosting."

"That's because we're your favorites, remember?" Lily grinned.

"It is true. My Suitcase Sisters are my favorite. Should I reveal to you that I also happen to have several other favorites in life?"

"No, don't tell us that," Lily said. "Let us keep believing we're at the very top of your list."

"And what do you think my fiancé would say to being replaced at the very top of my favorites list?"

We laughed and followed Wanja to the small airport café. "Before we sit down," she said, "I should tell you that your shuttle to Aberdare will not leave for another three hours. I would be happy to treat you to coffee here, or if you'd like to go into Nairobi, we can go to a coffee shop there."

I didn't have a preference.

"You know," Lily said. I could see her scanning her internal checklist. "Is there a possibility we could go somewhere for a few souvenirs? I know you might think we're not the souvenir-shopping type, but the truth is, I need to take home some gifts. I have a list."

"What kind of souvenirs?" Wanja asked.

"I don't know. That's the problem. We bought some carved giraffes at the Giraffe Manor, but I need more gifts. Some baskets, maybe. Or beads. I loved the Maasai beadwork. Can we get beads anywhere?"

Wanja nodded and turned to me. "And what about you? What would you like to shop for?"

"I don't know. Something for my husband and son, but I'm not sure what."

"A chessboard?" Wanja suggested.

"Great idea. They had a beautiful one at the Giraffe Manor with the pieces carved in the shape of animals." Another idea came to me. "This might sound ridiculous, but I'd love to buy some Christmas tree ornaments. Or anything little that could be hung on a string. The women in my family give each other ornaments every year."

"How lovely," Wanja said. "I should start doing that with the women in my family."

"Ooh! What about mugs?" Lily added. "I have a coffee

mug collection. Do you know a place where we could get one?"

"Yes. I know a place where you can buy everything on your list. But we will need some assistance. Let's get going."

We left the café and hurried outside to the van. Without explaining what we were doing, Wanja drove through the lunch-hour traffic and entered an area of Nairobi that had wide, two-lane roads going in each direction. Tall buildings and gorgeous, large trees with purple flowers lined the sides.

"What kinds of trees are those?" Lily asked.

"Jacarandas. Aren't they beautiful? This is the best time of year. I'm glad you get to see them."

"They look like they're raining purple," I said.

Wanja turned into an underground parking lot and pulled into a parking place next to a large van with the tour company logo across the side. "Would you mind waiting here?" she asked. "You will be safe. I would like to take your luggage with me up to our office. It's better not to have it with us where we are going."

We willingly surrendered to Wanja's instructions. We had every reason to trust her. The question was, where could she be taking us?

She left the windows open a crack, and from all the clicks I heard I had a feeling she locked us in. The underground parking area was cool, but we had noticed on the drive to Nairobi from the airport that the air was the warmest it had been since our arrival. I wished I'd let her take my sweater with the suitcase. If we were going to be tromping around a large indoor mall and going to lots of shops, I knew my sweater would be too hot to wear and a nuisance to carry. Bundling up and then walking around inside was one of the things I'd never liked about Colorado.

"It's kind of an adventure, isn't it?" Lily asked.

"What do you mean, 'kind of'? This is as much a journey into the unknown as any other part of the trip."

Lily pulled out her phone. "I'm adding a few things to my shopping list. Do you want me to start a list for you too?"

"No, I think I'll know what I want when I see it."

We had full service on our phones, so I used the time to text my guys and check messages. Micah had sent me a note. Short and sweet. I read it three times, grateful for every word. I was so glad he was in Colorado with Danny. Even though Danny hadn't sent me a message, I took it from Micah's update that they were okay. This could be an important time for the two of them and for Micah to privately mourn the woman who had given her all to fulfill the role of mother for the first thirteen years of his life.

An unexpected wave of gratitude washed over me. I was glad I wasn't there. Micah valued his private space. If I had rushed home, I had a feeling that in my jet-lagged state I might have reverted to my original attempts at motherhood by trying to insert myself into his method of processing.

Once again, the preciseness of God.

Wanja returned and opened the side door of the van. "Okay, please come with me. We have a driver. Titus agreed to take his lunch break early."

Once again we followed, even though I couldn't understand why she wasn't going to be our driver. She led us up to the street level, where we waited at the curb. A small blue car with rusted hubcaps and a dent above the front tire double-parked in front of us. Cars began honking.

"Hurry!" Wanja called to us as she opened the car door.

A middle-aged man in the driver's seat greeted us. Wanja put on her seat belt in the front seat and introduced us as the Suitcase Sisters before continuing to speak with him in

Swahili. We strapped in and held on as Titus darted into the traffic.

"How much money do you have?" Wanja asked us. "American dollars. How much do you want to spend?"

I instinctively put my arm over the shoulder bag that I'd been wearing across the front of me for days. I liked knowing where my passport and other important items were at all times. It felt odd that she was asking us such a thing.

Lily opened her wallet and pulled out an assortment of ten- and twenty-dollar bills. She handed it over to Wanja without hesitation.

"Nothing smaller? No ones or fives?"

Lily produced seven ones. Wanja folded the bills and put them in various places on her body. Three of the one-dollar bills were folded and tucked under the wide wristband of her watch. Others went down her shirt. The final bills went into her cross-body purse.

"How much for you?" she asked me.

I hesitantly surrendered eighty of the one hundred dollars I had in my wallet. The part of me that had read too many suspense novels thought the remaining twenty-dollar bill was important to hold on to. It might be our only hope if, in fact, Lily and I found ourselves in the middle of a bizarre kidnapping.

"I need to ask," I said cautiously. "Why do you want to hold the money?"

"You will see."

Her smile told me I should trust her. All the surrounding events indicated otherwise.

"Here is the plan, Suitcase Sisters. When we arrive, you stay close enough to take my arm at any moment. You do not say a word. This is important. Not a word. If you see something you like, simply tap my arm. Do not point. Do not stop and look closely. Do not speak. I know what you are looking for."

"How mysterious. Where are you taking us?" Lily asked with a chuckle. I could tell her laugh was nervous. Was she just now reading the room? Was she feeling the same cautions I'd been feeling since we were left alone in the underground parking garage?

"We are going shopping," Wanja said. "Now please place your purses under the seat. They will be safe."

She spoke to Titus again, and he pulled to the side, double-parking just long enough for us to scramble out of the car before the honking began.

We stood together, close enough to touch. I felt naked without my shoulder bag. I took note that in this run-down area of town, Lily and I were the only Whites in a sea of at least a hundred people coming and going. For the first time I felt a glimmer of what Micah must have felt from middle school till his sophomore year in high school. He was the only one in his classes with skin a noticeably different color than the other kids'.

The awareness was real. I understood now. The awareness that you are different stokes a strange sort of fear. It doesn't matter what anyone might have told me right then about being accepted or safe or just being myself. Lily and I were anomalies. I felt it.

"Remember. No speaking at all," Wanja murmured.

We moved as one, entering a marketplace that looked more like a humble, orderly village being rebuilt after a hurricane.

The vendors also moved as one. They rose from their tiny, three-legged stools and came to us in a circle. The stalls were dilapidated, and each small space was packed with African-crafted items. Lily and I glanced out the corners of our eyes at baskets, beads, carvings, fabrics, wooden bowls, and chessboards with carved pieces.

Wanja held her head high, undaunted. My heart was pounding wildly. I felt like poor little Simba in *The Lion King* when the hyenas encircled him.

Speaking Swahili, Wanja apparently made a specific request because all the vendors scattered to their stalls. We stood in the center of the marketplace as each one ran back, presenting their finest carved items to us.

Many showed us giraffes, which Wanja brushed aside, knowing we'd already purchased those. Others held up sleek, polished statues of African women. She scorned those offerings with a string of words that sent the hopefuls back for a second attempt at pleasing her. The vendors spread out like ripples in the water after a stone is thrown.

I was in awe. None of the men came near enough to touch Lily, Wanja, or me. All of them spoke with respectful tones. Clearly they wanted to make a sale.

I wasn't sure why, but my intrinsic fear began to dissipate. A new perspective came over me. These were salesmen, doing the best they could with what they had in a place of limited opportunities. Like with any open-air market in any city, it made sense to be protected from pickpockets. Wanja's insistence that we abandon our purses and make her guardian of the money made sense.

Within moments of her second request, every man's arms were dripping with strings of colorful beads. Both Lily and I touched Wanja's arm, and the haggling began. She pulled a single dollar bill from her watchband, and a cry rose from the vendors circling us. Some raised their arms, others seemed to bounce with their knees bent. It was killing me to not ask Wanja what was happening.

She appeared to select strings of beads from one man but

then turned her attention to another who was behind her. The circle shifted in the same direction, and it felt like we were the ones rotating, as if we were on a lazy Susan.

More words were exchanged with her favored vendor. He held out at least twenty strands of beads. She withdrew the dollar bill, turned, and handed it to the first man she'd bargained with. He handed her what looked like more than what the other guy had offered.

Both Lily and I tapped her arm again. I had a feeling we felt a mutual sympathy for the man who'd lost the sale. Wanja returned to him. He counted out the equal number of strands she'd just received and gratefully received the dollar bill.

Between the two of us, Lily and I now had far more beaded necklaces than we could possibly give away, but I saw Lily give Wanja another tap on the arm.

A man with a clever eye saw the clandestine move. This time he held the beads in front of Lily for her inspection. Wanja put up her palm like a school crossing guard and walked away. Lily and I had to hurry to get back in step with her. She exited the marketplace without a word and walked nearly a block in silence before the last vendor ceased to trail us.

"Stay close," she said calmly.

We walked another block before stopping.

"How many more bead necklaces do you want?" She handed a collection of strands to each of us. "Are you opening your own store when you return home?"

"I felt sorry for the guy," Lily said. "And they were only a dollar."

Wanja looked over our heads as if checking for traveling salesmen coming our way. I thought she might tell us this was the way things were done and we shouldn't be so

American in our ways. Instead, she said, "I need more specifics. Tell me your exact list and quantities. I will buy it
for you."

The word "list" was all Lily needed. She had hers memo-
rized and repeated the items and quantities as Wanja nodded.

"And you?" Wanja turned to me.

"I saw a nice chessboard with carved animals," I said. "It
was in the third booth from the entrance on the left side."

"Yes, I saw that too. Okay. What else?"

"There was also a round wooden game with marbles in
the booth next to the one with the chess set."

"How large?" Wanja asked.

I demonstrated with my arms.

"Anything else? Christmas ornaments?"

"If you see any, yes. I could use six or seven. And I'd like
a small bread basket. But you might need all the money I
gave you for the two game boards."

"I will let you know. And I will get everything you asked
for." She looked over our heads again and motioned with
her hand to her side. The rusty-hubcap mobile pulled up
behind us.

Once again, we did as we were told and slid into the back
seat of the car. Wanja left us and returned to the marketplace. Her long strides made it clear that she was a woman
on a mission. Lily and I had looped our excess of beaded
necklaces over our heads and remained wide-eyed at everything that was happening at such a fast pace.

Titus rolled down all the windows and drove. He started
to pass a man on a wobbly bicycle who was holding a chicken
under his arm. We had almost passed the man in the narrow
space allotted when the chicken escaped his clutch. It flapped
through the open window into the car and landed on my lap.

Lily shrieked.

The cyclist yelled something. Titus yelled something.

I circled my hands around the chicken as I'd done since I was a toddler and held it calmly as it pecked at the excessive assortment of colorful beads around my neck.

Titus stopped the car, waiting for the man on the bike to come alongside us. As cars honked, the man reached into my open window, and I successfully transferred the chicken to him. We drove on as if nothing had happened.

But something did happen. I looked at Lily. I shouldn't have done that because she let loose with the very best, impossible-to-stop belly laugh of all time. I thought I'd heard her laugh wildly in Costa Rica. Her African gully washer of laughter was a whole new level. And, of course, I had to let loose along with her.

Poor Titus.

By the time we'd circled the area long enough for Wanja to have completed her task and climb into the front seat with her arms full, Lily and I were awash in a puddle of receding laughter. We wiped our eyes and held our bellies.

Wanja turned and gave us a puzzled look. "What did I miss?"

19

Don't think there are no crocodiles just because the water's calm.

African proverb

My mom often said that God saves the best for last. I never understood what that meant, exactly. The line came to mind when our impromptu shopping spree and chicken kerfuffle was followed by coffee with Wanja.

She took us to the Java House. I loved the vibe from the moment we stepped inside the contemporary, artsy café. Wanja ordered an assortment of their bakery specialties for us to share and convinced me to order the Malindi chai latte instead of the masala chai offered on the extensive menu. She said it had the delicious spices of a masala chai but with an added shot of espresso. After all, the coffee beans were Kenyan grown and hand roasted. I needed to pay homage to the land I'd been treading, she said.

"So, what do you think?" Wanja asked after my first sip of the foamy, hot beverage.

"It's nice."

"But not as nice as Cheryl's masala chai," Wanja ventured.

"What can I say? I'm a tea drinker." I took another sip. "But this is nice."

Lily laughed. "That's like saying someone has a nice personality because it's the only positive attribute you can come up with."

"I will go order a masala chai latte for you," Wanja said.

"No, this is all I want," I said. "Really. I'm still caffeinated from our beautiful breakfast at the hippo pool. But if they have masala chai that I can take home with me, I'd like to buy a bag before we leave."

"I will tell you the secret to making the best masala chai," Wanja said.

"Yes! Tell me."

"Is it like your grandmother's *secret* banana bread recipe?" Lily asked.

"Of course. Because this is my personal recipe." She held her chin up. "And you might as well know the truth. I was the one who gave Cheryl this recipe."

I had my journal open and my pen ready.

"You must use two parts water and one part milk. Boil the water in a saucepan, then add all the spices. You must let this simmer for two to five minutes. Then you add the loose tea. Turn off the flame to let it steep. Then you add the milk and bring the liquid to a boil and turn off the flame. You must have a strainer when you pour it into your cup. And no respectable woman in my family would drink it without adding honey. Always use a wooden spoon for your honey. Never use metal with honey."

"How long do I let it steep? And what about the spices? What's the secret combination? How do you know how much to add?"

Wanja laughed. "No one has been as serious as you are about my recipe. I will email all the details to you. Never add lemongrass, as my mother does. I think it ruins the base notes of the cardamom."

"I wonder if the cardamom is what I taste in this Malindi chai," Lily said. "It's not a spice we often use. At home we'd call this a dirty chai."

"I heard that before from Cheryl's daughter-in-law. Malindi chai is her favorite. I was hoping they'd be back in time for my wedding, but it looks like they won't return until after Christmas. I hope you get to meet her one day."

"I do too," Lily said. "I don't have many relatives on my side of the family. I love the idea of connecting with a cousin I've never met and getting to know his family."

Wanja glanced at her phone. "Are you sure you don't want anything else to eat?"

"Not me," I said.

"You know," Lily said, "maybe I should order something. I understand the chicken in Nairobi is very fresh."

It took us a moment to catch on to her joke.

"I mean, they take the farm-to-table concept to a whole new level with delivery guys on bikes."

I gave Lily a courtesy chuckle. The chicken jokes had been abundant when Wanja settled into the car, and we'd told her what she missed while she was fulfilling our souvenir shopping lists. At this point, Lily's attempt at inducing a final giggle faded quickly.

"If you are sure that you do not want to order anything else, let's purchase some tea and coffee for you to take home," Wanja said.

"Are you driving us to the country club?" Lily asked.

"No, I'm taking you to a meeting point near the airport. My colleague will drive you to Aberdare."

"Does this mean we have to say goodbye again?" I gave her an exaggerated pout.

"Yes. Sadly so. This is our next goodbye," Wanja said. "I hope we will see each other again before heaven. If not, our reunion beside the River of Life will be all the sweeter."

The last sip of my drink clung to my throat as I felt it tightening. Mamacita was there now. At the River of Life. The reality continued to hit me in waves.

I wondered if Wanja knew about Danny's mom passing. He had called the hotel directly, not the tour company, when we were on safari. She probably hadn't received the news. I was glad she didn't know because that made the heaven part of her sentiment seem like a touch of honey to my heart. Eternity felt especially close. In the same way that Lily hoped to meet her cousin and his family one day, I hoped to be the one who would get to introduce Wanja to Mamacita.

My thoughts continued to run into deep rivers, but I kept them to myself as Wanja drove us to the meeting point. Lily had taken the front passenger seat, saying she wanted to see how it felt to be in the "driver's" seat and not be driving. They chatted about Wanja's upcoming wedding while I thought of home.

I texted Danny and gave him the name of where we'd be staying that night. I started to tell him about the open-air market and the chicken but deleted the text. That story would best be told in person. He anticipated I'd come home with stories. I knew he'd like this one.

When Wanja pulled into the meeting point for the shuttle, her colleague was already there. We said our goodbyes with hugs and exchanged promises to stay in touch.

"Safe travels, Suitcase Sisters."

Lily pulled out the handkerchief Cheryl had given her. She stopped before climbing into the shuttle and fluttered it in Wanja's direction. "You will always be our favorite, Wanja!"

The final blending of our laughter became our benediction.

"I'm going to miss her," I said as I adjusted my seat belt.

Lily didn't have a chance to reply because of the three young men who occupied the back bench seat. They leaned toward us, eager to converse in English and tell us they had just flown in and were going on an expedition to hike Mount Kenya. I felt relief that, after the initial friendly chitchat, Lily withdrew from the conversation. She leaned her head against the side window and checked her phone. She wasn't repeating her role as the friendly hospitality hostess as she had with our earlier tour companions, and I was grateful for that because it made it easier for me to do the same.

I thought about how Lily told me that morning she was ready to hear suggestions, not just receive sympathy. I felt the same way. If we'd been alone in the van, this would have been a great time to start talking solutions. We had a three-hour drive ahead of us. But knowing that the back-row trio would understand every word meant we'd have to wait. I was beginning to wonder when the time would be ideal. We were scheduled for separate flights home, so we couldn't count on those long hours to talk and process.

Soon we entered an area that was more rural but still filled with people. I watched the shops go by. Their names made me smile. Holy Ghost Auto Parts. Morning Dew Groceries. Happy Hallelujah Fashions. Abiding Faith Butchers. Shekinah Glory Hair Salon.

I thought of Wanja and smiled. I wanted to see her hair after she decided what to do with it for the wedding. Or should I say, what her sister decided to do with it. I wanted to see how she looked in the beautiful dress I heard her describe to Lily earlier.

Danny had told me one time that curiosity was my occupational hazard. He said my editor's brain was tuned to follow stories to their conclusion. I wanted to know what happens next, and I always hoped for happy endings. I wondered if that was why I kept pushing back thoughts about my inevitable job hunt. I wasn't ready to take a close look at my own real-life story until I had at least a vague idea of how it might conclude.

I realized I'd been wanting to do what any writer would be aghast that a reader had done. I wanted to read the last chapter. I wanted to know how everything turned out first, then go back and experience each chapter.

I'm sorry.

I reached for my journal. I needed to write a letter of apology to the Author and Finisher of my faith. If I was going to say I trusted Him, I needed to take this life He was composing in me page by page, chapter by chapter. As Njeri had spoken over me, I needed to wait for the Lord.

One of the guys tapped me on the shoulder, interrupting me in the middle of a long sentence I was writing.

"We have been talking," he said.

His comment was obvious because I'd heard them for the last ten minutes, but I didn't understand anything they'd said. My guess was that they were Scandinavian, but I'm not enough of a linguist to guess which country they were from.

"We think you girls should cancel your plans and come with us."

Lily was conveniently asleep with her head against the window. I scrutinized the three blond cuties. They were smiling and waiting for my reply.

"How old are you?" I asked.

"Eighteen."

"I have a son who is older than you."

They looked stunned. One of them pointed at Lily as if she might still be an option for their plan.

"Two sons," I said, holding up my fingers in a deliberately cheeky peace sign. "Her oldest just turned seventeen."

They expressed their thoughts to each other in their mother tongue and put their earbuds back in. I turned around, inwardly grinning over my Lorelai Gilmore moment. If Lily had been awake, she probably would have loved that they thought we looked young enough to still be so silly as to fall for them.

My phone vibrated, and I saw that Danny had replied to the texts I'd sent earlier that day. He said he and Micah were doing well, and he was glad the two of them had this chance to be together. He casually reported that they had gone to the funeral home to make arrangements. His last line said they both cried, but it had been a valuable experience for them.

For a moment I felt like the outsider in our little family. Yet the flutter of insecurity left quickly when I thought about how many times Danny and I had prayed that Micah would confide in us. Danny wanted to be close to him, but nothing he'd tried while Micah was under our roof had ever bonded them. This was their time. This was important for them. A sense of gratitude eclipsed all thoughts I'd had about going home ahead of plans.

This was the plan. This was the story that needed to be written on the pages of my life. More importantly, this was the plot twist for Micah and Danny that I'd hoped would come before the end of their blended tale.

While Lily rested and the athletes listened to their music, I filled seven pages in my journal with the flood of thoughts that kept coming over me like a waterfall. I went on to record the events of the past few days with a bumpy scrawl.

By the time we reached the Aberdare Country Club, I felt as if I'd expelled every thought that had been rising to the surface for days. I was also long overdue for a bathroom break.

Lily and I were the first ones out of the van. We went directly to the front desk to ask where we could find the restroom.

"That was way too close," Lily said. "I can't believe you even drank a bottle of water on the way here."

"Not all of it. But you're right. That was way too close."

We returned to the lobby, where a uniformed attendant approached us. He invited us to follow him to the dining room if we wanted to eat something while waiting for our room to be cleaned.

I asked if we could sit outside instead of in the dining room and have something simple, such as juice and perhaps a small snack.

"Of course," he said with a slight bow.

We were back in the world of British formality and opulent service. I almost expected his reply to be "As you wish."

"Time to act posh again," Lily whispered.

We followed him to padded outdoor chairs on the portico. The surroundings confirmed the cushiness of this place. We settled in and breathed.

"It's so beautiful," Lily murmured. "The temperature is just right. And this view . . ."

"I know."

The open veranda was made of stone and had supporting pillars that held up a finely crafted wood covering. In front of us was another soul-stirring vista of miles and miles of sloping green hills that poured into a wide valley.

The trees filling this up-country location were more

abundant than anywhere we'd been so far. Some of them were turning vibrant shades of red and orange as the deciduous leaves performed their swan song of the seasons.

Lily and I didn't say much to each other. We just breathed in and out, trying to take it all in. Two tall glasses of orange juice were brought to us on a tray along with a plate of crackers, cheese, and grapes. It was just right. All of it.

"I sent a text to Tim," Lily said. "And to both the boys."

"Did you hear back from them?"

She checked her phone. "No, not yet."

"Do you have phone service here? It seems like we're pretty remote."

"My phone says I do, but it said that before and I couldn't send or receive messages. I sent the texts when we were still close to Nairobi."

"It's early for them right now," I said. "How does Tim do with early morning conversations?"

"Good point. I'll wait till it's closer to lunchtime for him."

"I'm sure they're eager for you to come home."

Lily stared out at the lush world before us. "Would it be terrible if I said that I don't want to go home?"

"I'm glad we're not going home yet either. I've wavered on that, but I'm glad we didn't change our plans."

"I don't mean I don't want to go home *yet*. I don't want to go home ever."

"Ever?" I turned to see how serious her expression was.

"Well, I suppose I will have to return eventually."

"Yes, eventually," I repeated. "Like in two days. So, huzzah for two more days in this beautiful country."

"More like a day and a half. It's going to go so quickly." Lily made a little sandwich from two crackers and a slice of cheese and took a crumbly bite. "You know our word, fernweh?" She brushed the crumbs off her embroidered shirt.

"Of course."

"Well, I just decided that fernweh has a dark side."

"Don't say that."

"It's true. Once you've had a taste of faraway places, you long for more. I think the longing diminishes your fondness for everything you left behind."

I thought about her words for a moment and was glad we were the only ones on the veranda. It finally felt like we could have an uninterrupted conversation.

"Could it be," I suggested, "that the longing for faraway places has the potential to diminish our contentment rather than our fondness for what is familiar? It doesn't automatically rob us of our love for what we left at home."

"Are you saying familiarity breeds contempt?"

I nodded.

"My mom used to say that. Often." Lily turned to look at me instead of the tranquil countryside. "To be honest, that describes how I feel about my life. Everything about it is too familiar."

I put down my empty orange juice glass. "Are you ready for some suggestions?"

"Suggestions about my life?"

"Yes."

A hotel employee approached us with two keys in his hand. "I beg your pardon, ma'ams. Our manager asked me to inform you your room is ready. Would you like me to take you and your luggage there now?"

"Yes, please take our luggage," Lily said. "But we'd like to stay here a little longer. Is that a problem?"

"No," he said with a broad smile. "Not a problem. Nothing here is a problem. Hakuna matata."

Lily repeated the familiar phrase made popular from *The Lion King* and pulled some of her remaining US dollars from her pocket to tip him.

As he walked away, I had a feeling his words about how nothing was a problem here in beautiful Aberdare may have plunged Lily even deeper into her longing to never return home.

A shiver of fear went up my neck, the same way it had when we were at the hippo pool and I noticed the crocodile in the water coming toward us.

20

The best mirror is an old friend.

George Herbert

O kay," Lily said. "I'm ready for your suggestions. Go ahead. Pour out your wisdom on me."

I scooted my veranda chair a little closer and turned it so that I could face her instead of the outstretched grounds of the Aberdare Country Club.

"But first"—Lily held up her hand—"let me say that I've been thinking about your comment back at Brockhurst. You said Tim and I are at a crossroads. I don't think we are. We're not trying to decide which path to take next. We like our jobs. We're not going to move anywhere. Not when the boys are almost done with school. Plus, we love Nashville. The problem is that everything is the same. It's been the same for a long time."

"And that's why you want to go in another direction, right?"

"I don't know what I want. I just don't want to go back to my life the way it's been. And Fern, I meant it when I said I'm afraid of turning out like my mother. It's a true fear. Noah is the same age I was when my dad moved out. I don't want to drive Tim away, but I feel like he and I are so disconnected. Just like my mom and dad were. The inability for us to communicate on this trip has only emphasized that."

"You are not your mother, Lily. Listen to me when I say that. You are not your mother. Your life is not going to be like hers. It hasn't been like hers, and it won't end up like hers."

"How do you know that?"

"I just do."

Lily looked away.

"Remember how you told me, more than once, that I was going to marry Danny? You said you just knew. And the first time I heard you say it was soon after I met him, and I told you there was no hope for his son."

"You also told me Danny had, and I quote, 'the most sincere and alluring eyes.'"

I smiled. "He still does. My point is, you knew Danny was the one for me way before I agreed to go out with him. Way before I was willing to work through all the challenges it would take to make our marriage work. That's how I know you are not going to turn into your mother. Best friends know these things. We see what the other can't see."

Lily didn't comment.

"I know you, and I have seen how God works in your life. I believe you're going to continue to become the most complete version of you. I also know it will take some work. Just like marrying Danny and living with him and Micah and Mamacita took work."

"How do you suggest I do that?" She looked at me with tears in her eyes.

"Make a list."

Lily tilted her head. "Are you making fun of my lists?"

"No, not at all. I'm saying lists are the way you process. You even said when we were leaving Brockhurst with Wanja that lists are the way God directs you. Remember? I was telling her that I journal and you said—"

"I remember."

"Start some lists today while we're still together so we can talk about them before we go home."

"Lists of what?"

"I think you should start with yourself. List what was good and bad about your childhood. Micah's counselor had him do that, and it helped him so much. He needed to separate the truth from all the lies he'd held on to. She had him list ten things he believed about himself and his identity. When he and Danny went through them, seven of his core beliefs about himself were lies."

"Are you saying I should go to a counselor?"

"You could. You know what a fan I am of the family counseling we went through. Whatever way you address your mama trauma, I think you need to resolve it."

"My mama trauma?" Lily crossed her arms.

"You know what I mean. The unresolved issues you have with your mom. Since the day I met you, you've expressed a lot of hurt and anger over the choices she made and how it broke your family and severed your relationship with her."

"Why would I want to make a list of all that?"

"Because I think you've carried a lot of it into your adult life. I think you need to start the process of forgiving her. Then you can evaluate your own marriage without your mom's choices being the baseline for how you view your own life and your future."

Lily sipped her orange juice slowly and stared out at the pastoral landscape. "You know, I thought when I asked for suggestions, you were going to give me more honey ideas like adding sweetness to my words and scheduling a date night."

"Neither of those is a bad idea."

"Yes, but I don't think affirmations are enough to keep a marriage from falling apart."

"Is that the point you honestly believe you're at? That your marriage is falling apart?"

Lily didn't answer.

I leaned back in the comfortable chair and waited.

She sighed. "No, it isn't falling apart. It could. We're not in the best place. Mostly I feel stuck. And you're saying I'm stuck because I haven't made peace with my mom."

I nodded. I wasn't sure if I was right. I had no formal training as a counselor. But in my mind, that was what made the most sense. I was going off of gut feelings, the way she had often done when she gave me suggestions about my life choices.

We sat for a while in calm silence, the way close friends are comfortable doing.

"Hmm." The sound emerged from me involuntarily.

"What?"

"I was thinking of that African quote your uncle said when Njeri was leading me to the kitchen. Remember? He said, 'If you want to know the end, look at the beginning.' After you spent the day with Cheryl, it brought a lot of painful stuff with your mom to the surface."

"Yes, it did."

"Once you resolve that, I think your heart will have the space to fall in love with your husband all over again. It's too crowded in there right now for you to feel much of anything else."

Lily leaned back and uncrossed her arms. I thought of the many times she and I would get going on one of our long

236

sympathy-suggestion calls. We would have to hang up and think about everything alone before we could connect again and keep processing with each other. Rarely did we talk like this in person. We didn't always agree with each other's advice, but the time we spent talking always released whatever mental log jam we were struggling with.

"Lily, I truly believe you will be able to move forward when you're no longer carrying all this old stuff about your mom. It's weighed you down for too long."

She looked at her hands and quietly said, "I know."

"Once you resolve your mama trauma, you can make another list. A happier list of things you and Tim need to figure out. You'll be able to address your marriage as a single topic without all the added . . ."

"Baggage?" Lily completed my thought.

"Exactly."

Lily reached for the last cracker on our snack plate. "Because Suitcase Sisters travel light."

I smiled at my best friend. "Yes, we do. It's better that way, isn't it?"

"Yes. Thank you, Fern. I think you're right."

"Ooh. Wait. Say that again." I popped the last purple grape into my mouth. "I'm not sure I heard you. What was that? Something about being right?"

She ignored my teasing and picked up her phone. "I need three lists because I'm going to divide my assessment into three parts. Birth to age ten, ten to fifteen, and fifteen to twenty." She looked up. "I just realized I've lived with Tim longer than I lived with my mother. That's a sobering thought. Why has it taken me so long to deal with this?"

"Doesn't matter. You're starting a new chapter now. And may I add one more thought? You know how John said that Darla had been married to five husbands?"

"He was odd, wasn't he? I thought it was a strange thing to say about his wife."

"I took it as something he was saying about himself. They'd been married for a long time, and over the years people change. I thought he meant that with every new version of himself, Darla had chosen to remain his wife."

Lily nodded slowly. "It's like when Cheryl said she wished my parents had found a way to work things out. I know my dad has been at least three different men since I've known him. My mom changed a lot too. She was different when I was young."

"What if your crossroads is more of a pause so you can make a new choice? Or a renewed choice. You can choose to fall in love all over again with the version of who you are now. And who Tim is now."

"Interesting thought." She looked beyond me and seemed to fix her gaze on something. "Are those peacocks?" She pointed. "They are, aren't they?"

Two large birds leisurely made their way from under the shade of one of the voluptuous trees and strutted across the grass. Their bodies were a vibrant, royal blue, and the little plumes on top of their heads looked like airy crowns.

As we watched, one of them stopped and suddenly spread its tail feathers, revealing the beautiful colors and design.

"Wow," I said. "I don't think I've ever seen a peacock before. Have you?"

"No. And I want one."

I laughed. "And where will you keep it? I've seen your backyard."

"We'll have to move because I need a peacock in my life. Aren't they beautiful? Let's go down there. I see other people taking pictures. I need pictures."

"For all your followers?" I teased.

"Stop."

Lily managed to come within a few feet of the peacocks, and we both took a steady stream of photos. If she'd had the right kind of feed in her hand, I was sure she could have fed the peacocks the way we had fed the giraffes.

I thought again how God-orchestrated some of our experiences on this trip had been. I had strolled through a tea field. Lily had fed a giraffe, and now we were making friends with a peacock. There was a sweetness to it. Like God's way of adding honey to our trip.

The peacocks strutted off down the hill, and Lily and I decided to do our own strutting around the grounds.

"I feel like we should be wearing flowing Victorian dresses," I said. "And holding twirling lacy parasols."

Lily laughed. "I hope you're writing all this down. I saw you writing in your journal on the way here. When we're ninety and end up sharing a room at the nursing home, will you pull out your journal and read it to me so we can remember everything about this trip together?"

"Sure."

"Promise?"

"Yes, I promise. And don't forget that I'm counting on you to send me every single photo you've been taking, and I'll do the same for you."

"Deal."

We kept walking across the sloping green lawn and saw a sign leading to the pool.

"What do you think?" Lily attempted her silly British accent. "Do you fancy a dip in the pool before supper? I believe that is what all the posh ladies here at the country club do on evenings such as this."

"Indeed. Lovely suggestion." I hadn't meant to attempt an

accent, but it came out that way. My comment sounded as silly as Lily's.

As we came around the side of the pool area, we could see that no one was in the pool. We'd have it all to ourselves just as we had at the Giraffe Manor. I liked the idea even more.

On the hilly side was a large deck with multiple lounge chairs tucked under sun umbrellas. It looked so inviting. I wished I had my suit on under my clothes so I could peel down and jump into the water right then.

"Just keep swimming. Just keep swimming," Lily repeated in a low voice.

"What are you saying?"

"I'm being Dory."

"Who?"

"You know. Nemo's friend."

I kept staring at her, shaking my head.

"I forget that you missed the season of watching animated kids' movies with Micah." With a tilt of her head to whatever she had just noticed behind me, she said, "Oh no! Flirt alert at two o'clock."

I turned to see something neither of us would now be able to unsee.

The boys from Scandinavia were stretched out on the lounge chairs, fresh from the pool. Their fair skin glistened in the late afternoon sun. Two of them were smoking, and their swimming apparel was . . . well, it left very little to the imagination. None of the men or boys in Lily's life or mine would be caught dead wearing something so scant in public.

"Change of plans on going to the pool." I picked up my pace and headed straight back to the main building.

Reverting to her British intonation, Lily said, "Dear girl, did you think I was referring to that sort of pool? I meant billiards. Forgive me for using the lower-class term and calling it pool."

"Do you think they have a pool room here?" I asked in a normal voice. "I mean—pardon my slip—a billiards room?"

"Highly probable, dear Watson." Lily's accent had changed, and it was terrible.

"Wait. Are we doing Sherlock Holmes now? Why do I have to be Watson?"

Our playful banter continued as we followed a walking trail that led us back to the veranda. The grounds were gorgeously inviting, the way Brockhurst had been. But this place felt different. It wasn't just the boys at the pool. The purpose and the people of this place were different from Brockhurst. It didn't feel like hallowed ground to me.

I think that realization may have added to our fish-out-of-water feelings at dinner. We were simply guests here. We didn't know anyone, nor did we strike up conversations with anyone. We were no longer trying everything for the first time. We were becoming familiar with the rhythm of Africa, and with her various moods.

Our room was as comfortable as we expected it to be. The bonus was that we had a fireplace. A fire was lit and waiting for us when we returned after dinner. Like elderly spinster sisters, we sank into the two chairs in front of the fire and quietly went about our evening engagement of choice.

The popping of the wood in the fire was accompanied by another one of Lily's carefully curated playlists. This one had no words. No lure to dance. No invitation to sing along. It was a soothing stream of instrumental music. I wondered why I didn't listen to music more often. It had such a calming effect. Music like this had to be Lily's haven the way baths were mine. Another facet of her life that had been unknown to me due to our being long-distance besties.

Lily was tapping away on her phone, composing her lists. I considered if this would be the right time to interrupt her and say I was ready for her to give me suggestions on my job dilemma. The extensive journaling I'd done on the way here had settled much of my sorrow over the loss of my job. I felt prepared to take the necessary steps when I returned home. After everything was settled with Mamacita, I was sure Danny could help me apply for other jobs. Maybe a local bookstore had an opening. It would soften the blow if I could at least be around books every day and talk to people about books. I wondered what the going salary was for librarians in our corner of Colorado.

Even though I had some ideas, I wanted to hear Lily's thoughts, lists and all.

"Lily?"

"Hmm?" She didn't look up from her phone.

"I'm ready. Finally. Advice, please."

"Oh! A text came through. From Tim." She read it silently, and I watched her lips curl upward in her Cheshire cat grin. That was a good sign. "I told him how much I appreciated his taking care of everything at home so I could come on this trip. I added a little honey, like you said."

"And?"

"He said he misses me." She read the text to herself again. "He said he had no idea how much I do to keep our family running and appreciates me more than ever. He added some sweet stuff too. I'm going to try to call him."

Lily stood and went into the bathroom. She closed the door, and a few minutes later I could hear bits of her muffled conversation. I was so happy for her. Then I remembered that I had been about to ask for her suggestions to my job conundrum. It was a good thing I was comfortable with my birth order as well as where I fit in the hierarchy of urgency when I first married Danny. I knew how to wait for my turn.

I wondered if I should try to call Danny. Instead, I opened my emails. I'd only checked them once on our trip. Maybe Danny had emailed me since the phone hadn't been as reliable as we'd expected.

I quickly cleaned out the unnecessary mail. The ones I decided to open were good and bad. Five authors I'd worked with had heard about my layoff, and as writers, they had a lot of eloquent things to say about the way it was handled. I knew this wasn't a good time to respond to any of them.

Two emails were from the HR department of the new publishing house. Apparently, I hadn't filled out all the necessary forms to finalize my exit. The forms were attached for me to complete and return. I couldn't bring myself to open them and force myself to search for a box I had failed to check or a place where I'd missed providing my electronic signature.

I wished I'd done anything other than open my emails. The exercise jarred me back to my real life, and I decided not to check them again until I was home.

Then I saw one from my mom and gladly opened it to see photos of their new puppy. She asked how I was doing. I tried to remember when I'd updated my family during the whirlwind of the last few weeks. My mom knew I'd been let go and that I was going to Africa. She'd told my sisters. But I hadn't told any of them yet about Mamacita. I wasn't sure Danny would have thought to do that.

I wrote a group email to my mom and sisters, telling them about the passing of my mother-in-law and how I was heading home in a day and a half. I also told them my phone service hadn't been dependable. I overexplained, as is my habit, and told them Lily was convinced we didn't have the right phone plans, even though she was assured the additional services we both paid for were supposed to work.

Only minutes after I hit send, my eldest sister, Anne, wrote back. She said I was in her prayers and added a paragraph asking if I knew that Queen Elizabeth had also been in Kenya when she heard the news of the passing of her father, King George VI. In true Anne style, she asked a riddle.

Who was the princess that went up a tree and came down a queen?

I googled to find that Elizabeth and Philip had been staying in a game-viewing hotel in 1952 when her father died. The hotel was no longer operational, but it sounded similar to where Lily and I would go tomorrow to spend our last night in Africa.

I had to smile. Of course Anne would know such a random fact. She had written letters to both Prince William and Prince Harry when she was a little girl. She'd named her eldest daughter Elizabeth and hosted tea parties for her book club that were fit for royalty.

Anne may have been attempting to compare the news I'd received of Mamacita's passing with the news Queen Elizabeth had received, but the striking difference was that I had not descended any stairs or received any new titles the morning after I heard. When I awoke, I was still Fern. Fern, the unemployed princess who hadn't even managed to fill out her termination forms correctly.

While Lily spoke honeyed words to her husband, I crawled into bed. Tonight, I would be the first one to fall asleep.

21

Let your love be like the misty rain, coming softly but flooding the river.

African proverb

My sleep was fitful that night at the country club in the Aberdare hills.

Lily was vibrant the next morning. For the first time since we'd arrived in Kenya, she was up before me. She hummed and made coffee in the in-room coffee maker while I turned the other way and pulled the blankets over my head.

"Tea," she said cheerfully. "It's English breakfast because that's all they have here in the room. And no milk. I hope you like it without milk. I'll put it on your nightstand."

I tried to play possum, as my dad called it, and act like I was still asleep.

"I know you're awake." Lily tried to recite the poem I'd rattled off for Samburu on our morning game drive. "The morning is due pearls, and all's right with the world."

I pulled back the cover enough to give her a raised-eyebrow glare. "Due pearls?"

"Isn't that how it goes? Like everyone deserves to be given pearls on a beautiful morning?"

I groaned and burrowed back into my cave.

"At least I recited the other line right. Didn't I? God is in His heaven and all's right with the world. That's a good reason to get up on our last full day in Africa, isn't it?"

I rolled over and propped myself up. "Yes, it's a very good reason." I growled playfully. "Thanks for the tea."

"You're welcome, Lady Lioness. Now tell me. How did you sneak in during the night, and why did you eat my sweet petunia of a friend?"

I took a sip of the hot tea, promptly burning my tongue. In a way, I felt like I deserved it. "I have a headache."

"Hope the tea helps." Lily brought her coffee back to her bed and slid under the covers.

Our beds had been our cozy spots at Brockhurst the same way they had been in Costa Rica. Here we were again, being "us." The comforting thought brought a glitter-size dot of brightness to my mood.

"So, dear friend of all friends, tell me what you were going to say last night before I called Tim. But wait. Before you tell me . . ." She adjusted her position in her bed and reached for her phone. "I have to say thank you, again. I know I wasn't very receptive yesterday to your suggestion about the lists, but Fern, you have no idea how much it helped. It was like looking in a mirror for the first time. Or pulling back a curtain to another world. I saw it. I mean, I haven't sorted it all out yet, but I can see where the lies are coming from. They're from the accuser of the brethren, I know, but I can see where they started and I can pray them outta there. I see my mom in a different light too."

"Good." I hoped I sounded less snarly.

"It's really good. And my talk with Tim was really, really good. I asked him to forgive me for not being all in on our marriage for a while now. He didn't understand my big confession at first. I told him I needed him to know that I loved him. I've always loved him. I always will love him. I needed to remember that our vows and our marriage are sacred. It's of irreplaceable value."

"Wow," I said.

"I know. I think it was a wow for him too. He hasn't heard words like that from me in a long time. I'm a slow learner, but once I get it, I get it." She sipped her steaming coffee, peering at me over the rim of her mug with her eyebrows raised. "Your turn. I'm talking too much."

"No, you're not. I'm happy for you and, to be honest, a little relieved that you and Tim had such a great conversation." I sipped the last bit of tea and slid back under the covers, stretching out my legs and pointing my toes.

"I also told Tim about the odd guy, John, and what you said about changing as we get older. I said I liked your theory that we get the chance to choose to fall in love with the current version of each other."

"What did Tim say?"

"He said he agreed." She smiled. "And he said he loves me. I hadn't heard him say it like he meant it in a long time. Apparently, a little honey goes a long way."

I smiled at my contented friend. This was all so good. I didn't want to deep-dive into my work issues now. Last night the topic felt right. This morning I wanted to put my issues aside and enjoy the glow that had settled on Lily.

"Are you hungry?" Lily asked. "Because I looked at the schedule and breakfast is served until 9:30. We need to be out of our room by 10:30. They have dancers in the lobby at 10:00 and our ride will be here at 1:00, so we have time for lunch or a swim or whatever you want to do."

"Could we just stay in bed and sleep all day and then have tea where we sat on the veranda yesterday?"

"Sounds like you're the one who doesn't want to go home now."

"I want to go home. Eventually. But I have so much to face as soon as I get there. I haven't heard back from Danny. I think he and Micah are doing okay, but it's frustrating to not be able to talk to him. You know what that's like."

"Yes, I do. Now, tell me what you were going to say last night right before I called Tim."

I sighed. "Last night I made the mistake of going through my emails and I got depressed about my job. Or, I should say, my lack of a job. I feel adrift. Denial is good for only so long."

Lily nodded. "True."

"Do you want to hear something pathetic?"

"I want to hear everything."

"The only two job applications I've ever filled out in my life were the one for Brockhurst when I was eighteen and the one for the intern position at the publishing house."

She looked confused.

"I don't have a résumé," I said plainly.

"So? That's easy. I can help you with that if you want. What else is bothering you?"

"I kept thinking about what a joke it was for me to give you advice when I'm the one at a crossroads. I think I projected my issues on you, and I apologize for that."

"No apologies, remember? And I told you, your advice was great. It was exactly what I needed."

"Well, I don't feel like I can take any credit for that."

Lily lifted her chin and looked as if she was about to make

one of her declarations, like when she greeted the gnus by their proper name. "You know what you are, Fern? You're a peacock."

"A peacock? You mean I act proud and strut around?"

Lily returned the scrunched-up-nose look I had just given her. Maybe she'd never heard the term "proud as a peacock" or thought anything but adoring thoughts about them.

"No, what I mean is that you appear calm and mild until just the right moment, and voilà! Your hidden gifts come out in a stunning fan of beauty. Others look at you and are in awe. But you stand there, stunned, because you don't see it. It's right there. It's part of you. It's amazing, but you can't see it."

I had no words, grumbly or grateful, to give Lily in response to her analogy. I felt my spirit softening, though. Her voice softened too.

"That's why you will always need me as your best friend. I can see the marvelousness of you. And I will always tell you when your awesomeness is showing."

"Thank you," I said softly, feeling humbled.

"Karibu," Lily replied with a small grin.

"I'm ready for your advice," I said. "That's what I was going to say last night. I want your suggestions. No more sympathy. Tell me what you think I should do about a job."

"Make a list." Lily grinned. "But then, you knew I was going to say that, didn't you?"

"Yes, and I started on that."

"I think you need to make two lists. The first one should be about all your experience and what you love in your field of expertise. The second should be all the possibilities that are open to you. Possibilities for a new job, a future place to live, and how many babies you want to try for."

"Whoa, babies?"

"It's a possibility."

I gave Lily a friendly scowl.

"Just be open to the possibility. Now's the time to think about it and pray about it. Seriously. Think about it. Ten years from now it probably won't be a possibility."

"I don't need to make a list of future places to live or babies or anything else. I just need a job. And the options are very limited where we live."

"Fern." Her voice was tender. "Has it dawned on you yet that the only reason you and Danny have stayed in Colorado was because of his mom?"

Her words hit me hard.

I felt the squeeze that came every time I remembered Mamacita was gone. With her departure had also gone all the daily visits and caregiving obligations. We had no more expectations on us or additional expenses. Lily was right. We didn't have to stay in Colorado.

"You hadn't thought of that, had you?"

I shook my head.

"Well, I did. And I don't mean to be disrespectful by bringing this up so soon, but you are once again a woman of possibilities. Not only with your job, but with the options of where you and Danny live."

The concept was still sinking in.

"Micah wants you to see him in California. You said he never wants to return to Colorado. Why don't you consider moving to California?"

My first thought was of Danny and how much he loved the place we'd stayed for our honeymoon near the beach in Southern California. My next thought was that it was too expensive to live there. Especially when I didn't know if I could find a job there. And where would Danny work?

"No," I said. "We couldn't move to California."

"Why not?"

"Because." I had no immediate answer for her and punted with a diversion. "I think my headache is coming back."

"Then I'll make you another cup of tea in a minute," Lily said. "Stay with me on this. You and Danny have a wide-open, unwritten future ahead of you. The possibilities are abundant. Just think about it. Pray about it. Baby steps."

I noticed that she emphasized the word "baby" and said, "I saw what you did there. You're back to the baby pitch again."

"You noticed. Okay. So? What are you afraid of?"

"I'm not afraid."

She cleared her throat. "This is an important question. Did you not allow yourselves to dream about having a baby because of Micah?"

"No, I don't think so. We haven't tried, and we haven't not tried. We just haven't gotten pregnant in the natural flow of our lives."

"But if it happened, what would you think? What would Danny think?"

"We'd be okay with it."

"Just okay with it?"

"I don't know. We haven't talked about it in a long time."

"Fern, having a baby is a privilege. Creating a new life together is a gift. Future generation and all that."

"I know."

"Then open yourself to the possibility, pray about it, talk to Danny about it, and try, try, try. That will be the best part. The trying."

"I don't think I've dared to feel anything one way or the other about pregnancy."

"I know. And as you said, denial is good for only so long."

Lily must have been too energized to linger in bed as I

poured out my heart to her. She had popped up and efficiently prepared a second cup of tea for me while we were talking.

"Lots for you to process," she said.

I nodded and sipped the tea.

"I'm going to get my shower, if you don't mind me getting in there first."

"It's all yours," I said.

She left me sitting in the afterglow of her words after she closed the bathroom door. I drank the tea slowly and returned to the thought that Danny and I were no longer tied to Colorado. How had that escaped me? The options now open to us were as wide as the Masai Mara, with endless directions to go. I wondered if Danny had thought about leaving Colorado. He'd lived there his whole life and seemed content not to go anywhere.

I unplugged my charging phone and checked my messages and emails for any news from him. Nothing had come through during the night. I missed him more than ever.

My still-spinning thoughts told me to ignore the three new emails in my inbox, so I did. That two of them were from the editor at the new publishing house didn't escape my notice. I couldn't read them now. She knew I was out of the country. Whatever files I'd failed to send her would have to wait until I was home and could access my laptop.

I reached for my journal on the nightstand and wrote what would probably be the last love letter I wrote to Jesus while I was in Africa. I began with exactly what was on my mind. I might as well. He already knew. I had a feeling I was the one who needed to see the words on paper.

Here I am, thousands of miles from home, and "home" as I once knew it will never be the same. The tectonic plates have shifted, and there's now this great

rift in the center of my life. A great valley of possibili-
ties. Mamacita is with You, Micah is with Danny, and
I'm here. At least for one more day. Why? What are You
doing? What do You want me to do?

A sweet thought, like a drizzle of honey, covered my anx-
ious thoughts. I felt my lips inching upward in a grin.
You're saving the best for last, aren't You?
Jesus felt so close. I had sensed His nearness in this same
quiet way when I was in the tea field, adrift on an emerald
sea. Peace was coming to me. I didn't have to chase after it.
I was drawing near to God, and He was drawing near to me.
When my turn came for the bathroom, the hot shower
took care of my headache. The belly-filling breakfast in the
restaurant, followed by the local dancers, brought my heart
back to Africa. The steady rhythm they danced to in their
colorful outfits was like a heartbeat. It was also melodious like a chorus of birds in a tree. A tree that extended its
embracing branches over a waiting bench. An invitation to
come. To take heart.
One more day. One more location to visit—a hotel in the
treetops. One more coming down the stairs in the morning
and facing whatever was next.

22

Return to old watering holes for more than water; friends and dreams are there to meet you.

African proverb

*L*ily and I did not expect that the lodge on the slopes of Mount Kenya would look the way it did. The description on the itinerary said it was built in the treetops. I pictured something like the Swiss Family Robinson treehouse in which each room was in a different part of a very old, very large tree.

After Anne told me the story of Queen Elizabeth, I thought our hotel would be grand and very British. I expected something from a children's book inspired by Hobbits from the Shire, only built in the arms of ancient trees instead of burrowed into hillsides.

The mountain lodge in front of us was huge, all one building, and constructed from dark wood that had been laid in vertical strips. We approached, rolling our suitcases over a long ramp, also crafted from wood but cut in short, narrow strips. The railings were made of wood too. Rising up and stretching over us were scrub-like trees and green jungle foliage.

I felt like I was about to enter the remains of Noah's ark right after it had come to rest on Mount Ararat.

The interior was another surprise, a blend of African decor accentuated by accoutrements of British influence. We checked in, took our room key, and climbed the stairs, carrying our suitcases to the next floor. Lily didn't have to say she was once again proud of us for traveling light.

We were puffing too much to say anything.

Our comfortable room continued the theme of wood paneling and had twin beds with two armchairs by the large window. We migrated to the window as soon as we entered and looked out on a large pond. Around the perimeter of the watering hole was green foliage. Beyond that, the edge of a densely wooded area was visible.

Lily plopped on one of the beds, and I realized that every night we'd selected where we slept in the same pattern. As we faced the beds, Lily always took the one on the right, and I automatically went to the one on the left.

"Isn't that how our beds were in Costa Rica?" I asked after sharing the fun fact with her.

"I think they were. Do you mind that I'm closest to the window?"

"No. Of course not."

"Did you see the paper they handed me at check-in? It lists the animals that typically come to this watering hole at night. We can check off what we want to see, and someone will come wake us in the night to look out the window. We can sit here and watch them from our treetop view."

"You're kidding."

"Nope. Any favorites I should check for you? More elephants, perhaps?"

"Yes, please. I would love to see an elephant or two."

I followed Lily's example of kicking off my shoes and stretching out on my bed. The lure of an afternoon nap was hard to resist after my rocky night's sleep and our winding ride up the mountain road. "If we're going to be woken throughout the night, I'm going to need a nap. Are you tired?"

"No. Not really. I'm going back down to the desk to see what time we're supposed to be ready to leave in the morning. It's missing from the itinerary, and the event planner in me won't be happy until I have a time set in writing. I might take one of the guided walks if one of their guides is going out now."

I pulled the folded blanket at the foot of the bed over me. "I wish I didn't feel so wiped out. I'd go with you, but I don't think I'd make it very far down the trail."

"Don't worry about it. Traveling is tiring. We've both experienced that."

"I know, but I think what I'm feeling is tied to grief. Does that make sense?"

"Absolutely. You lost your job. And then you lost your mother-in-law. Those two life events are huge, even if you weren't traveling."

"True. I feel like I'm turning into a blob, but I don't want to slow down yet. I can sleep on the plane on the way home tomorrow."

"You're not a blob. You just need rest." Lily blew me a kiss. "Sweet dreams."

She shut the door behind her, and I found it easy to drift off. I slept deeply and woke with a start when I heard the room door open and Lily come back in.

"What time is it?" I asked, squinting.

Lily walked to the window and looked out at the watering hole. "Almost tea time. Are you interested?"

"Yes, please." I sat up and tried to get my eyes to focus. "How was the walk?"

"Great. Did you know this hotel is built on an ancient migratory route for elephants? I hope we see some. I asked the guide if he'd seen any baby elephants around here, and he said a pregnant elephant stopped coming to the watering hole a couple of weeks ago. He hopes she's okay."

"Are any animals out there now?"

Lily glanced out the window again. "Just some of those antelopes like we saw before with the swirly horns. I think the guide said they were kudu. They have a lot around here." She came over and sat on the end of my bed, looking wistful. "I really miss Tim. And the boys too. I kept thinking of them on the walk. I wish Tim could have experienced all this. It's been amazing. So much better and more fascinating than I imagined it would be."

I reached over and patted her leg. "Look at you, falling in love with Tim Graden all over again."

Lily smiled. "I can't believe I was so lost when we got here and was doubting everything about our marriage. I want it to keep getting better."

"It will. What was your uncle's African saying? 'If you want to know the end, look at the beginning'?"

"Tim and I did have a lovely beginning, didn't we? Remember how he wrote songs for me?"

"Yes. And I remember how excited you were every time he left one of his sweet love notes on the windshield of your car."

"I used to always fold back the covers on his side of the bed and leave the light on in the bathroom if I went to bed before him. I should start doing that again. Those little things meant a lot to him. I had so much anger toward him when we arrived. All the little annoyances felt amplified, as if he was the one pulling away. But I was the one who was shutting down emotionally. Then all the stuff came up about my mom."

"Your poor little heart was crowded."

"It was. And not with good stuff. That's all gone now."

I smiled. "It's a good look on you."

"What's a good look?"

"Your uncluttered heart. Your falling in love with Tim again. I can't help but think that God still has lots and lots of goodness ahead for you guys, Lily."

She nodded. "You said it was a crossroads. It is. I can see why my mom thought the unknown path would lead to new and better stuff in her life when she was my age. But staying on the familiar path and taking the time to clear out all the weeds and trash is going to be so much better. I just know it."

"Do you remember how you told me that Danny and I would have a different marriage once Micah went to college? Well, I think you and Tim are going to find the same is true for you in just a few years."

Lily's expression lit up. "Hey. Maybe the four of us could go somewhere."

"Back here, maybe?"

"Or Ireland. Or Italy? Where's the list we made on our last night at camp in Costa Rica? Did we keep that list? You and I had a dozen places we wanted to see together."

"I think you should start a new list for us," I said. "Of course, traveling with our guys will be a different kind of trip than this has been."

"I know. But don't you think it will be fun in other ways?" Lily sat up straight. "It feels so good to dream again."

I scooted closer and wrapped my arms around my tender-hearted, starry-eyed friend. "Thank you."

"For what?"

I pulled back and made sure she was looking me in the eyes. "Thank you for inviting me to go on this trip with you and for always being there for me. You're the best friend a woman could ever have."

"I feel the same way about you, Fern. You see me in a way that no one else does."

We both were a little teary-eyed.

"Shall we go up to the top floor and toast our friendship with a cup of tea?" Lily asked.

"Why the top floor?"

"I didn't tell you yet. This is the time of day when animals come to the watering hole. We can watch them from the top floor. The best part is that they serve tea."

"The animals serve tea? That's unique."

"Stop. Don't edit me. You know what I mean. The hotel serves tea on the highest level, up in the treetops, so to speak. And service starts in a few minutes."

"Is it high tea?" I got up and tried to smooth the wrinkles from my slept-in shirt.

"Is that supposed to be a joke, or do you mean is the tea service fancy?"

I unzipped my suitcase and peered inside, even though I knew I no longer had anything truly fresh to change into. "I was asking if we're supposed to dress a certain way. But that was a clever joke, wasn't it?"

Lily ignored my last question and went over to the mirror, where she ran her fingers through her hair. "I think what we have on is fine. We're at a mountain lodge, after all."

"With all the British ways of doing things here, along with my sister's pictures of her high tea events, I think we might need to dress up a little. Here." I tossed Lily one of the two sheer scarves I'd packed. "We can take these in case we need them."

"Is this silk?" Lily slid the scarf between her fingers.

"I don't know. Maybe. Anne gave it to me, so probably." I brushed my hair and thought about how my mom always made my sisters and me wash our long hair on Saturday nights and wear it down with a bow on Sundays when we went to church. I left my hair down for the first time on our trip. It fell over my shoulders, and somehow I felt as if it added a Sunday-best touch to my limited wardrobe of khaki jeans and a crumpled, long-sleeve blue T-shirt. It was challenging to feel tea-party ready when wearing a jacket and hiking boots.

As we left our room, Lily said, "I love this scarf." She practiced swishing the long tail of the pink and ivory scarf over her shoulder before arranging it around her neck. "We are turning into the Posh Suitcase Sisters. We'll have to update Wanja."

I laughed, but not much because climbing the stairs to the top of the lodge at that altitude was no joke. At the end of the hall, we opened a door marked "Terrace" and stepped onto a long lookout area that was open to the view of the watering hole and woods. Lily and I were the only ones there.

"Do you think this is the right place?" I asked.

"I think so. Let's sit over here."

I tapped Lily's arm and pointed to the sign attached to the thick wooden post above the chairs. "Do not feed the monkeys."

"No chance of that happening," she said. "They are the only animal I didn't take a liking to on this trip. And the gnarly warthogs."

"Or the hyenas," I added.

"Definitely not the hyenas."

"I thought the wildebeests were a bit unnerving. And smelly."

Lily laughed. "I liked the gnus. At least we're far enough away from the animals up here. I doubt we'll smell any of them."

We pulled the cushioned chairs closer to the edge and gazed down on the watering hole as if we did this every day and knew what we were looking for. Several kudus, which Lily had seen earlier, were gathered at the far end, dipping their necks down and raising them to look left and then right. Lots of birds fluttered around, and a couple of weasel-like critters zipped across the dirt and into the greenery.

"I should tell you that I worked on my job possibility list during our drive here," I said.

"You did? I thought that whole time you were writing about the Scandinavian boys by the pool."

I shook my head at my mischievous friend. "No. Definitely not."

"Okay, go on. You were saying you made a list. You have my complete attention."

"The most obvious possibility would be to work as an independent contractor and do content editing for various authors and publishing houses. I don't know if I could make enough, though."

"What kind of salary do you need? I mean, we've never talked about our finances in specifics, but it's not like you're single and yours is the only income. Could you get by on less than what you used to make?"

She had a good point. "Danny and I haven't talked about it yet."

"I know this might be too soon, and I don't want to sound disrespectful, but I have to ask. Is Danny going to keep Mamacita's house? Could you rent it for additional income? If he wants to sell it, how many people would he have to share the profit with?"

"No one. Danny's dad and sister passed away, you know, so it's just us and Micah."

"Micah was her only grandchild," Lily murmured. "I hadn't thought of that."

Something felt stuck in my throat as I realized that Danny's lineage could end if Micah never married and had children. The contrast between his extended family and mine was glaring. My parents had sixteen grandchildren. I hadn't thought of any of this before.

"So, if the house is yours free and clear, you could sell it, and at least that would give you a financial buffer so you could try doing freelance work and see how it goes. Or you could live somewhere else. Lots of possibilities." Lily picked up the binoculars on the side table and scanned the expansive view in front of us. Beyond the watering hole was a forest of trees that were different from ones we'd seen elsewhere on our trip. She seemed to be looking for something to fix her attention on.

I felt the same way. I wanted to find the right thing to focus on too. But my search was internal.

"Lily, how are you managing to come up with all these options I never thought of?"

"Peacock," she said with a grin.

I got her reference immediately and smiled back.

"It's all right there, Fern. You just can't see it. What's the saying about not seeing the forest because of all the trees? Your life is filled with possibility trees. I think of it as best friend job security for me. Someone must tell you these things. I commit myself to remain your mirror of irreplaceable value. Just as you are to me."

I leaned back in the chair. "Thank you."

"Karibu. And may I give you one more suggestion?"

"Yes, please."

"Have you considered what a big job you and Danny are going to have clearing out his mom's house? How many generations lived there?"

"Just two. Well, Danny and Micah would be generations three and four."

"You told me once that she saved everything."

"She did."

"So, consider yourself employed full-time for at least a month, if it falls on you to be the one to get the house ready to sell. I know it's not the work you expected to be doing, but it's important work. And it would have been a lot harder to do if you were still working full-time at the publishing house."

"You're right."

Lily took a page from my book of teasing. "Excuse me? What was that you just said?"

"I said you're right, and you are. Asante sana for once again enlightening me on the obvious."

"Peacock," she said once again.

The door opened, and a uniformed attendant pushed a tea service trolley toward us.

"Put on your scarf," Lily whispered.

I unraveled my long, multicolored scarf and draped it around my neck, giving it a proper swish, the way Lily had. I stifled the urge to giggle as if we were two little girls playing dress-up.

With a slight amount of clinking and muffled sloshing, our server prepared two cups of freshly brewed tea and handed them to us on saucers. Two shortbread cookies balanced on the edge of the saucers. He then offered us cream and sugar on a silver tray.

Lily added both to her cup of steaming tea. I wanted to be a purist just in case this was a local Kenyan tea. I wanted to believe it had come from the fields of Limuru. In the same way I couldn't take photos when we were watching our majestic lion at the golden hour, I didn't want anything to cloud my cup of local tea.

Without a word, our efficient server slipped away, leaving the silver teapot and cream and sugar on the tea service cart parked behind us, along with another plate of shortbread cookies.

Lily lifted her cup and playfully put up her pinky. I matched her posture.

My first sip was just right. Not too hot. Not diluted with milk or embellished with sugar. It was pristine and perfect. Slightly malty undertones typically found in a rich Assam, but with a lingering finish that carried hints of red earth in the rain.

I considered sharing my tea snob evaluation with Lily but decided some things don't always translate well between tea aficionados and coffee drinkers.

We settled into one of our quiet pockets. Neither of us needed to say anything to assure the other that this was where we wanted to be, and we were with the person we wanted to be with. I knew we were both at the highest level of contentment possible at that moment.

Above us, a long streamer of ivory clouds, as sheer as our scarves, had unfurled, softening the same blue skies we'd strolled under yesterday on the Aberdare hills. The light of the day was slowly dimming, softening the shadows between the trees.

I watched closely as the shadows directly across from us

seemed to wave as if a singular breeze had visited that corner of the woods. Lily saw it too. She pointed.

We watched without words as a single bold elephant lumbered out of the hiding place, swinging her trunk back and forth and checking out the watering hole. She was grand. Grand and matronly. I loved her.

Two more elephants followed. The grand dame raised her trunk, and another sister emerged from the deep woods. A moment later another plump friend joined them. They formed a gorgeous gathering of the women at the watering hole. I hoped they were all pregnant.

The trees swayed once again, and Lily stood up, reaching for the binoculars. I joined her, still holding my china cup and narrowing my sight to the movement in the wooded area. The large ladies formed an uneven circle between the trees and the watering hole. Their ears flapped, and they stomped the moist soil as if trying to kick up some dust. They reminded me of bodyguards falling into place, looking like they were a force to be reckoned with. And they were.

Into their circle, another elephant emerged. She approached slowly, cautiously. One of the elephants made a loud snorting sound. The final guest came forward with a surprise.

"Is that . . . ?" Lily whispered.

We drew in our breath in unison. Hidden between the tree-stump legs of the last guest at the watering hole was what we'd dearly hoped for.

A baby elephant.

The little one was small enough to fit all the way underneath the thick body of the mama. We caught only glimpses of the baby among the many stomping aunties. They protected the newest member of the herd by escorting the mother and child down to the edge of the watering hole, ears flapping and feet stomping.

Lily and I reached over and squeezed each other's arms. We were witnessing fresh hope for Africa. A promise for the future, packed into the miracle of new life plodding forward on stumpy, clumpy legs.

"I think she's a baby girl," Lily said.

"I do too." I swallowed back unexpected tears. We had no way of knowing if we were looking at a boy or a girl baby elephant, but the cuteness was endearing, and I loved that Lily and I both thought it was a girl.

At the water's edge, the mother stepped slowly into the mud. The bodyguards continued to flap their mighty angel-wing ears. One of them—the primary matriarch, perhaps—raised her trunk, and out came a trebled trumpeting sound. An announcement, it seemed.

The princess and her entourage were in the house.

With protection and apparently her mother's blessing, the adorable little one bumbled toward the water, ears waving, skinny little tail up, and trunk swaying back and forth. She explored every sensation of rocks, mud, and water with a zest for life. Then she charged into the watering hole the way a toddler would pounce into a puddle. We had a clear view of her once she was in the shallow water and the shenanigans began. The discovery of sloshy mud and tickling water seemed to elicit pure joy.

I laughed softly as she continued to roll in the shallow water and splash around. The sisterhood surrounding her took long drinks and kept their protective enclave in place. The baby had room to be at play. She was well protected, just as we had been at the hippo pool.

Lily and I settled back in our padded chairs, our view unhindered. We soaked in the extraordinary moment, sipping our tea with elephants.

"I can't imagine a better final act for this trip, can you?" Lily asked.

"My mom always says that God saves the best for last," I whispered.

Lily grinned. "You know why she says that, don't you?" I waited.

"She means you. You were her last daughter. God saved you for last. And you're the best."

I didn't know how to respond. A lump formed in my throat. I'd never seen that as my mom's meaning. All I could think was what a generous thing it was for Lily to say in comparison to the many things her mom had said or not said to her.

"If I see your parents again," Lily said, "I'm going to thank them for not stopping after four daughters. I'm glad they brought you into the world and loved you so well. I don't know what my life would have been like without you."

I blinked quickly. "Nor mine without you."

"Look at the sky," she said. "What color would you call that?"

"I don't know. My vocabulary isn't advanced enough to name it."

"That's saying a lot for someone with a vocabulary like yours. Aren't any poems coming to mind?"

I shook my head. This moment did not remind me of any other familiar moment in my life. It didn't bring to mind a poetic quote or a vivid description from an accomplished writer. This moment was all its own. Fresh, singular, primal, and somehow marking in my spirit the starting point of some unknown next chapter in my life.

It was, as Lily said earlier, the final act on our impossible-to-fully-describe adventure. I didn't want the curtains to close.

"Would you consider doing something for me?" Lily asked.

I glanced at her and waited for a little more explanation before offering a resounding commitment to a Lily-style unknown of unlimited proportions.

"When you finish writing about this trip in your journal, would you share a copy of it with me? I don't want to wait until we're in the nursing home. I want to remember everything now."

"Okay," I agreed. "I can do that."

"It doesn't have to be fancy. You could just take pictures of the pages that I'm sure will have your beautiful descriptions of things we saw and the fun details of what we did."

"I can type it up. That's not a problem."

"It doesn't have to be a whole book." Lily paused. I didn't look at her, but I knew the kind of smile that was rising on her face when she added, "Unless you *want* to write a whole book. Because you could, you know. Being a woman of possibilities and all that."

To my surprise, I didn't argue with her. I let the thought rest on me the way the waning sunlight on the Masai Mara had rested on the upturned face of the golden lion. This was a holy moment of communion for me too.

Creator of this beautiful world, what would bring You joy in this next season of possibilities in my life?

A clear thought came to me, bringing with it a sweet peace. I put down my teacup and saucer and reached for Lily's arm. The words I spoke were ones I had not dared to think, let alone say aloud.

"Lily."

"Yes?"

"I want to have a baby."

She lowered her teacup.

"Or at least try." I lifted my chin, smiling and feeling the tears streaming down my face.

"Ah, there she is. My woman of possibilities. Well, don't tell me. Tell that guy you're so crazy about. You know, the one with the sincere and alluring eyes."

23

May the African sun always shine through your eyes and the sound of its drums always beat in your heart.

African proverb

Our departure from Nairobi was on time. Lily and I moved through the airport crowds without saying a word. I think both of us were caught off guard at how sad we felt about leaving and yet not surprised at the emotions that filled our hearts. The sadness brought me to tears once we were in our first-class seats and the plane lifted off from the sacred soil we had been traversing.

Surprisingly, the amenities of first class didn't feel as joyous and lush as what we'd experienced on our flight from Heathrow. We had been pampered everywhere we went during our travels, and I was embarrassed to realize that having plenty of legroom, tasty food, soft blankets, and a warm washcloth somehow felt normal. Expected. I'd prepared myself to rough it on this trip, but the whole experience had been cushy and lovely.

"Fern, does any of this feel real to you?" Lily had the aisle seat this time. I was gazing out the window as the last lights of the city of Nairobi faded behind us and the great darkness of the undeveloped regions of Kenya loomed below. Regions I now knew to be alive with animals, tea fields, fascinating people, and luxurious hotels.

I turned to her with tears in my eyes. "No, it's been a dream. Nothing like I thought it would be."

"I know. I feel the same way. Everything was different than I expected."

"Thank you, Lily. Thank you for being my closest friend for all these years and for inviting me to share this adventure with you."

She reached over and gave my arm a squeeze. "I don't think we'll ever be the same, do you? I feel like Africa gently pushed me, pushed both of us, into the next season of life."

I nodded.

"I don't want to forget any of it."

"I have an idea." I pulled my notebook out of my bag and found a pen. "Let's make a list."

She laughed. "I never know if you're making fun of me when you say that."

"No, I'm serious. While everything is still fresh in our minds, let's make a list of our favorite moments."

Lily began with her memory of standing in line at Heathrow, nervously watching every passenger go by, hoping I'd be one of them and we wouldn't miss our flight. We listed the highlights of our first-class "flight of delight," as Lily called it, and went on to our ride with Wanja to Brockhurst and settling into our beds that first night by candlelight. We continued adding to the list as we flew through the night toward Amsterdam.

"Be sure to write down 'Suitcase Sisters,'" Lily said.

I smiled as I wrote the two words and thought of how Wanja had rebranded us in the same way Lily had rebranded me all those years ago in Costa Rica when she whispered the mysterious word "fernweh."

A sweet sense of wonder along with a dose of resolve settled on us as the list grew. We had done it. We had gone to Africa and experienced remarkable moments as well as settled significant life issues we'd brought with us.

Lily was already coming up with ideas on how she could fully enter into her marriage and refresh the deep love she'd once felt for Tim. I had a plan in place for what I was going to do next. It was decided late in the night in between the animal viewings.

The hotel staff had knocked on our door throughout the night, alerting us to the arrival of wildlife at the watering hole. Lily and I scooted to the window and looked down on the various nocturnal animals that had gathered. The first few sightings were interesting, but around 2:00 a.m. our slumber-party conversation became the true value of our last night together. Lily camped on a career option for me that Danny had first suggested the day I told him I'd been let go. It had been too soon for me to hear his advice then. The solution seemed obvious now.

I would set up my own business as a freelance editor.

"When you get to the end of the list," Lily said now, adjusting her airplane seat, "write your new goal to start a business and add my goal."

"How do you want me to summarize your new goal?"

"Just put 'fall in love again.'"

I added those two goals to the end of the list, and Lily was on to the next topic we hadn't yet exhausted.

"I think you should add something about settling your mother-in-law's estate."

"No, I don't think so. That's at the top of another list I need to make when I'm back home."

"I have a feeling you'll be busy until the first of next year. At least."

"You could be right," I said. "Danny texted me this morning that they went ahead and scheduled the funeral for next Saturday. Micah is going back to school for the week and returning on Friday for four days."

"Would you like me to come for the funeral?" Lily asked. "I'll come if you want me to."

"Thanks, but no. I'd love for you to come see me another time, though. What do you think? Next summer?"

"Or sooner. Or you can come to Nashville."

"Or we could meet somewhere. Should we make a list of possibilities?"

"Later," Lily said, reclining her seat. "Our lack of sleep from last night is catching up."

Both of us slept for nearly the remainder of the flight. The local time was 7:00 a.m. when we landed in Amsterdam, and once again I was having a hard time holding back the tears. This was where Lily and I would go our separate ways.

We hugged and said our teary-eyed goodbyes. Then, with our suitcases wheeling behind us, wearing our crumpled and slightly dusty not-so-skinny jeans, we went to our gates.

I felt Lily's absence immediately. Especially when I wedged into a middle seat near the back of the plane for my flight to Denver. I kept wondering how Lily was doing on her first-class flight to Nashville. Then I thought about how much I missed Danny and how eager I was to see him.

When I landed in Denver, he was waiting for me with tears in his eyes. The tough coach was always a softie with me. His arms held me for a long moment, and our kiss was tender and lingering.

My misty eyes tried to focus on his handsome face, his sincere eyes. Behind him, I caught a glimpse of our tall son approaching with beverage cups in a cardboard tray. His dazzling, wide smile lit up his face. I blinked to make sure I was seeing correctly.

"Micah!" I embraced him.

In my ear, he whispered, "Welcome home, Mom."

That was when the tears went from a mist to a downpour, flooding the river of my heart. He had never called me "Mom" before. For a long time, I was "Hey." When he introduced me to anyone, I was called "my dad's wife." But that moment in the airport I became his mom, and I knew I'd never be the same.

Micah's flight was scheduled to leave in three hours, so we had enough time to find a place to sit and talk and enjoy our coffee and tea. Yet again I was grateful that none of that precious time would be spent at baggage claim.

"I want to hear everything," I said. "How are you guys?"

"Good," Danny said.

"We want to hear everything from you," Micah said.

"I brought some gifts." I reached for the full shoulder bag that held all the extras that no longer fit in my small suitcase.

"Later," Danny said. "Tell us. How was it?"

"Incredible. I wished so many times that both of you had been there. You would have loved all of it. The food. The people. And oh, Danny, the lion." I teared up, and so did he. "I wish you could have seen the lion. We saw him at sunset. This big, bronzed lion with a full mane, and he turned his face to the west, and the wind . . ." I reached into the pocket of my jacket for a tissue. "I have pictures."

"You can show us all of them later," Micah said, echoing Danny's sentiment.

"Okay, it will all come out eventually. The gifts and photos and all the stories. They will probably be in pieces. Chapters, you know, because it was so much. So rich and full." I took a breath and dabbed my happy tears. "I want to hear about you guys. I missed you so much. I wanted to come home a dozen times."

"You did the right thing to stay." Danny's lips turned up in a wobbly smile. "We have some news for you. I was going through some drawers and files at my mom's, and I found money. She had a way of squirreling away cash for years. Micah went on a treasure hunt, and so far, we found a lot of cash."

"A lot," Micah echoed.

Danny reached for my hand. "You don't have to try to find a new job right away. I hope that takes some pressure off you. We'll be fine."

Micah laughed. "It was bizarre. Every drawer had a hidden envelope with money. Including a coffee can in her freezer that had more than a thousand bucks. Mamacita was one of a kind, that's for sure."

I sat back, trying to process what my men were saying. I'd felt the Lord telling me to release the pressure about my job when I was in Kenya but had no idea then why I should feel so confident and peaceful about simply waiting on Him. This was why.

"The other reason you can't start a job search," Danny said, "is because I'm going to need you to help me get everything settled. It's going to take weeks to sort through everything and see if we can sell any of it."

"Of course. I'm all yours."

Danny gave me his best, humblest, and most endearing smile. "And I'm so glad you are." He leaned in and gave me another kiss.

"So, here's my news," Micah said. "Not that your kissing reminded me of it or anything."

I looked into his warm brown eyes and put my hand over my heart. "There's more? Wow. I should go away more often."

"No, you shouldn't," Micah said, pointing to Danny. "This guy was lost without you. Pizza every night. Never did the laundry. One of your plants, the one in the bathroom, died."

Danny pretended to give Micah a punch in the arm for ratting on him. Micah laughed. It was the best sound on earth.

"Tell me your news," I said.

"I met a girl."

My hand reached for his. "You did?"

He looked so happy. "Her name's Shawna. She's amazing. I want you guys to come to California as soon as you can so you can meet her."

"Yes. Absolutely." I hugged my two gorgeous men and told them how much I loved them. All our years together before this moment seemed small. Distant. The closeness I now felt with them loomed large and dazzling. Endless possibilities had opened to us.

For the next few days I moved as if I was one of the elegant giraffes striding through the morning mist. I moved forward on all the things that needed to be done but soon found the fog of jet lag was real. I secretly loved spending long hours at Mamacita's. Everything I touched was soaked with sweet and often quirky memories of her.

Danny was right about it being a treasure hunt. The funniest place where I found some of Mamacita's hidden stash was in a maternity girdle. I'd never seen such a thing, but she had one. It had probably been her mother's or even her grandmother's. The pouch in the front that was supposed to stretch as the baby grew was firm and lumpy. I snipped the stitched edges and out tumbled money. So much money.

I checked the tiny dates printed on the bottom right of the bills and had a feeling Mamacita's tradition of squireling away cash had been passed down from her mother because some of the bills were almost a hundred years old. One of the ten-dollar bills I found was odd. It had a bison on it and was dated 1901. I smiled, thinking of the gnus and Shotgun and Samburu. I sent a photo of the bill to Micah, and he excitedly called to tell me he found one like it on eBay that was for sale for more than a thousand dollars.

A new list began. We needed to sort all the cash. Not just to get a final total. We needed to find the hidden gems in the stacks that were worth more than their face value.

The best companion I could have hoped for accompanied me on every one of the sorting, cleaning, and packing days that winter. It was the playlists I'd loaded to my phone. My favorite was the one Lily sent me that she had played at the Giraffe Manor. Outside, the snow came down from the Rockies in great gusts, riding on freezing winds, but inside, the African sun warmed my thoughts, and my heart fell in sync with her familiar beat.

The past and the present danced around me during those first few months after I returned from Mother Africa. I began to dream about the possibilities of the future both in my waking hours and in my nights of deep sleep. Having the luxury of not needing to work quite yet was a gift I hadn't experienced before. Danny and I took a close look at our finances, and with the sale of the house, we were fine.

I saw my pause in working full-time as a self-imposed sabbatical and wasn't nervous about telling friends in my former publishing circles that I was available for freelance editing. I had two projects already scheduled for next summer. Both were from authors I used to work with. They wanted to pay me to do an edit on their novels before they turned them in to their new publisher. It was the highest compliment I could have received.

For Christmas, Lily gave me a new journal. She said I shouldn't write in it yet but should save it for our next Suitcase Sisters adventure. On the cover was a quote inscribed in gold script: "The world is a book and those who do not travel read only one page."

I loved it. But I didn't know if I could wait until she and I went on another trip before filling the pages with notes.

With everything else going on, I'd put aside my idea to compile all the notes from our trip and turn them into a book for Lily. But at Danny's insistence, I started a file on my laptop and transferred into it all my journal entries about Africa. After I had coached authors for so many years and helped them through their individual writing process, Danny was now the one coaching me. He said I had to get all my journal entries into a single document before I could tell if it was just a collection of memories for Lily and me or if it should be bound into a book. A book about Lily and me and Africa. The only way to find out was to do the work and start typing.

So I did.

Danny and I went to Southern California for a long weekend in February. We met Shawna, and I quickly understood why Micah cared about her so much. She was lovely. They'd had some on and off stretches over their first semester but seemed to be settling into a steady friendship, which is what they decided they wanted to develop first.

What linked them during a freshmen meet and greet was that they found out they were both adopted, and neither of them knew their birth fathers. It touched me to see how God was showing that He cared about every detail in our son's life.

The details of Mamacita's funny-money surprise took weeks to organize. Several months, actually. It made Danny and me laugh whenever we brought it up. We found a realtor who sold the house as is for a fair price. The new buyers had plans to knock out walls and fix it up. At one point I considered telling our realtor that the new owners shouldn't be surprised if they took a sledgehammer to one of the walls and dollar bills came fluttering out.

Danny and I decided not to say anything. If the new owners happened onto their own trove of blessings, let them have it. We hadn't done anything to earn the unexpected inheritance we'd encountered. Why not let someone else possibly be blessed with a sweet surprise as well?

We were able to bless Micah with money for a more reliable car. He was thrilled. One of our donations from the bounty went to the clean water ministry run by Jim and Cheryl. We thought Mamacita would love knowing that her tucked-away treasure would bring a cup of cool water to someone on the other side of the world in Jesus' name.

All the financial transactions went smoothly and swiftly. Mamacita's will was simple. She'd signed it after her husband died, which was a few years before Danny and I were married. It stated that everything should go to Danny. In her handwriting, in Spanish, she wrote that she hoped her only son would share the inheritance with Micah because he was her only grandchild, and she loved him.

It was true. Micah had been her only grandchild.

However, to our surprise and joy, it looked like that fact was about to change. On the Monday after Easter, five months since I'd returned from Africa, I woke up and realized I was nauseous for the third morning in a row. I picked up a pregnancy test when I was buying groceries that afternoon. I called Lily before I took the test.

"It will be positive," she said. "I just know it. This is God's gift to you guys, Fern. Promise you'll text me after Danny knows."

"I will."

"What do you think? December baby? Or maybe sooner?"

I laughed. "You always think further ahead than I do. Let's wait and see what the test says."

"Whatever month it is, I'm coming. You came for me when Noah was born, and I promised myself then that I'd come when it was your turn."

"I'd love to have you here. But again, can we hold off on the plans until we know?"

"Sure. But I already know. You're pregnant, Fern."

I held her words like a fragrant little bouquet until Danny got home. I wanted him to be there so we could find out at the same time.

He roared when we saw the plus sign on the test.

That was the only way to describe the wild and joyous sound that came from his lungs. The lion I saw at the golden hour hadn't roared, so I couldn't make an exact match to Danny's exuberant roar, but in my heart, I heard a roar. The roar of the One who was calling His children. The next generation depended on their arrival.

Lily said she couldn't wait, so she came to see me for three days in early June. She wanted to put her hand on my belly and feel my "baby elephant" move.

Lots had happened to her, too, since Africa. The best change was how she and Tim were closer than ever. She'd connected with her cousin, Cheryl and Jim's son, who was still in California with his family. He went to see her in Nashville, where she set up a big fundraiser in January for the clean water ministry. The event went so well, Lily was invited to work full-time setting up more fundraising events by a separate organization she'd long admired. The hours were fewer and the salary was higher than what she'd been making. It was remarkable. An unexpected career move for her and one that gave her more time to be with her family.

The second wonderful outcome of meeting her cousin was that he and Tim hit it off, and Tim asked if they could go to Brockhurst as a family for their next vacation. He and Lily wanted their boys to have an international experience before going to college. Tim's dad volunteered to go with them, and Lily couldn't wait for their trip in early July. Her mother-in-law planned to stay home by the pool and read a book.

My pregnancy went smoothly, and I loved being home, working on a few editing projects with authors I adored. I even worked on my book. Every time I checked the list of memories Lily and I had compiled on our flight to Amsterdam, I was grateful. Grateful for the adventure that had been given to us at just the right time, and grateful for Lily and her list-making talents. Otherwise I might have forgotten some of the highlights.

I didn't tell anyone I was working on a book. Danny was the only one who knew. His coaching skills weren't always appreciated, but if he hadn't urged me to keep going, I have a feeling I would have put it off until the once-vivid images had faded.

Micah and Shawna spent the summer together on staff at a Christian conference center in Oregon. He wanted us to come to Glenbrooke and visit them, but we weren't able to pull it off. Our summer was swallowed up by fixing up our condo to rent it and moving into a three-bedroom condo in our complex. I was eager to prepare a nursery, and Danny wanted me to have a separate office. When the three-bedroom unit went on the market, we bought it the same day. It needed some upgrades, which we had done before we moved in.

Lily came to see me the last week of August. The timing was perfect because we'd only been in our new condo for a few days, and she helped me set up the nursery. My office was large enough for a couch, so I picked out the best couch I'd ever had. It was perfect for afternoon naps, of which I'd become a pro, and for overnight guests. It made me happy that Lily was our first guest to sleep on it.

"Let's start with the list of names," Lily suggested within an hour of her arrival.

We were trying out my office couch and sipping the sweet tea she'd brought with her. She told me it was her favorite, and we laughed.

"But before we go down the list," she said, "have I told you how excited I am that you're having a girl?"

"Yes. Many times."

"Just wanted to be sure. So? Where's your list?"

I pointed to the side of my head.

"Are we doing charades? You want me to guess?"

"No. We don't have a list. Danny and I narrowed it down quickly. Her name is Carolyn Rose."

Lily seemed to swish the words around in her mouth before swallowing them. "I love it. Not too modern. Not too old-fashioned. Wasn't Mamacita's name Rose?"

"Rosa. Yes, we wanted to tuck in a remembrance of her in the name. Carolyn doesn't connect with anyone either of us knew, or any famous name."

I put down my glass of sweet tea. It was way too sweet for me.

"Danny and I were going through a baby-name book, and when we got to the Cs and I read 'Carolyn,' we looked at each other and smiled. That was it. We just knew it. She can go with Carol or Lynn or even Rose. She will be a woman of options when it comes to her name."

"Rosie," Lily said thoughtfully. "What do you think of her Auntie Lily calling her Rosie?"

"I love it."

"And I love that you and Danny found it in a book. That's a nod to your mom."

"Speaking of books," I said slowly. "I have something for you."

I pointed to one of the many unopened boxes in my new office. This box was small. It contained only ten books, and one of them was for Lily.

"Would you open that box for me?"

Lily took the pair of scissors off my desk and gingerly sliced through the tape.

"It arrived yesterday, but I wanted you to be the one to open it."

Lily folded back the cardboard flaps and removed the brown packing paper. Her eyes grew wide as she stared at the contents. She didn't touch the top book. Instead, she turned to me with a perfect expression of amazement and delight.

"Did you . . . ? Is this . . . ? Fern . . . ? Are you kidding me?"

I nodded, barely holding in my joy. "I haven't seen it yet. Could you hand me one?"

Lily lifted out two copies of my hot-off-the-self-published-press book. It was our book, really. The story of us. Two besties on a life-changing adventure in *Ahh-free-kaa*.

She cried. Then laughed. Then she cried again. I went to the refrigerator and pulled out two big, fat slices of Njeri's banana bread I had made before we moved to the new condo. I'd been saving the treat in the freezer for a moment like this. That morning I had put the slices on two fancy little plates and covered them with a napkin.

Presenting the banana bread to Lily by pulling off the napkin with a swish, I grinned as she laughed and cried again.

We did zero unpacking for the next few hours as we skimmed through the chapters together, remembering, laughing, smiling. I was pleased and proud of the end result and glad I'd taken Danny's advice to keep going and finish the final chapters so I'd have it done and some copies printed before the baby came. Neither of us knew then that they really needed to be ready before Lily's spontaneous visit.

"It's beautiful," Lily said, hugging our little treasure. "Please tell me you're going to send one to everyone you know in your publishing circles. You'll have a bidding war over who ends up publishing it."

"I don't know about that. It's really just for us. I promised you I'd put it all together before we become neighbors in a retirement home. So I'm way ahead of schedule."

"Fern, if you don't do it, I will. As your dear bosom friend and kindred spirit, I will become your Diana Barry and send it in for you!"

"My Diana Barry? I didn't know you read *Anne of Green Gables*."

"I didn't. I saw the movie."

Lily was on a roll and tried to come up with more ways to convince me that I should go all out and try to publish the book through my connections. She said I should hire Mia to do book promotions for me. We conjured up images of Mia finding an elephant somewhere, positioning her slender body on its back while pretending to read a copy of the book with a cup of tea in her hand. She would be doing all this in an evening gown with a long slit up the side, wearing stylish glasses and a great hat. We agreed that her red hat would work nicely.

"Oh, and she'd need a peacock feather tucked into the side band," Lily said.

"Absolutely."

Lily pointed at me. "Remember, this is why God put me in your life. You're a peacock, and you need me to tell you how magnificent you are. You just can't see it."

That night, when I pulled up the covers of the cozy bed in our new bedroom and listened to my husband slowly breathing in and out, I wrote a little love letter to Jesus in my head. I thanked Him for the abundance He had given me with Danny, Micah, baby Carolyn Rose, and this new condo, and for the gift of my kindred-spirit friend who was sleeping on the couch in my new office. It was all so lavish.

I whispered the conclusion of my letter into the quiet of the night.

"I don't know what's next, Lord, but I know You. And You are so good. If You've chosen to bless me and grace me in all the ways You already have, what else do You have in mind? Whatever it is, I know it will be grand because my mom was right. You always save the best for last. I love You, Lord. For now and for always, Your girl, Fernweh."

Njeri's (Secret) Banana Bread

5 tablespoons unsalted butter or coconut oil, melted

½ cup honey

1¾ cups mashed ripe banana (about 3 or 4 bananas)

2 eggs, at room temperature

1 teaspoon vanilla extract

2 cups flour

1 teaspoon baking soda

½ teaspoon salt

1 teaspoon cinnamon

½ cup dark chocolate chips, chopped walnuts, or raisins (optional)

Preheat oven to 350°F. Grease a 9×5-inch loaf pan, or line with parchment paper, and set aside.

In a large bowl, combine the melted butter or coconut oil with the honey and mashed banana. Whisk in the eggs and vanilla.

In a separate bowl, mix the flour with the baking soda, salt, and cinnamon. Whisk until well combined.

Fold the flour mixture into the wet ingredients. Blend all ingredients, but don't overmix.

If desired, stir in chocolate chips, walnuts, or raisins.

Pour batter into prepared loaf pan.

Bake for 55–60 minutes or until a toothpick inserted in the center comes out clean.

Check on the banana bread after 35 minutes and loosely cover with foil if needed to prevent overbrowning the top.

Drizzle a small amount of honey over the top of the loaf as it cools. Cool for 10 minutes before removing from pan.

Wanja's (Secret) Masala Chai Latte

Serves 2

¼ teaspoon ground cloves
1 tablespoon ground cinnamon
a pinch of ground cardamom
a pinch of freshly ground black
  pepper
1 teaspoon ground nutmeg
½ teaspoon ground ginger

2 cups water
2 tablespoons loose-leaf black
  tea (more if you like a stronger
  taste of black tea)
1 cup whole milk
2 teaspoons honey

Combine all the spices.
Pour 2 cups water into a saucepan and bring to a boil.
Add the spices.
Simmer for 2–5 minutes.
Add loose-leaf black tea.
Immediately turn off the heat and let mixture steep for 3–6 minutes
  based on preference.
Add milk.
Bring liquid just to a boil.
Remove from heat.
Strain immediately and serve with honey.

Some of Robin's Favorites in Kenya

TheWaterProject.org

Brackenhurst.com

JavaHouseAfrica.com

SerenaHotels.com/Mara

AberdareCountryClub.com

TheSafariCollection.com/Properties/Giraffe-Manor

SheldrickWildlifeTrust.org

Robin Jones Gunn is the bestselling author of over one hundred books and is best known for the Christy Miller, Glenbrooke, and Sisterchicks series. Four Hallmark Christmas movies were created from her Father Christmas and Glenbrooke novels.

Robin's memoir, *Victim of Grace*, along with *Praying for Your Future Husband*, coauthored with Tricia Goyer, are the most popular of her ten nonfiction titles, which include giftbooks and devotionals.

Her books have appeared multiple times on the ECPA bestseller list, and her work has been both a finalist and a winner of the Christy and Gold Medallion Awards. She is a frequent keynote speaker at international and local events. Robin cohosts the *Women Worth Knowing* podcast with Cheryl Brodersen.

After living on Maui for a decade, Robin and her husband moved to California to be closer to their two grown children and four grandchildren.

Learn more at RobinGunn.com, and download discussion questions at RobinGunnShop.com.

Ready for more Suitcase Sisters?

Your next armchair adventure is coming in 2025!

In the next Suitcase Sisters adventure, two friends travel to Italy on a lark—what's not to love about gondolas, villas, trains, pasta, Vespas, and gelato? In the beauty and chaos of their journey, they grow closer to God and to each other.

In the meantime, visit
RobinGunnShop.com
for more Suitcase Sisters fun!

Connect with Robin

Visit Robin's website to sign up for her newsletter, browse her online shop, listen to her podcast, and more.

RobinGunn.com

 AuthorRobinJonesGunn   RobinGunn   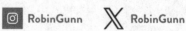 RobinGunn